ALSO BY ALLEN ESKENS

THE
QUIET
LIBRARIAN

ALLEN ESKENS

MULHOLLAND BOOKS
Little, Brown and Company
New York Boston London

Mulholland Books / Little, Brown and Company
Hachette Book Group
1290 Avenue of the Americas, New York, NY 10104
mulhollandbooks.com

First Edition: February 2025

Mulholland Books is an imprint of Little, Brown and Company, a division of Hachette Book Group, Inc. The Mulholland Books name and logo are trademarks of Hachette Book Group, Inc.

The publisher is not responsible for websites (or their content) that are not owned by the publisher.

The Hachette Speakers Bureau provides a wide range of authors for speaking events. To find out more, go to hachettespeakersbureau.com or email hachettespeakers@hbgusa.com.

Little, Brown and Company books may be purchased in bulk for business, educational, or promotional use. For information, please contact your local bookseller or the Hachette Book Group Special Markets Department at special.markets@hbgusa.com.

ISBN 9780316566315
Library of Congress Control Number: 2024943531

1 2024

MRQ-T

Printed in Canada

AUTHOR'S NOTE

Between May 25 and May 28 of 1995, at the height of the Bosnian war for independence, the Serbian army, or the Army of Republika Srpska (VRS), fired multiple rounds of artillery into the city of Tuzla, a Bosnian-Muslim-held city. One of the shells exploded in Kapija Square, where young civilians had gathered to enjoy a break from bad weather. The shelling—which came to be known as the Tuzla Massacre—killed 71 people and wounded 240 more, most of them between the ages of eighteen and twenty-five.

In July of that same summer, the Serbian army entered the Bosnian-held city of Srebrenica, where men and boys as young as twelve years old were rounded up and killed, a genocide that ended more than eight thousand lives. This novel is set against the backdrop of that summer in Bosnia, bookended to some degree by those two massacres.

I owe a great debt to two people who helped me understand the culture, the times, and the circumstances of the war in Bosnia. The first is Dr. Erma Nezirević, a Bosnian-Muslim woman who grew up in Banja Luka, a Serbian-held city in northern Bosnia. Her survival during those war years is truly an inspiration. The second is Elvir Mujić, who escaped the Srebrenica massacre by fleeing into Serbian territory and surrendering to Serb forces just before the killing took place. I cannot thank these two people enough for making it possible for me to tell the story I wanted to tell.

I dedicate this book to them and to all the innocents whose lives were forever changed—and for those whose lives were taken—during the Bosnian War.

THE
QUIET
LIBRARIAN

1

Minnesota

AFTER EVERYTHING

The man steps through the door and into the library, no coat despite the late-spring rain. He stops to cast his gaze around the room. Maybe it is the way he focuses on people and not books that first catches her attention. Or maybe it's the question in his eyes despite his confident demeanor, the look of a seasoned hunter in an unfamiliar wood.

Whatever the pique, it is enough to hold Hana's attention.

The man pulls a small notepad from the pocket of his tweed jacket, a pencil slid into the wire spirals, old-school in this world of cell phones and apps. He opens the notepad, reads something, and looks around the library again, pausing on faces, holding for a few seconds on Deb Hansen, the president of the Friends of the Library, who sits in the reading room. He glances at his notes, gives an almost imperceptible shake of his head, and moves on. She is not the one he's looking for.

Hana slips into a row of histories, pulling her cart of books behind her, keeping one eye on the man as she reshelves a tome on the Crusades. The man passes his gaze over a young mother and then a twenty-something girl looking through the DVDs. There are no other patrons in the library, yet he continues to scan.

The man is tall with sleepy eyes that droop at the edges. Dark hair sprinkled with gray puts him in his late forties maybe early fifties, Hana's age or thereabout. His chin looks weak but probably hadn't been so in his youth. He wears a jacket but no tie, and his khaki pants are creased at the hip as if he had been sitting—maybe in a car—before coming into the library.

When he sweeps her way, Hana holds still—a rabbit frozen in her tracks. She immediately feels foolish for reacting so. No one comes to the library looking for her. She has been invisible for far too long now, walking through the rows with her cart and her drab clothing. The Sweater Lady—that's what the children call her when they think she cannot hear them. She tugs at the sleeves of her cardigan, an unconscious tic that she can't seem to shake even after all these years.

She likes the history section. It is quiet there, and the aging books smell slightly of old wood, a scent that can sometimes whisk her back to the mountains of her youth and the peace of those days before the war. It had been a desire to find that sense of peace that drew Hana to the library in Farmington, Minnesota. That had been thirty years ago, and she still finds herself looking over her shoulder for those who might hunt her. Thirty years and she can still see the faces of the dead when she closes her eyes at night.

She peers over a collection of Civil War histories and watches the man make his way to the circulation desk, where Barb snaps on her best can-I-help-you smile. The man is probably in sales, hustling cleaning supplies or new software for the computers. He leans down and says something to Barb, who looks confused at first but then stands, scans the library, and points at Hana's cart, which sticks out into the aisle.

Hana pulls the cart into the row with her. Maybe Barb was directing the man to a book. Hana picks up a treatise on the fall of the Roman Empire and places it on the shelf.

No, that can't be it. Barb wouldn't need to look around the library before pointing. She knows the placement of every book in the building.

The man walks toward the history section. Hana pulls her cart deeper into the row and picks up a book on the Louisiana Purchase, raising it toward the shelf as the man draws closer. When he enters her row, the book in her hand sinks slowly to her side. This man is not a salesman. A salesman would have no business with her.

He offers a weak smile, a gesture that seems forced. Practiced. Up close, his eyes seem more sad than sleepy, and his features are stronger than they appeared from a distance. He stops a few feet away and asks, "Are you Hana Babić?"

He pronounces her last name wrong, ending it with a hard K the way most Americans do.

"Bah-bich," she corrects quietly, doing her best to hide what remains of her accent. "Hana Bah-bich."

"Sorry." He reaches into his breast pocket and pulls out what looks to be a wallet, then opens it to show her a gold badge. "I'm David Claypool, a detective with the St. Paul Police Department. Is there someplace where we can talk?"

It is then that Hana notices the gun holstered on his hip. How had she not seen that when he first walked in?

Memories—of men carrying guns, of bodies covered in white sheets stained red with blood—flash through her mind. Hana opens her mouth, but no words form. She wants to know why this man has sought her out, but she doesn't want to hear what he might say. She wants to ask if she's done something wrong, but that is not the right question either. The better question is, *Does he know?*

The book she holds slips from her fingers and falls. "I'm sorry," she mutters.

Before she can bend to pick it up, he squats, lifts the book, and puts it on the cart, his dark eyes meeting hers again; she sees kindness in them or maybe pity. "Can we talk?" he asks again.

"Yes," she says, "in the conference room."

She leads him to a small room reserved for book clubs and school projects, walking like a child being escorted to the principal's office, passing by the circulation desk, where Barb watches them. At the conference room, Detective Claypool opens the door for Hana, and she passes within a few inches of him, his tweed jacket smelling old, but the scent mixed with something clean. Soap. Maybe bodywash.

Detective Claypool gestures Hana to one of the four chairs at a small table, his anemic smile gone now. He takes a seat next to her but turns his chair to face her. When he opens his notepad, Hana tries to read the hen scratching, certain that hidden within those pages are the secrets of her past, embers of a life that Hana has worked hard to escape. The words on the pad flash by too quickly for her to see.

He looks at his notes and asks, "Do you know a woman named Amina..."

He pauses as if he needs to practice before attempting her last name, and in that pause, Hana's world folds in around her. No breath comes in. No breath goes out. Her tongue becomes bone-dry. It feels as though her body is being pricked with tiny needles.

Detective Claypool tries again. "Amina Jun..."

How could he not make the effort to learn Amina's name before plodding forward so clumsily? His delay is torture, and when she can no longer endure it, Hana swallows the dust from her throat and whispers. "Amina Junuzović."

"Yes," he says, in a heavy tone. "I'm sorry to have to tell you this, but Amina has passed away."

At first his words float in the air like wisps of smoke, impalpable, formless, the gibberish of a foreign tongue. Hana repeats them in her head, trying to give them texture and edges. *Amina...passed away.*

"I'm sorry," Claypool says. The kindness in his eyes makes Hana want to believe that he means it.

"When?"

"Yesterday."

"She has a grandson—Dylan. He lives with her."

"He's safe."

Hana breathes a small sigh of relief, but there is a terrible pain in her chest. Amina is dead. "What happened?"

Claypool slides the pencil from the spiral of the notepad. "Were the two of you close?"

"Close?" Hana ponders the ambiguity of the word for a moment before answering. "Amina is...the only friend I have in the world. I would like to think that I was her friend as well."

"Where were you yesterday at about four p.m.?"

Hana stands and backs away from the table. "Why would you ask me such a question?"

"It's routine," Claypool says, and there is a hint of embarrassment in his eyes.

"I was here...at the library, working. You can ask Barb—the woman at the circulation desk." Hana is about to say more when it hits her that Claypool had dodged her question. She asks again. "What happened to Amina?"

"You may want to sit down," he says.

Sit down? Is he worried that she might faint—wilt like some delicate flower? He sees her as weak, but how could he know; she has hidden the truth well.

Hana is thin. Her clothes, a simple gray skirt that reaches to her feet, a white blouse, and of course the cardigan sweater, all hang loosely on her frame. Her hair, once as black as onyx, holds veins of silver that streak back from her temples, contrails that lead to the bun on the back of her head. It all works to age her beyond her forty-seven years. She has gone out of her way to look older than she is, duller, plainer, cultivating an appearance to make her invisible to the world. Of course he would see her as weak.

He asks, "Do you know of anyone who might want to do her harm?"

"Was she . . . killed?"

"I'm afraid she was," Claypool says.

His answer does not cause Hana to faint. It is the one answer that makes sense of Claypool being there and asking the questions he is asking. Still, bile roils in Hana's stomach. Her mouth turns wet with spit, nausea building with every shallow breath. She walks to the window that looks out over the old grain elevator by the railroad tracks. It's raining, and she leans her forehead against the glass to cool the heat of her skin.

"Your name was listed as a contact on some documents we found," he says. "That's why I came here. I was hoping you might be able to help."

"What happened?"

Again he dodges the question. "Is there anyone you know who might have wanted to harm Amina?"

Hana returns to the table and sits in a chair across from Detective Claypool, holding his gaze for a second before saying, "I want you to tell me what happened to Amina." She can see in his eyes that he is wavering, so she searches her memory for his first name and finds it. "David, if you want answers from me, you are going to have to tell me the truth. What happened to Amina?"

His eyes soften in surrender. "Yesterday," he begins, "someone broke into her condo. The intruder . . . tied Amina up."

"Was she—"

"No. We found no indication of that. We don't know how long the intruder was there, but we think maybe a couple hours. The place was torn apart, like he was looking for something."

"He?"

"A man was seen on her balcony just after..." Claypool seems to get twisted in what he wants to say.

"After what?"

Claypool takes another breath, a beat to collect his thoughts. "At four fifteen yesterday, Dylan's bus dropped him off at the corner near Amina's condo. He was walking with two other children, both older."

Claypool pauses. He gives Hana a look as if to appraise her grit, assessing whether she might be able to handle the details he is about to tell her.

"Go ahead," Hana says.

"There was a crash. The sound of breaking glass. The sliding door to her balcony. What happened isn't clear. The kids saw her fall, but they didn't see how she came to go over the railing. We believe she was pushed. She might have been trying to escape, or... maybe not. The children said that they saw a man on the balcony. He stepped back into the condo before they could get a good look. They weren't able to give a description beyond believing it was a man."

"I saw that story on the news last night. I had no idea..."

"We haven't released her name to the press yet."

Hana closes her eyes and sees her friend fall four stories to the ground. "And Dylan saw her fall?"

Claypool nods.

Hana folds her hands together on the table. "Did she die from the fall... I mean... was it instantaneous?"

There is a gentleness in Claypool's voice that makes Hana forget about his badge and gun. "A couple of guys working across the street heard the commotion. They tried to help her. She died from internal injuries before the ambulance could get there."

Claypool waits to let his words settle before continuing. "Do you know of anyone who would want to harm her?"

Hana shakes her head no. "Amina was a gentle, forgiving soul."

Claypool flips through his notebook, landing on a scribbled page. Hana tries to read it but can't. "Do you know a man by the name of Zaim?"

"Zaim? Amina dated a man named Zaim—not for very long though. She broke up with him about a week ago."

"Do you know his last name?"

"I...I don't remember if she ever told me. Like I said, it didn't last long, maybe a couple months."

"Did you ever meet Zaim?"

"No. They weren't serious. Do you think—"

"Did she talk about him—say anything to make you think she was afraid of him?"

"What did he do?"

"Maybe nothing. It's just a name we have."

"How do you know about him...if you don't know his last name?"

"Dylan told us. What did Amina tell you about Zaim?"

Hana tries to remember. "Amina said that he smiled too much— like a salesman...like he was putting on a show. She didn't trust men who smiled too much."

"Was he ever rough with her?"

"Not that she said."

"And she never said his last name?"

"She may have, but I don't think so."

Claypool flips to a clean page of his notebook. "Before Zaim, had there been anyone else in her life? Another man maybe?"

"Not for a year or more. She wasn't big on dating."

Claypool taps his pencil on the empty page as silence builds between them. He is contemplating something. Then he leans in as if to study her reaction and says, "When those two workers got to Amina, she was conscious—barely. Amina grabbed her necklace...a pendant..."

A sudden dizziness sweeps over Hana. "A marble." Her voice is shaky despite her effort to sound calm. "Blue like the waters of the Adriatic Sea."

"Yes, blue. Does that necklace have some significance?"

"Significance?" Hana steadies herself, hoping to give away nothing.

Claypool says, "Her last act in life was to hand that necklace to those men. Given how badly she was injured, that last act took strength...I can't help thinking that she was trying to say something."

"It was her favorite necklace."

"It might be important."

Hana wants to look him in the eye but she cannot do it. "I'm not aware of any special significance." Lying to Claypool isn't easy. She's out of practice.

"You have an accent," Claypool says. "Are you from Bosnia as well?"

Claypool's question is a dangerous one. Too much digging and he may discover that Hana Babić—the real Hana Babić—died thirty years ago on a mountain in Bosnia. A strange suffocation tightens in Hana's throat. She needs to get out of that room and away from Claypool. She needs time to think.

She stands. "I'm not feeling well."

Claypool stands as well. Politeness, or does he plan to block the door? "I have a couple more—"

"I'm sorry." Hana puts her hand to her lips to feign illness. "I can't talk right now. I need air."

Claypool opens the door for Hana. "I understand."

As she passes, he pulls a card from his pocket and hands it to her. "When you're feeling up to it, I'd like to talk. Please call me."

Hana takes the card, but does not answer. She walks to the women's restroom without glancing back.

In the restroom she holds on to the sink as visions of Amina pass before her. They had been through so much together, yet Hana has no tears, nor the power to conjure them, having cried her last so many years ago. Instead Hana breathes slowly, intentionally, calm on the outside but spinning on the inside. She wets her face with cold water, the swell of emotion making her angry. She's stronger than this—or she had once been so.

She dries her face with a paper towel. When she finally peeks out of the restroom, Claypool is gone.

2

Bosnia

1977

Nura Divjak drew her first breath on a cold night in 1977, in the upstairs bedroom of a small farmhouse northwest of Tuzla, Yugoslavia. Her father—her babo—had been the one to deliver her because there wasn't time to get a midwife. Babo had hands of granite, but was a loving, gentle man, his hard eyes softening to tears as he first held his daughter—or at least that is the story that Mama told Nura.

The three of them lived on a weathered mountaintop surrounded by forests of spruce, and oak, and beech trees that stretched for several kilometers in every direction. Babo's older brother, Reuf, lived across a small gravel courtyard from them; beyond that, they were alone.

Babo and Reuf had inherited the mountain from their father, dividing it between them with a handshake after he passed away, Reuf taking the tillable land on the northern slope and Babo the southern woods. Reuf, a man who wore thick glasses and fancied himself something of an intellectual, sometimes bragged that he had outmaneuvered his younger brother to get the cropland.

In truth, neither man had a heart for farming. Reuf preferred reading and spending time in Tuzla, where he drank coffee and discussed world affairs with other men. Babo had wanted nothing of the farm other than a barn to stable a handful of cows and some woods in which to hunt. His true passion lay not in corn, but in stone and mortar, taking up masonry as a trade.

Nura's earliest memories of Mama were of sitting on her lap on their front porch, looking out over the mountains, the autumn beech trees catching the sun to paint the horizon a vibrant orange. Mama would tell her stories of the woodland faeries who walked through the trees at night, beautiful creatures with long hair and mellifluous voices who protected children from bad men. She remembers looking up at her mama and wondering if she had once been a faery with her round apple face, a slender nose, and long black hair that caught the sun.

As a little girl, Nura dreamed of being like her mama, of taking control of a house, raising children, and sitting at the side of a man she loved. More than that, she dreamed that one day she would be beautiful like her mother, but with every passing year, Nura's mirror revealed more of her father's features than her mother's: the angular face, the hard cheekbones, and a nose just a touch too big for a young girl. She whispered her disappointment to her reflection but to no one else.

The nearest village of any size, Petrovo, lay three valleys away, and when Nura was old enough, that was where she went to school. Nura knew that a great big world lay beyond her woods, beyond Petrovo and Tuzla, beyond the mountains and the sea, a magical world that seemed to her as make-believe as the faeries of Mama's stories. But in 1984, when Nura was six years old, the great and magical world beyond the sea came to her little mountain. That was the year that Sarajevo hosted the Winter Olympics.

Babo bought a television set that year, erecting an antenna up the side of their cow barn, the metal spire grabbing colors from the sky and casting them into Nura's living room. She and Mama watched as ice skaters from England named Torvill and Dean danced so beautifully that it made Nura want to cry. Babo, however, preferred to watch hockey. And, because he loved to hunt, Babo became captivated by a strange sport called the biathlon, in which men skied through the snow and shot at tiny targets.

Her country—her Yugoslavia—had offered this beauty to the world. She and her people were the epicenter of all things wonderful. Nura was sure that nothing more amazing than the Olympics could ever happen in her lifetime.

But then, almost three years later, something more amazing did happen.

On her ninth birthday, after a meal of beef stew capped with a chocolate cake, Babo and Mama gave her a new coat—brand-new, not secondhand. Nura had been wanting a coat because her old one no longer fit and had stains at the cuffs from wearing it when she did her chores. She promised herself that she would never wear this new coat out to the barn.

But when they finished the cake, Mama sat beside Nura at the table, put her arm around her, and said, "There is something else." Mama and Babo shared a look.

Babo said, "It is a present, but it is one for all of us."

Nura tried to read the secret in their eyes, but couldn't. Then Mama said, "In the spring, you are going to become a big sister."

The words didn't sink in right away, but then Mama placed her hand on her belly—on her womb—and Nura leapt into her mama's arms and cried with happiness.

* * *

Danis came to them on the third Sunday of April, 1987, his face plump and red, his tiny hands perfect as he wrapped his fingers around Nura's pinky. It was as though she could see entire galaxies shining in his eyes. And when she held him for the first time, he looked up at her as if he were studying her face, memorizing it. She was so happy she wanted to cry. Instead, she leaned in and gave him a gentle kiss on the cheek and whispered a promise.

"I am Nura, your big sister," she said. "I will always love you and take care of you."

True to her word, she had been the one who taught him to dance when he was barely old enough to stand. It was more of a silly little bounce than a dance, but he would do it whenever she sang to him. She taught him to say Nura, which started out as "Nono" but grew into a proper name by the time he reached his second birthday.

In the summer when he was two, she took him to the pond for the first time. The land behind the barn sloped gently to a creek, where Nura's great-grandfather had dammed up the water to make a pond for watering cows. Not much bigger than the footprint of their house, the pond was Nura's favorite place on the mountain. Danis dipped his toes into the cool water and squeezed mud through his fingers. She showed him how to make ripples on the water by throwing small stones. And though he was easily distracted—as most toddlers are—something about the way the light danced on the surface of the pond held his attention and calmed him.

Those years had been the happiest of Nura's life. In the winters, she pulled Danis on her sled. In the springs, she taught him how to find mushrooms and wild blackberries. In the summers, she took him to the pond, and read him books, and told him stories about the woodland faeries. They picked apples and pears in the fall and rolled down hills full of leaves. And even though Danis grew fast, he always seemed the perfect size to fit on Nura's lap.

* * *

The first time that Nura saw an image of war on her television, it had been in the summer before her fourteenth birthday: tanks in the streets of Slovenia and Croatia, bloody sheets draped over bodies, and burning houses. She held her breath as she watched soldiers battle in villages that were part of what had once been her country. When Danis, who was four, wandered into the room, she turned the television off and with a smile on her face, asked him if he wanted to go to the pond.

They returned that evening, hungry for dinner, their pant legs wet from walking in the shallows. As they approached the house, Nura heard Babo and Uncle Reuf inside, engaged in a heated discussion. She held Danis's hand tightly in hers and snuck onto the porch to listen, the men's voices hitting hard against the window above her.

Reuf said, "If we declare independence, Bosnia will no longer have a communist fist beating us into submission."

"Do you think a piece of paper means anything to Milošević?" Babo said. "Do you think a referendum will end our problems? You see what the Serbs are doing in Croatia. Declaring independence will bring violence to our door."

"We are in the middle of nowhere," Reuf said. "No one cares what happens on this little mountain. They would not be able to find us if they tried."

"You are wrong, brother," Babo said. "War has a way of finding everyone."

"All our lives, we have dreamt of independence, and now it is here," Reuf said. "The hour has come at last."

"Independence from whom?" Babo calmly asked. "Why do you think that a new government will treat us any better or worse? All men have ambition. All men seek power for their own gain."

"But it will be men like us who make the laws, not some tyrant in Belgrade."

"Men like us? Farmers? Is that who will be making the laws?"

Nura could hear sarcasm in her father's tone and anger in her uncle's reply.

"Muslims," Reuf said. "We will control our destiny."

"My brother, when is the last time you saw me in a mosque? Does my wife cover her beautiful hair with cloth? No. I am a mason...a farmer. I want to build houses and raise my family and my cows. I want to be left alone. I do not care about your politics."

"You are a child," her uncle fumed. "You cover your eyes with your hands and think that the problem will go away. To say that you do not care about politics is to be a man adrift on the ocean who says that he does not care about water."

Nura loved her uncle. He was kind, like Babo, although he sometimes walked with his head a little too high in the clouds. He had given her a new book every year on her birthday and had taken her to Tuzla to explore the Salt Museum and get lost in the collection of books at the library. But in that moment when Reuf called Babo a child, she hated her uncle for treating her father that way. The two men were not just brothers—and neighbors—but friends. Babo had told her stories of the two of them as children, boys in search of adventure in the woods, each looking out for the other. How could something now make them argue that way?

"I have a wife and children to think of," Babo said. "What would you have me do?"

"We are forming counsels and militias—pockets of men who can act when the time comes. The steel is hot and ready to be forged. Plans need to be made. I want you at my side. I want you there when we raise our flag over a country that we will build together."

"Will I be able to raise my cows under this new flag of yours?"

"Of course you will."

"Will I be able to ply my trade as a mason?"

"Yes."

"So I would gain what I have now."

"Don't you want to be free?"

Babo sounded tired, or maybe sad, as he gave his reply. "Brother, the freedom that I seek is the freedom to be left alone . . . to build things with my hands . . . to raise my cows. I have a son and daughter to think about. I'm sorry, but I will not join you. I will not invite trouble to my home."

Before another word could be spoken, the porch door opened and Mama looked down at Nura sitting with Danis. "What are you doing?" she asked.

"Nothing," Nura said, her voice cracking slightly.

"Come inside."

Nura stood and led Danis into the house, her eyes cast down as they passed Babo and Uncle Reuf. Danis didn't understand any of what was happening and asked Mama what she was making for supper.

Mama placed a hand on Nura's shoulder and, in a gentle voice, said, "I'm making burek. Would you like to help?"

Nura smiled at Mama's forgiveness. She loved her mama's quiet ways, how she kept some things between the two of them. And she loved her mama's burek. Danis jumped and squealed with delight. Burek was his favorite.

Then to the men, Mama said, "Reuf, you are welcome to stay and eat with us, but there will be no more talk of politics. Is that understood?" Her words were like iron.

Uncle Reuf wilted as he gave his answer. "There will be no more talk," he said.

As they ate their meal that night, Nura couldn't help replaying the argument between Babo and Uncle Reuf, one of Babo's comments echoing louder than all the others. *War has a way of finding everyone.*

Was there going to be a war?

3

Minnesota

AFTER EVERYTHING

Hana comes out of the restroom in search of mooring, her gait made unsteady by a tumult of memories. It is Amina's hand, of all things, that finds its way through the muddle, the way Hana held it on that darkest of nights so long ago—and again later, on the brightest of days when Amina gave birth to her only child, Sara. Years later, Hana held Amina's hand as Sara walked down the aisle at her wedding. Hana sat with Amina the day Sara gave birth to Dylan, and she held Amina's hand as they lowered Sara's casket into the ground two years later. She and Amina were supposed to grow old together, share the aches of time over coffee and cake. Now she will never be able to touch the hand of her friend again.

Claypool had asked about the significance of the blue marble; he may as well have asked the significance of rain in a time of drought. But why had Amina handed the marble to those men? If the blue marble had been a message, it was one meant for her alone. But what had Amina been trying to say?

Hana slips into a row of books to get away from Barb's watchful eyes and to steady herself against a shudder of grief. Poor Amina. A lifetime ago they survived a crucible that would have laid waste to the strongest of men. Why now? Why Amina? Unlike Hana, Amina had left no wake. It doesn't make sense.

Hana tries to put herself in Amina's head after the fall, enough strength for one last gesture. In Hana's mind she watches Amina pull the necklace off, hold it in her hand. But nothing comes to her.

Claypool said that Amina's killer tore her condo apart like he was searching for something. Or had he been searching for *someone?* After all these years...could it be possible? Why not? Hana knows all too well how the bitter taste of revenge can linger on the tongue.

She composes herself, steps out of the stacks, and makes her way to one of the library's computers. She opens an incognito search so that the computer won't hold on to the information, then types the name *Nura Divjak*. She finds the site she's looking for. It ends with the suffix ".rs"—Republic of Serbia.

She clicks on it, steadying her breath as the page fills her screen.

It's a rendering of what they believe she should look like now that she is nearly fifty years old. They have the nose wrong. She has grown into it over the years so it doesn't look as big as it had when she was a teenager. Thirty years ago, they had used an old school photograph. Now it's an artist's sketch of a woman who has no smile. That part, at least, they got right.

Hana looks around. No one seems to be paying attention to her; still, her heart beats hard in her chest. She scrolls down to read:

REWARD—EIGHT MILLION DINARS
For the capture of
Nura Divjak—the Night Mora
Wanted for the murder of innocent civilians
In Bosnia Herzegovina—1995

The first time she saw her Wanted poster it had been a worn piece of paper handed to her by a friend, back when the reward had been only three million dinars, not eight. That older poster also promised the reward for either her capture or her death. They had removed the death part; apparently the international community frowns upon such assassinations. Still, the people who might hunt her would know that the money—about seventy thousand dollars—will be paid either way.

A rustle of shoes on carpeting pulls Hana's attention. Deb Hansen is wandering toward her, a book in her hand, her finger pressed between pages to mark her place. Hana closes the computer window, and Deb takes a seat in the chair beside her.

If the Farmington library had a patron saint, it would be Deb Hansen. She had been the director when Hana got the job, back when Hana could barely speak English. Of all the people who applied for the position, Deb had taken on the one with no degree in library science, no high school diploma. She had gone with a refugee whose past was a mix of half-truths and forgeries. She had hired a girl who hid terrible secrets beneath her drab cardigan sweaters. Deb had given Hana a break when she didn't deserve one, and Hana never forgot that kindness.

Now Deb serves as president of the Friends of the Library, which makes sense because, even in retirement, she spends more time at the library than she does at home. And if Hana ever needs reassurance that kindness exists in this world, she need only think of Deb.

Deb leans in to Hana and in a low voice asks, "Are you okay?"

"Is it that obvious?" Hana says.

Deb shrugs and then nods.

"A close friend has died," Hana tells her.

"Oh, I'm so sorry. It wasn't one of our patrons, was it?"

"No."

"And that man ... who was talking to you ... he's a relative?"

"A detective."

"Oh my." Deb clutches a hand to her collar. "Was your friend...I mean, was she...?"

"She fell from a balcony," Hana says. "He wanted some background on her, that's all."

"You should ask Barb for the rest of the day off," Deb whispers. "Hell, take the rest of the week. You've earned that much."

"I think I'd rather stay here. I don't want to be alone with my thoughts right now."

Deb puts a hand on Hana's shoulder. Gives a pat. "Just...don't lock it away," she says. "Grief needs to be felt—expressed. When my Arnold died, I bottled it up to the point that I couldn't eat or sleep. Then one day I cracked. I just started crying and couldn't stop. All day from sunup to sundown. I had said goodbye to him at the funeral, but it wasn't until that day of crying that I said goodbye to him in my heart."

Deb takes a moment to herself before continuing. "All I'm saying is don't be afraid to take some time off if you need it."

"Thanks." Hana gives Deb's hand a pat.

Deb stands. "And if you need a friend to talk to..."

"I will," Hana says.

After Deb leaves, Hana's thoughts return to Amina. She had once said that their friendship had been chiseled from marble. Hana liked the sentiment, even though she saw relationships more as water. Marble is inflexible, solid, unchangeable unless the stone splits apart. On the other hand, water can join and separate. It can be large and turbulent like a sea or small and placid like a puddle. And if relationships were capable of high tides and low tides, she and Amina had been on a low tide over the last few months, the lull born of history. Amina's grandson, Dylan, had reached an age that brought back too many painful memories for Hana, and rather than face them, Hana had pushed Amina—and Dylan—away.

Maybe that was why Hana knew so little about the man named Zaim. Occasional phone calls, a few texts here and there, were no substitute for an afternoon of deep conversation. Had she asked more questions, talked to Amina more, maybe she would have seen the danger coming.

Their last conversation had been a week ago. Amina called Hana to tell her that she had ended her relationship with Zaim. At the time, Hana had been relieved, because all she knew about the guy was that he liked to flatter Amina and then borrow money.

"I don't trust him," Amina had said. "He's not the man I thought he was."

"All men say nice things when they are trying to take something from you," Hana said. "Some men just cannot be trusted. It's good that you found this out early."

"There's no doubt, he is not to be trusted," she'd said.

Hana pressed for more, but Amina gave a wistful sigh and said that it was a long story best told over a cup of coffee.

They never had their cup of coffee, and now they never will.

Zaim wasn't the man Amina thought he was. She didn't trust him. Those offhand comments now take on immeasurable weight.

Hana opens a new search on her computer and types *Zaim* into the box. How many men named Zaim can there be in America? She gets eight million hits. She narrows the search by adding the word *Minnesota* to the query and gets just under one million hits. Amina must have mentioned his last name at some point, but try as she might, nothing comes to Hana.

He was from Bosnia, though. Hana remembers asking Amina if he had been in the war.

"We haven't talked about that," Amina had said. "Questions like that open doors that I'm not ready to walk through."

After twenty minutes of dead ends, Hana closes her search window.

She doesn't know his last name or what he looks like. She may as well be searching the internet with her eyes closed.

If the blue marble had been meant as a warning, the message was garbled. All Hana could think was that someone from a place far away and a time long ago had found their way to Minnesota. If someone from the war had at last killed Amina, it made sense that they would also be here for her, too.

Hana had learned long ago that it was better to be the hunter than the hunted. But she had been a very different person then, a girl forged by tragedy and rage, capable of acts that would stun her current coworkers. Still, the vestiges of that girl must reside within her somewhere, relics buried beneath thirty years of ash and rust. The time has come to dig.

Detective Claypool must suspect Zaim of having a role in Amina's death. Zaim had been the only name he asked about. He must know more. If she could get him to reveal something—anything—it would at least give her a bread crumb to follow. It would be a place to start.

Hana pulls his card from her pocket. Hesitates. Then types his number into her phone.

"Detective Claypool here."

"Detective, this is Hana Babić…from the library. I'm sorry for how I acted—"

"Please, don't be sorry. I have never been good at breaking bad news to people."

"Um…you said that you'd like to talk some more…when I am feeling up to it."

"Yes."

"I think I'm feeling up to it."

4

Bosnia

1992

B abo had been right about the war finding them, but when it came it did not arrive with the thunderclap of shells or the roar of tanks—not at first. Rather, it came with hard stares and whispers in dark corners.

Nura attended a small school in Petrovo, a village of two thousand people, the vast majority of them Serbian. There were few Muslims in her school and only her in her class, but such things didn't matter to Nura. For her, school was an opportunity to leave her mountain and be with other kids—to make friends. And by the time she was a teenager, Nura had two of the best friends a girl could want: Jovana and Tanja.

As children, the three of them had spent their recesses together: hopscotching, running, and playing with dolls. They grew up talking about boys, and music, and things that weighed heavily on a young girl's mind. Nura had stayed the night at both of their houses, shared meals with both of their families, and slept in the same bed with them.

For her fourteenth birthday, Tanja gave Nura ten beautiful blue marbles, a color that Tanja said reminded her of the Adriatic Sea, her family having spent a week in Dubrovnik a few years earlier. Nura had never seen the sea, but the marbles matched the picture she had in her mind. They were mere bobbles, yet Nura cherished that gift.

That night, she slept at Jovana's home, a small cottage in the country outside of Petrovo. They ate a spiced chicken that melted on Nura's tongue, and for dessert they had soćni kolaći, a rich cake with raisins and walnuts that Jovana's mother made. They watched romantic movies on Jovana's VCR. Jovana's little brother, Ratko, who was ten, sat with them and made puking sounds every time the people on TV kissed.

When they finally climbed into bed, Jovana gave Nura a friendship bracelet she had made, strings of red, green, and gold tightly woven into small diagonal lines. Jovana tied it around Nura's wrist and Nura promised to never take it off.

Two months later, Nura spent New Year's Eve at Tanja's home, a house as nice as any in Petrovo. It had been the first time that Nura counted down the final seconds of the year. But the moment that stayed with Nura wasn't the clang of noisemakers when the clock struck midnight. It was when Tanja's older brother, Luka, kissed Nura on the cheek to celebrate the passing of the year, a small peck that made Nura feel like she was falling.

He was four years older than Nura and had locks of golden hair that danced as he walked. He was the kind of boy she pictured when reading stories about heroes and princes. Slavic mythology spoke of a god of thunder named Perun, usually pictured as a man with a long beard and flowing white hair, but Nura liked to imagine that if Perun had ever existed, he would be young, and strong, with piercing blue eyes, like Luka.

But other than that New Year's Eve peck, Luka never acknowledged Nura, the gangly girl with the nose a little too big for her face.

Two months later, Bosnia declared its independence from Belgrade. The next day, Jovana and Tanja stopped talking to Nura, turning their backs on her whenever she came near. By April, the two began calling her Yak, a shortened version of Bosniak, a word meant to suggest that she smelled bad. Jovana's brother Ratko started calling Nura "the Muslim whore."

One day, Jovana and Tanja caught Nura behind the school and threw her to the ground. Tanja sat on Nura's chest, pinning her arms down, while Jovana cut the friendship bracelet from Nura's wrist with a knife. That same evening, a convoy of Serbian soldiers were ambushed leaving Tuzla. Ninety-two members of the Yugoslav People's Army were killed and another thirty-three were wounded, shot by soldiers from the Bosnian Territorial Guard.

The next day, Mama and Babo told Nura that she would not be going back to school.

* * *

After that, Nura's world shrank. Babo and Uncle Reuf felled a dozen trees where the trail to their houses left the highway, hiding the turnoff from strangers. The only remaining path to civilization was a tractor groove that twisted through the woods behind Uncle Reuf's house, cutting its way down the back side of the mountain to a pasture. Beyond the pasture lay the blacktop that went north to Petrovo—a Serbian town—or south to Tuzla, which was under the control of the Bosnians.

Uncle Reuf had an old truck that could make it down the rough trail, and he sometimes snuck into Tuzla for supplies, but Babo's Yugo remained parked in the machine shed.

After the Serbs cut electricity to the mountain, Babo built a generator from an old mortar mixer and used a waterfall in the creek to power it. The generator produced enough electricity to run refrigerators and a few lights in both houses.

Babo and Uncle Reuf also began spending their days in the forest hunting deer or boar. Sometimes Nura heard gunfire in the distance, not the single report of a man shooting at game but sporadic exchanges that lasted hours, faint echoes that reminded her that somewhere out there men were fighting a war. And even though she feared for Babo and Uncle Reuf on those days, it didn't stop her from wanting to go hunting with them.

On a calm night in July, when the sound of gunfire had been absent for weeks, the family sat for a dinner of beets and potatoes. Babo and Uncle Reuf lamented their bad luck in not having brought home meat for a while. Nura mentally prepared her pitch. When she thought the moment was right, she said, "I can help you hunt."

Both men looked at her as if she had just asked to sleep on the roof. Then Babo smiled and put his hand on hers. "We are not starving just yet. We have five cows for meat if we need them."

"But if I go hunting with you, we can spare the cows until later. I'm a good shot." Babo had taught her how to shoot his squirrel rifle, although she had never actually shot at anything more than a tin can.

"It is too dangerous," he said. "Reuf and I can take care of it."

"There hasn't been fighting in a long time," she said. "Besides, I'll be with you and—"

"It is not for girls," Uncle Reuf said.

Babo gave him a stern glance before looking into his daughter's eyes, his face clouded with apology. "I love you, my sweet daughter. And I appreciate that you want to help, but I would not be a good father if I let you follow us. We go beyond our mountain, where the woods are not safe. You help me by taking care of the cows and the farm while I am gone. That is more than enough."

Babo had spoken and that was the end of it. They finished their meal without another word on the matter, Nura hiding her disappointment in silence.

The next morning, Babo asked Nura to accompany him to the machine shed. There he picked a coil of thin wire from a nail on the wall and handed it to Nura. She looked to Babo for an explanation.

"You cannot join us for the hunt," he said, "but I can teach you to set snares. It is still hunting, but you will make the prey come to you."

Nura tried to be appreciative, but her effort fell short. Babo smiled and led her into the woods. They walked until Babo pointed to a rabbit run, a trail in the grass that showed where the rabbits liked to travel. Nura had walked past that spot a hundred times but had never noticed the tamped grass.

"If you were a rabbit, would you walk along that path or fight through the thicket?"

"I would take the path," Nura said.

"Then that is where we will set our snare."

Babo knelt beside the path with the wire and a set of pliers. He unspooled about half a meter of wire and clipped it off. "We're going to start with a simple slipknot snare. Someday, if you want, I will teach you to make more sophisticated snares with triggers, but for now this is all you will need."

He twisted one end into a tiny loop and slid the wire through to make a slipknot. Then he anchored it to the base of a sapling next to the trail.

"Make the loop about the size of your hand," he said. "And place it..." He took Nura's hand and touched the tip of her fingers to the ground. "Just above your knuckles. That's about where the head of the rabbit will be."

"What if he ducks under?" Nura asked.

Babo smiled with pride. "You are a smart one, my Nura."

He found a twig nearby, broke it to the size of a pencil, and jammed it into the ground beneath the loop. "With this stick here, the rabbit will raise his head as he passes."

Babo got up off his knees with a mild grunt, and stepped back to inspect his work. "Now, it is very important that you check your trap every day, because if you catch a rabbit, you do not want it to suffer. Do you understand?"

Nura nodded, even though she had assumed that they would be leaving the woods with that day's supper in hand. As they stood together, admiring the snare, Nura asked, "Babo, why do the Serbs want to hurt us?"

Babo thought for a bit, and said, "I don't think Yugoslavia was ever meant to be a country. There are faction—"

"No, I mean us...our family. We have done nothing wrong. We are not soldiers. We are not even Muslims—not really. We do not observe salat. We do not pray at the mosque. Can we just tell them? Maybe they will leave us alone."

Babo put an arm around her. "Like it or not, my child, we are at war. It doesn't matter that we are not soldiers. The Serbs have such hatred for us that they will not look for uniforms. They will not ask if we are observant in our faith. They will see us as their enemy and do us harm."

"Why?"

Again, Babo gave her question considerable thought before he answered. "Men have the capacity for good as much as they have the capacity for cruelty. What is right and what is wrong is written on our hearts. But when there is war, men follow what they choose to follow and rationalize the evil they do. The Serbs see this as their country. They see us as a blight. They are told that the only way to have peace is to expel us or kill us. When such are the words they hear every minute of every day, it becomes too loud for them to listen to their hearts. They will do terrible things and believe they are doing what is right."

Nura wanted to tell her babo how proud she was to have him as her father. She wanted to say that he was the wisest man in the world. Instead, she leaned her head to his shoulder and said, "I will be the finest hunter in all the land...even if it is only with snares."

*   *   *

That evening, she caught her first rabbit, carrying it home with enough pride to fill the barn. She hid her queasiness as Babo led her through the task of cleaning the meat. She had seen him and Uncle Reuf butcher cows before, but only from a distance. She had never held a knife to flesh, but if she was going to be a hunter, she would have to do such things.

She used Babo's knife, a folding knife with two blades and a worn black handle. He had carried that knife in his front right pocket for as long as Nura could remember. When she finished skinning the rabbit, she cleaned his knife and handed it back to him—but he didn't take it.

"I think it is time that you have a knife of your own," he said.

The thought of Babo giving her something so personal, something so much a part of him, almost made her cry, but she held her tears back. She was a hunter and hunters don't cry.

The rabbit offered far less meat than she had expected, but Mama cooked it into a stew and everyone praised her for the meal she had provided.

* * *

By 1995, they were down to three cows despite Nura's growing proficiency as a trapper and Babo's daily hunting trips.

When Danis's birthday came that spring, Nura made him a slingshot, cutting the handle from an oak branch and slicing strips of rubber from a used inner tube for the bands. The pocket was a patch of leather sawed from the heel of an old boot. To make the present extra special, Nura wrapped the ten blue marbles that Tanja had given her when she was fourteen—ten perfect little balls he could use for ammunition.

Of all the presents he opened that year, her slingshot was his favorite. He fired stones, nuts, bolts, and ball bearings that he stole from Babo's machine shed, anything small that had weight. But the marbles he treasured. He only shot the marbles at a paper target that he pinned to the wall of the barn, being careful to find each again before having another go.

One day, they were sitting at the pond, Nura teaching Danis about fractions as he shot stones at a nearby tree. Danis stopped shooting and stared blankly at the pond.

"What's wrong?" Nura asked.

He didn't answer at first, but then said, "Will I ever go to school?"

"Someday you will."

"Promise?"

Nura smiled to hide her doubt. "Yes, my little tadpole. I promise."

"Will they make me be a soldier?"

"What?"

"I don't want to be a soldier."

Nura patted her leg and Danis sat. That was the thing about Danis: He was eight years old, an age when other boys would recoil at the notion of sitting on their big sister's lap, but Danis never seemed to outgrow being her baby brother. He was smart and beautiful, with dark eyes that danced when she told him Mama's stories about the woodland faeries that walked through the trees at night. And she hated how the sound of gunfire in the distance sometimes caused her little brother to curl up and hide his face.

"It would make me sad to hurt anyone like that," he said.

She wrapped her arms around him. "I will never let them take you away. I will never let them make you a soldier."

"The war scares me."

"You don't need to be scared." Nura held Danis tightly to her. "I will protect you."

"Promise?"

"I promise." She kissed the top of his head. "The war will be over soon," she said.

"And I will be able to go to school?"

"Yes...and you will get to play with the other boys. It will not be long. You will see."

Nura hated how easily she had lied.

* * *

When they emerged from the woods that day, they saw Uncle Reuf's truck, a beat-up old monster he called the Torpedo, parked in the courtyard, suitcases loaded in the back. Inside, Mama shooed them upstairs, which always meant that the men were talking politics. Nura was seventeen and wanted to stay with the adults, but Mama was firm. It didn't matter, because Nura could listen through the heat register.

"These are very dangerous times," Uncle Reuf said. "Very few Muslims remain in these hills. Most have gone to Tuzla to the refugee camp near the airport."

"If we keep our heads," Babo said, "we will outlast the war."

Reuf then spoke with a heaviness that Nura had never heard from her uncle. "I am leaving. They are calling for men to go defend Srebrenica. The Serbs are tightening their siege."

"What good will you be to them if the city is under siege?"

"I cannot speak of independence and then not heed the call to help my brothers. And you...should take your family to Tuzla," Reuf said. "It's safer than staying on this mountain."

"What do they care about our little farm?" Mama said. "We have no strategic value to them."

"They intend to drive us from the land by any means," Reuf said. "They expelled the Muslims from Foća, and Zvornik, and Višegrad."

"Expelled?" Mama asked.

"A man from Foća told me that they murdered civilians there. Hundreds, maybe thousands. But that is not all. The man said that Serbian soldiers...took advantage of the women. They created...I can't..."

"Say it," Mama said. "We need to know what is happening."

"The man called them...rape camps," Reuf said. "Special prisons where the women are..."

"That cannot be true," Babo said.

"I wish it were not," Reuf said. "They treat us worse than animals to spread fear so that people will run and not fight. But things will turn around, and when they do, we will bring them to justice—every last one of them. We will not let them get away with such inhumanity. That is why I must go."

Nura couldn't sleep that night. She had always envisioned war as men in uniforms standing on opposing hillsides firing their weapons at each other. Civilians were supposed to be off-limits. Women were supposed to be left untouched—*she* was supposed to be left untouched.

*   *   *

A month later, as Nura spread straw bedding for their three remaining cows, Uncle Reuf's story of the man from Foća came back to her—for it was in that moment that she heard the hum of the truck engine climbing up the back side of her mountain.

5

Minnesota

AFTER EVERYTHING

Detective Claypool suggests that Hana come to the police station in St. Paul to continue their discussion, a mere thirty-minute drive for her, but she has no desire to go to a place with interrogation rooms and locked doors.

She declines his invitation with the lie that she doesn't feel up to making the drive. He offers to come to her house, but she declines that even faster. Finally, he suggests a restaurant in Rosemount, ten minutes for Hana and twice that for Claypool. Neutral ground. No locked rooms. No phalanx of people with badges and guns. Hana agrees.

The restaurant squats in a strip mall between a nail salon and a hockey training center. Parking is easy, and when she gets inside Hana is pleasantly surprised by the decor: faux tin roof, red chairs tucked up against dark wooden tables. There is a bar in the middle, but the seating is spread out to give a pretense of intimacy. She spots Claypool seated at a table near a stone fireplace, the flames low enough to be a source of ambience but not heat. He waves her over.

He stands when she approaches his table. He has taken off the tweed jacket. His white shirt is clean. No tie. No sweat stains on the collar. Sleeves rolled to the elbow to show solid forearms, arms like her father had, firm from all those years of working with stone. His shoulders seem bigger and broader than she would have expected for a man his age. The tweed jacket he wore to the library did him no favors.

Hana wears the same gray skirt and blue cardigan that she'd worn to work. The sweater has a small moth hole in the right sleeve near the elbow, a flaw that had been absent from her thoughts when she'd met with Claypool at the library. She folds her arms and covers the hole with her fingers.

"I've never been here before," he says as he waits for her to sit.

Hana has never been to that restaurant either, and the place is only ten minutes away from the library. She's gone out of her way to make her world small.

"You're looking better," Claypool says. Then to clarify, he adds, "Than when I left you."

"I feel better."

A waitress stops at the table and asks if they want to order drinks. Claypool looks to Hana.

"No thank you," Hana says.

"Just water," Claypool says.

When the waitress leaves, Claypool laces his fingers together, appraising Hana as he had at the library. "I was hoping you might be able to fill in some details that we're missing," Claypool says.

"About?"

"Gaps in Amina's history."

Hana tightens her jaw before catching herself. Claypool's eyes are soft and brown, and hold to her like he's studying something complex. Hana does her best to not look away.

"We know she was the legal guardian for her grandson," he says. "Are you familiar with how Dylan's parents died?"

"A boating accident. Sara—Amina's daughter—and her husband

were on the St. Croix in a canoe. A friend of theirs was on a Jet Ski. He wanted to splash them. The friend lost control and hit them."

"Did you know Sara well?"

"I was there when she was born."

"You've known Amina for a long time."

"Yes."

"And Sara was born just after Amina came to the States, right?"

Hana's jaw tightens again.

"Did you know her before she came here?"

"You asked me that already."

"Did I?"

"Yes. And I told you that I didn't know Amina before she came to America." She holds eye contact with Claypool to sell her lie. "Amina was alone. She needed a friend."

"Dylan's parents died when he was, what…two?"

"Yes."

"So, Amina's the only parent he's ever known?"

"He called her Mama Mina. I don't believe Dylan has any memory of Sara. There are pictures, of course, but a picture cannot tuck a little boy into his bed at night."

The waitress comes with waters and asks if they are ready to order. Hana hadn't looked at the menu, but figures that the restaurant likely serves chicken Caesar salad, and asks for one. Claypool gives the menu a quick glance and orders the same.

After the waitress leaves, Claypool asks, "Was Amina pregnant when she came from Bosnia?"

"What does that have to do with her death?"

"Maybe nothing, but maybe something. With this kind of investigation—where there is no clear suspect or motive—we have to keep our minds open. Anything could be important."

"I thought you had a suspect."

"I do?"

"That guy, Zaim."

"Let's just say he's on the list."

"Am I on the list?"

"Should you be?"

Claypool's eyes don't seem soft anymore. But then he smiles. "I don't really have a list. I'm just trying to figure this thing out."

Seeing an opening, Hana says. "Tell me what you have. Maybe I can help."

Claypool looks at Hana for a long moment before his face turns serious and he nods.

"There's something I didn't tell you before. Amina had been gagged when she... Well, one of the workers loosened the gag. When Amina handed those workers that necklace, she was trying to say something. She managed a single word before she lost consciousness. One of the men thought she said 'please,' but the other man was sure she said..."

"She said...?"

"It makes no sense, but he thought she said the word 'bliss.'"

Hana works to hold her expression in check. She knows the word, and it is as befuddling to her as the necklace itself. She considers what she might tell Claypool and what she must never reveal.

When she is ready, she says, "The word is 'Iblis.'"

"Iblis? Is that a name?"

"It is."

"First name or last?"

"Iblis was an angel, formed by Allah out of fire. You would know him as Satan or the devil."

"Why would Amina say that name as her final act?"

Hana takes a sip of water, her throat suddenly dry with the dust of old memories. She says, "How much do you know about the war in Bosnia, Detective?"

"Um..."

"You saw it on TV, maybe? Footage of old men and women being forced out of their villages? Soldiers riding around on the tops of tanks waving flags that held no meaning for you?"

"I guess."

"Do you know about the genocide? Thousands upon thousands of innocent Bosnians killed for being Muslim?"

"I heard about that, but I guess I can't put much meat on the bones."

"Did you ever hear about the rape camps?"

Claypool swallows, but otherwise gives no reaction.

"Bosnian women, picked off the streets and taken to abandoned hotels, gymnasiums, barns, and raped by Serbian soldiers. Burned with their cigars. Beaten."

"Amina had two small, round scars on her back. Were those...?"

"Cigar burns."

"I had no idea."

"Rape was a tactic of war. They needed us to fear them so that we would run from them. Leave the country. Their strategy was to expel us. And those who didn't leave were starved or shot. The soldiers were told that our expulsion—our death—was needed for the protection of the Serbian people. But I believe it was much simpler."

Hana's words grow in volume as she speaks, and she leans over the table to make sure that Claypool is paying close attention.

"They did it because they wanted to. We have both light and dark within us, Detective Claypool. We can search for our better angels or we can give in to Iblis. Those men had the desire to hurt us. They had the power to hurt us. And when the war started, they were given permission to hurt us."

Hana jabs a finger into the tabletop to accentuate her final words. "They raped us...and tortured us...because they could. Iblis raped Amina. She never referred to him by any other name."

Claypool glances up, looking beyond Hana's shoulder. She turns to see their waitress holding two plates and an expression of horror. "Um...your dinners are ready," she says.

Hana leans back to give the poor girl room to serve the salads.

"Will there be anything else?" the waitress asks timidly.

Hana offers an apologetic smile. "No, thank you." The waitress leaves.

"Do you know who her Iblis was? If he's still alive—"

"He is not alive."

"Are you sure?"

"Yes, I am sure."

"How would you know? I mean—"

Hana's mind swims with the image of Amina's rapist—Iblis—as he lay dying at Hana's feet, his blood dripping from her hands. Again, Hana lies. "Amina told me that he is dead...and she wouldn't lie about something like that."

"So why would she use her last breath to say 'Iblis'?"

"Her rapist—her Iblis—wasn't the only monster in Bosnia. Iblis lived in every camp. He roamed the mountains killing innocent women and children."

"So you believe that Amina's killer is someone from her past—someone from Bosnia."

Hana wants to kick herself for letting that slip. "I have no idea who killed Amina or why."

She takes a bite of her salad and waits for Claypool to say something. When he doesn't, she can't help but fill the silence. "My father once told me that what is right and what is wrong is written on our hearts—that we need only pay heed. Still, I have come to believe that the world is overpopulated by men who will take the path of cruelty far too easily."

"I can't disagree with that. As a homicide detective, I see it every day. But...I hope you don't think all men are like that. Some of us are the good guys."

Hana looks at Claypool's left hand. No ring. "Would I be wrong in assuming that you are divorced?"

Claypool sits up like a man caught off guard by the snarl of a dog. His shoulders ease and his eyes fall in surrender. "Yeah, I am divorced."

"If I asked your ex-wife, would she say you were a good guy?"

Claypool picks up a fork and sifts through his salad, but doesn't take a bite. They sit in silence for a minute before Claypool says, "Is that why Amina was seeing a therapist?"

"How do you know about that?"

"I'm a detective. It's what I do."

When Hana doesn't respond, he says, "We found a letter from a Dr. Ellsworth in her condo, also some bills and canceled checks. We know she was seeing a therapist. Was that to deal with . . . all that happened to her?"

"It is not unusual that a refugee might seek help to deal with the traumas of war, is it?"

"No. But I have to look into everything if I'm going to be thorough. Do you know what she talked about in her sessions?"

Amina had promised to never utter the name Hana Babić to her therapist. Still, the thought of Claypool digging through those notes— the possibility that Amina may have let something slip—sends a chill through Hana's veins. "Is the therapist important to the case?"

"I've told you more than I should have already," he says. "I can't discuss the details of an ongoing investigation." Claypool lifts his jacket off the seat and reaches into its pocket, pulling out a piece of paper. "But I can share this." He unfolds the paper and hands it to Hana. "We found it when we searched the apartment. It's a page from Amina's last will and testament. Read that bottom paragraph."

Hana reads:

Having no living relative, I nominate Hana Babić as legal guardian of the person and estate of my minor grandson Dylan Greene and as custodian under the Minnesota Uniform Transfer of Minors Act.

Hana reads it again, then looks at Claypool. "I don't understand."

"What's to understand?" Claypool says. "She wants you to raise Dylan."

"But, I'm not...Amina never said anything..." She pauses to collect her thoughts, and her mind flashes to Danis, to the promises she had made but never kept. She closes her eyes to wipe away the memory.

"The law doesn't bind you," Claypool says. "You're Amina's choice, but you have no obligation."

"And if I refuse?"

"If you refuse? Dylan stays in foster care. Maybe gets adopted, maybe not. Sometimes foster care works out, but a lot of times it doesn't."

Hana lays the paper on the table and slides it to Claypool.

He slides it back. "It's a copy. I wrote the attorney's name and number on the back. Think about it, and when you decide, give him a call."

Hana folds the paper until it fits into the pocket of her sweater. She thinks about how she sat at her kitchen table that morning, eating a breakfast of oatmeal and blueberries. Her friend Amina had been alive then—at least as far as Hana knew. Dylan had been just another carefree little boy. Hana's biggest concern that morning had been whether to carry an umbrella to work. She hadn't prepared for any of this.

But Hana had learned long ago that living was like walking atop an old fence rail. Get too comfortable, too trusting, and you invite the fall.

6

Bosnia

1995

That day, Danis had been helping Nura muck the barn, at least to the extent that an eight-year-old can be helpful in such a chore. His shovel weighed almost as much as he did, and he could do little more than scoop a lump or two at a time. When he spied a stray cat that had moved into their hayloft, he dropped his shovel and ran to the ladder to chase it.

"What are you doing?" Nura said.

"I want to pet it," Danis called over his shoulder as he climbed.

"She is too fast," Nura said. "You will never catch her."

He stopped on the ladder to look at Nura, the disappointment in his eyes unmistakable.

"If you want to pet her, you will need to tame her first."

"How do I do that?"

Nura beckoned him with a finger. When he was close, she knelt to be eye-to-eye with Danis. "You must make her trust you. If you feed her every day, she will see that you have a kind heart. It will take time."

"What should I feed her?"

"There is leftover rabbit stew in the refrigerator. Get a small piece of meat—but don't let Mama see you."

42

She gave him a wink and he ran off.

She had been listening for his returning footsteps when she heard the rumbling cadence of the truck engine in the distance. It started small from somewhere far down the mountain, the sound climbing the tractor path behind Uncle Reuf's house. At first, Nura thought it was her uncle returning despite his vow to make his stand in Srebrenica, but something about the low growl of the engine as it crept up the slope told her that it was not Reuf's truck.

Nura stepped through the barn door, pitchfork in hand, ready to run to the house, when she saw Babo come around the far side of the machine shed, his hands black with grease from working on the tractor. Babo waved her back into the barn and ran to meet the intruders.

The truck engine grew louder, and although Nura couldn't see it on the other side of the house, she could hear it crest the hill behind Uncle Reuf's barn and pull into the courtyard.

That's when the yelling began.

A man with a very deep voice hollered an order to "Find Reuf Divjak." Then he called out, "You! Come here!"

Nura wanted to go to her family, but Babo had wanted her to hide.

"On your knees!" the man barked.

Nura couldn't stop herself. She snuck to the house to where the back porch climbed four steps to the door. She was about to sneak up the steps when she remembered the loud creak that would make.

The house had no basement. Rather, it stood on wooden piers that lifted it off the ground, creating a crawl space barely three feet high at its tallest point. There were gates at the front of the house and the back so that animals couldn't get at the potatoes and plum preserves Mama stored under there. Nura slipped under the porch and eased the gate open, entering on her hands and knees and closing the gate behind her.

She wore denim overalls, her work clothes, which made crawling easier than it would have been had she been wearing a dress. Thin spikes of light fell through the slats of the front gate on the far side of the house, illuminating the space enough for Nura to see her way. As a child, she had played in the crawl space, oblivious to the cobwebs and dust, which she now swatted away as she crept toward the front of the house.

At the front gate, she lay on her stomach and peeked through the slats.

A small truck, drab green and boxy, sat parked in the courtyard. She didn't see the soldiers until she moved to look through a knothole in one of the slats—the sight stopping her breath.

Her father knelt in front of a large man who held a machine gun. Babo's hands were raised behind his head, his fingers laced together. The large man had a thick beard, black with prominent streaks of gray on either side of his chin, as though drool from the corners of his mouth had stained his whiskers. He smoked a thick cigar as he jabbed the barrel of the gun into Babo's chest.

A clatter rose from across the courtyard at Uncle Reuf's house. Two soldiers, one old and one young, stepped back out of the front door. "He's not here," the younger man shouted.

When the two men drew near, Nura realized that she knew them. The old one was Stanko Krunić, the father of her friend Jovana. A thin man, he wore the green coat of a soldier, but beneath the coat she could see a checkered shirt, and on his feet he wore the rubber boots of a dairy farmer. His cheeks and chin were dark with stubble, and a cigarette dangled from his lips. He held his machine gun loosely, the way one might carry a dirty shovel.

The other soldier was Luka Savić, the older brother of her friend Tanja, the boy with the golden hair. Nura felt an overwhelming sense of betrayal to see him in a soldier's uniform, a machine gun slung over his shoulder.

These men had been her friends. She had eaten at both of their houses. Stanko's daughter, Jovana, and Luka's sister, Tanja, had been to this very house, played in her barn, eaten at her table, watched television while sitting on Nura's couch. Surely these men could do her family no harm.

The large man with the striped beard turned back to Babo. "Where is your brother?"

"I do not know," Babo said.

The man ordered Stanko, "Bring me this man's family."

"No," Babo cried. "If there is a price to be paid for being a poor Muslim farmer, I will pay it. My family is innocent."

The man cracked the muzzle of his rifle across Babo's face, dropping her father limp to the ground. A gasp escaped Nura's lips, and she bit into the cloth of her sleeve to stop herself from calling out.

Babo rolled to his side and then onto his stomach. Blood trickled from his nose. He struggled to open his left eye.

The porch door above her slammed open, and she heard Danis scream, "Babo!"

No, Danis.

She could see his legs as he charged down the steps toward his father, but he stopped short. He held his slingshot in his left hand, and with his right, he reached into his pocket and pulled out a blue marble.

"No!" It was Mama running out the front door. "Danis, no!"

He fitted the marble into the pocket of the slingshot and drew back the rubber bands. Before Mama could stop him, he let the marble fly.

It sailed true, hitting the bearded man in the face. Luka raised his gun and fired. Three bullets ripped through Danis's chest, opening large holes in his back. Bits of shirt, and blood, and tissue sprayed the air behind him. Danis fell backwards, landing hard on the grass, his head tipped toward Nura, his eyes open and still.

"Danis!" Mama screamed, and dropped to her son's side, his lifeless body slumping as she tried to lift him. "No. Please...no."

The man with the beard muttered something to Luka and then walked over to Mama, grabbing her by the arm and lifting her off the ground. Mama swung her fist at him, but the man took her punch as though it was made of feathers. When she reared back to hit him again, he slapped her across the face so hard that she went sprawling to the ground. She seemed dazed as he grabbed her arm again and— half lifting, half dragging—pulled her to the house, tossing her up the porch steps like an old rag.

His heavy-booted footsteps carried along the floor above Nura to the living room. Nura strained to listen and thought she heard a whimper from her mother. "Please..." And then came music from her father's stereo. The man had turned up the volume to drown out her pleading.

Outside, Babo had worked his way to his hands and knees.

Luka and Stanko snickered as they watched him struggle. They talked quietly. Stanko held up five fingers. Luka shook his head no and held up three fingers. Stanko seemed to consider something before nodding and holding up three fingers.

Stanko stepped in front of Babo, looked at Luka, reared back, and drove his right boot into Babo's face as hard as he could. Babo's head snapped back and he went to the ground like a clod of mud. Stanko laughed and held up one finger.

Nura screamed into her shirtsleeve, her wail drowned out by the loud music coming from above. Her eyes filled with tears. She blinked them away and looked again.

Stanko paced two steps back from Babo and put his gun on the ground as if that was needed to focus his effort. He charged Babo and kicked him in the head with all the power he could muster. Again Babo's head snapped back, and he fell motionless to the ground.

Luka approached and put two fingers to Babo's throat, waited, and then smiled and shook his head no. Stanko flexed his hands into fists as though psyching himself up. He took two deep breaths and drove his foot into Babo's head a third time, the effort seeming to take Stanko to the edge of exhaustion. Luka knelt, put his fingers to Babo's throat, and again shook his head no in obvious delight.

Stanko pulled out his wallet, dug out some money, and handed it to Luka, who received it with smug satisfaction. Then Stanko pointed his gun at Babo and fired a single round into his head.

Nura surrendered to the dirt beneath her. She closed her eyes and prayed for the earth to swallow her. Behind the muffled sound of the music, she heard the crack of a gunshot. Heavy footsteps leaving the house told Nura that her mother, too, was dead.

Tears streamed down Nura's face as she rose to her elbows to again look through the knothole. The man with the beard stepped off the front porch and gave instructions to Stanko and Luka, orders drowned out by the music and the anguished screams that filled her head.

Stanko, the father of her friend Jovana—a man whom she had broken bread with, a man who sometimes hunted on her father's land—picked Danis up by his shirt collar and carried him into the house.

"There's a daughter," Luka said. "She went to school with my sister."

Nura ducked, even though there was no way for anyone to see her through that small hole.

"Search the barn," the man with the beard said. "And kill the cattle."

Luka jogged off, his gun at the ready.

The man with the beard reached into the back of the truck and heaved out a large gas can, unscrewing the top.

Stanko trudged out of the house, grabbed Babo by his boots, and dragged him back to the house, yanking him up the porch one step at a time, Babo's head flopping limp as it hit each riser.

The man with the beard followed with the gas can.

A gunshot sounded from behind the house and one of her cows cried out. The cry was silenced by a second shot.

The smell of gas seeped through the floorboards above her.

Another gunshot and another cow moaned her pain. Two more shots and the moans died away.

The footfalls above her made their way toward the front door, pausing for a moment before—

Whoosh!

The combustion hit her in the back, the heat from the fire wedging its way between the floorboards. Out front, Stanko and the bearded man watched the fire with quiet delight. Nura turned and began scurrying toward the back gate.

The back porch was already engulfed in flames by the time she got there. Beyond the flames, Luka stepped out of the barn, his eyes scanning the property for her. The last of the three cows sauntered out of the woods, pausing at the back edge of the barn before Luka saw it and fired a burst of bullets into the cow's head. She fell dead.

Above her, fire punched through the floor, the heat licking at Nura's back and neck. Smoke rolled through the crawl space, so thick that Nura could no longer see. Her eyes burned. Her throat felt like she was breathing broken glass.

A crash from above sent sparks raining down on her. The floor was alive with fire, the heat unbearable. Beyond the gate, the back porch fell to the ground, cutting off her only supply of air. Her skin felt as though it was being peeled from her body. A bullet was better than burning to death.

She punched the gate open, shoving hard to push it past the burning lattice that once surrounded the back porch. Blinded by the smoke, she felt for the opening.

A piece of burning debris the size of a shoe hit her in the back, spurring her forward. She lunged through the opening, landing on her forearms, the burning lath frying her skin.

She dove ahead, churning with her legs until she cleared the opening and rolled away from the flames. She expected a bullet from Luka's gun—hoped for it. She wanted to join Mama, and Babo, and her beloved Danis. She coughed and gasped, the pain in her arms more than she thought she could endure. Yet when she opened her eyes and blinked away the sting, she saw no Luka.

By now, every inch of the house was ablaze, flames reaching through the windows and licking holes in the roof. Nura struggled to her feet and stumbled toward the courtyard, where the soldiers had been. Surely one of them would have the decency to put a bullet in her. But when she came to the courtyard, they were gone.

She walked to the woods, fighting to stay on her feet, her mind an explosion of pain and grief. One step then another, down the hill until she came to her pond. She took two steps in and fell forward, the cold water bringing the burns on her forearms to life.

Her scream echoed through the mountains.

7

Minnesota

AFTER EVERYTHING

H ana sits on the edge of her bed, her thoughts muddled. The blue
marble had to be Amina's warning to her: Iblis had come. But
who is he? Is he here alone? And how is she supposed to take on a child
when she carried a target on her back?

She is tired of thinking, so she relies on muscle memory to remove
her shoes. Stands. Walks to the dresser. She takes off her cardigan
sweater, touching a finger to the hole in the sleeve. Frayed at the cuffs, it
has outlived many of her other sweaters and probably should be tossed,
but the hole can be mended, the frayed cuffs trimmed and cleaned. She
folds it and lays it on the dresser, her hand lingering on the soft wool.

Her sweaters have been her comfort—her disguise. They make her
invisible, just another middle-aged woman. How could her enemies
find her if they can't see her? But now, it seems, someone is getting close.

She unbuttons her blouse, slips it off, folds it, and lays it on top of
the sweater, then works her hair out of the hair tie, letting her locks fall
past her shoulders. Her cheeks are high and thin, accentuated by mar-
ionette lines that crease the sides of her mouth. She is slim, but there is
definition in her arms, lines of sinew and muscle that she hides beneath

the frumpy clothing. She is only forty-seven but she looks—at least to her eyes—much older. If it is true that a hard life can age a person beyond her years, then Hana deserves credit for not looking older than she does.

She touches the scars, parallel lines that crisscross her forearms, wrinkled like old parchment, a pattern left behind by the burning lattice. She hears her mother's scream, watches Stanko Krunić kick her father in the face. Danis falls as three bullets rip through his heart. She can feel the heat from the fire on the back of her neck.

Hana puts her palms on the dresser to steady herself. It seems she sealed her past behind a wall far too thin to serve its purpose. She waits as the memories pass.

After pulling off her work bra—white and practical—she slips into a running bra, black and tight. She exchanges her gray skirt for a pair of leggings, and her running shirt is long-sleeved and blue. Her shoes are a singular indulgence in her muted existence. She paid two hundred and fifty dollars for them at a store that caters to long-distance runners. She completes her transformation by pulling her long hair into a ponytail and putting on a bandanna to catch the sweat.

It is misting outside, but not yet raining—not that it would matter. She needs this run. The news of Amina's death and her dinner with Claypool have thrown her for a loop. Her ghosts are unrelenting and need to be quieted. Tonight, Hana needs her run the way a dying sinner needs absolution.

She lives in a farmhouse much like the one on her little mountain northwest of Tuzla: two stories, painted siding, wooden floors that creak when you cross them, doors that no longer fit properly in their jambs—although this house has a basement where her childhood home had only a crawl space.

She owns ten acres of land, a mixture of pasture and trees, and behind the house is an old barn that had once been red but has grown gray with age. She raises cows like she did in Bosnia, three of them, just like on the day her world went up in flames. When one grows old, she sells it to a meat locker in town and buys a new calf. Always three.

She steps into the drizzle and starts her run as she does every day, a slow jog out to the end of her long gravel driveway. On the black-top, she begins her three-mile route, which takes her past a handful of farmhouses hidden behind pine windbreaks. Dark clouds gather to the west, the falling rain obscuring the horizon. If the rain is headed her way, she won't make it home before it hits.

Why hadn't Amina ever mentioned that she wanted Hana to be Dylan's guardian? But Hana knows the answer. It was because Hana would have said no.

When Hana held Danis for the first time, she whispered into his ear that she would always protect him. That day at the pond, she'd told him that he would go to school, that he would play with other children. She'd promised to shield him from the war, and then did nothing as Luka Savić shot him to death. Amina knew this and yet bequeathed to Hana a responsibility for which she is woefully unprepared.

Hana's feet clap the wet pavement as she runs. She makes her first turn and, as is her habit, picks up the pace. Her fingers are cold and wet, but the rest of her body is sweating. She wipes the mist from her eyes with the sleeve of her shirt.

How could Amina think that Hana would be a good choice for guardian? If Hana had been more convincing, there would have been no Dylan, because his mother, Sara, would not have been born.

Amina had been sick on the long journey from Bosnia to America. Hana had chalked it up to the ordeal they had survived, or maybe to air sickness, as neither of them had ever been on a plane before. It wasn't until a month into their new lives in America that Amina confessed her condition. Hana had urged Amina to end the pregnancy—argued for it—even offered to pay the expense, but Amina refused.

The day Amina gave birth to Sara, Hana searched her friend's eyes, her smile, her words, for evidence of deceit. How could Amina be happy to have given birth to the aftermath of such an evil act? To carry a reminder of her rapist in her arms. Nurture it. Did she not understand?

"How does she not remind you of what happened?" Hana had asked.

"She does...if I look for that, but I do not. This is Sara," Amina said with quiet pride. "She is my beautiful daughter. She is not Iblis. She carries none of his evil."

"I know you are right, but...I cannot change the way I feel."

"Hatred is a bitter herb," Amina said.

"Sometimes I think that hatred is all I have left."

"That is because you have chosen to live in your memories."

"I live in my memories because that is where my family lives."

Hana has lost track of her pace and is running too fast. Her heart pounds in her chest, and her breathing is labored. As she rounds her second turn, she resets her gait to the internal metronome that guides her runs.

Taking Dylan in would put him in harm's way. If Amina died at the hands of someone from the past—someone now searching for Hana—the last place Dylan would be safe is in her home. Surely Amina would understand this. Leaving him in foster care is the best way to protect him. The foster care system can't be as bad as they say, can it? He is an eight-year-old boy. Smart. Cute. How could someone not adopt him? At least he would be far away from her. He would be safe.

But what if he didn't get adopted? What would happen to him then? A patron at the library once told Hana her story of growing up with foster parents who made her sleep on the floor as punishment for not cleaning her plate at the dinner table.

"It was hell," she had said. "There were nights when I cried myself to sleep. No blanket. No pillow. Winter, summer—it didn't matter."

Surely that is the exception and not the rule. Dylan might find a home with love, and warmth, and siblings. He might grow up in a home where he could want for nothing.

Or he might not.

Again, Hana finds herself far above her pace. She turns the third corner. Only one mile left. Dark clouds have moved in and now hover overhead, the mist turning into a rain that soaks her clothing but feels good on her skin. The sun has fallen, taking with it the last bit of gray from the sky.

She picks up her pace to a full run.

If she had Dylan, though, she would have an excuse to talk to Detective Claypool and get updates on the case. Any tidbit might help. If there is a bounty hunter on her trail, she must find him first. She won't sit around and wait for fate to play its hand. She did that in Bosnia and it cost her a family.

Her lungs burn as she turns the final corner. Heat lightning flashes in the distance, silhouetting the trees at the end of her driveway. A cloud opens above her and the rain falls like it's being poured from a bucket. Thick droplets pelt her face. She sprints the final two hundred yards.

Her legs burn. Her lungs are on fire. Her feet pound. She runs. Harder. Faster. Driving home.

Then she hears Danis whisper, *The war scares me.*

You don't need to be scared, Nura had told him. *I will protect you.*

Promise?

I promise.

She sees Danis lying on the ground, bullet holes in his chest, his cold eyes turned to her.

I will protect you. I promise.

Hana turns into her driveway, spent, her legs trembling. Heaving breaths of chilled night air, she slows to a clomping walk, looks skyward, and opens her mouth to drink the rain that peppers her face.

If Danis were here, he would tell Hana to take the child. Mama and Babo would want that as well. She hears their voices mixing with the tapping of rain on the leaves around her.

She will take the boy, and she will not fail him the way she failed her family.

8

Bosnia

1995

When Nura returned from the woods and the pond, she looked upon the ruins of what had been her home and could barely stay on her feet. Flames still flickered in pockets, but the great conflagration had died away. The second floor had collapsed into the downstairs, and sticks of wood—rafters and wall studs—poked up from the pile like overcooked bones. Veils of smoke lifted from the embers, whipping in the light breeze. Somewhere in that rubble lay her family, tossed and burned like trash.

She had eaten breakfast with them that morning, Mama worrying about the dwindling supply of flour, Babo picking dirt from beneath his fingernails with a toothpick. Danis had told a story of a turtle he'd found that had fallen on its back. When he'd turned it over, the turtle stuck its head out as if to thank Danis for his kindness.

She could not leave them like this, but her mind was too numb to hold a thought.

She walked to Uncle Reuf's house and found the door kicked in by the soldiers. She had been in that house a thousand times, but never when it was empty. Nor had she ever been in Uncle Reuf's bedroom, which is where she went in search of dry clothes. His room smelled of wood oil, and dust, as well as something familiar—old sweat mixed with the dirt from his boots, a scent that had lingered in Babo's closet as well. Nura took a moment to wrap herself in that scent.

She found a short-sleeved shirt and a pair of athletic pants, both too big for her, but they were dry and warm. She unhooked the buckles of her wet overalls and let them drop to the floor. It was then that she noticed that parts of her shirtsleeves had become fused to her skin.

She carefully lifted Babo's knife from her pocket, opened the blade, and cut her sleeves away, her wounds coming alive as she peeled, the pain nearly causing her to pass out. Pustulous burns crisscrossed her forearms, the distinct outline of the burning lattice laid out in shades of white and red. The edges of the wounds hurt the most, the fire having burned away many of the nerve endings in the middle.

Her hair on the left side of her head had been burned short so that it no longer covered her ear. But on the right side her hair still fell to her shoulder. Her left ear and neck were tender to the touch and in the small of her back she had a burn from where the flaming wood had fallen on her.

She put her uncle's clothes on, rolling the pant legs up and cinching the drawstrings at the waist, bunching the fabric into small pleats. A pair of his wool socks for slippers and she was ready to go back downstairs.

Nura had once watched her mama care for a burn on Babo's hand and thought she remembered the protocol. First, she searched Uncle Reuf's bathroom for a first-aid kit, finding one in a cupboard beneath his sink. The kit had a tube of antibacterial ointment and a little gauze but not enough to wrap her wounds. She went to his kitchen and found two thin cotton towels and cut them into strips. A pair of safety pins and she was ready for the hard part.

Nura turned on the kitchen tap and worked lather from a bar of soap until she had her hands covered. Dipping her left arm under the water first, she wetted it and began gently working the lather over her burns. Despite the care she took, her fingers felt like a wire brush against her skin, sending jolts through her chest and up into her teeth.

Her heart pounding, tears dripping down her cheeks, she rinsed her left arm and repeated that torture on her right. When she finished, she dabbed her skin dry with a clean towel, smoothed a layer of the ointment over the burns, and wrapped both arms in cotton cloth.

The sun was about to sink beyond the mountains. This would have been the time of the evening when she and Mama would be cleaning up the dinner dishes. Danis would be pestering Nura to play a game. The sun was about to set and take with it the life she had loved, pulling it deep into some dark underworld from where it could never escape. She wanted to follow the sun to that dark place. Instead, she went up to her uncle's bedroom, laid on his lumpy mattress, and felt certain that she would never find sleep, Babo's knife open and ready just in case the men returned.

But somehow, when she closed her eyes, exhaustion pulled her beneath a cloak of slumber so thick that her sleep held no nightmares.

* * *

Nura woke before the break of morning, the pain in her arms pulling her up from the heavy bliss of sleep.

The blooming dawn cast an impotent glow into the room, giving shape to the world around her. Staring at the light fixture above her uncle's bed, the memory of where she was and why came back to her. Rain fell against the windows in heavy taps, adding to the chill in the air, yet behind that tapping the house was eerily quiet. In those silent minutes, she tried to understand why she hadn't crawled from her hiding place when her family was being murdered. Why she hadn't charged at Luka, a stone raised above her head. If she had done that, someone would have shot her and she would be with her family now.

She lifted the covers back and eased herself up to sitting, working her way out of her uncle's bed, being careful not to use her forearms for support. The floor was cold beneath her feet, despite her uncle's wool socks. She grabbed the quilt off her uncle's bed to wrap around her shoulders, sure that no blanket would ever assuage the chill in her bones.

Nura padded to the stairs, dark and brown, decades of wear making each step smooth to the point of being slippery. The rail creaked near the bottom where the newel had been worked loose.

In the kitchen, she found a box of crackers, filled a glass with water, and crushed the crackers into it, making a paste. The first spoonful was the hardest to swallow. Her throat still burned from the smoke, but she needed strength for the task ahead. Her family lay in the rubble across the courtyard. She could not leave them there.

After breakfast, she scavenged through the house and found blankets to use for shrouds and string to tie them shut. Her shoes were still wet from floating in the pond the day before, so she found a pair of boots that were far too big, but would work if she wore enough socks. From a hook near the front door, she grabbed a coat that had a hood to keep the rain off her neck.

Outside, the rain beat a steady rhythm against her coat, although it had lightened a bit from the heavy droplets of that morning. In her uncle's barn she found a spade and a pickaxe. She would likely not have the strength to swing the pick, but she took it anyway.

Blankets in one hand and tools in the other, she headed across the courtyard.

The front porch was gone. With no steps to climb, Nura pulled a wheelbarrow from the side of the house, turned it upside down, and used that as a step, climbing up and into the house: no door, no jamb, just the jagged remnants of a wall that rose to her waist on either side of where the door had been.

Beyond the threshold, fallen floor joists and roof trusses littered her path. Large sections of the upstairs and roof blocked her way, all of it made slick by the rain. She climbed into what had once been the family room where she and Mama had watched the Olympic figure skaters dance to beautiful music, a place where she and Danis played games and where Babo talked of a future beyond the war.

A section of wall from the hallway had fallen into the family room, balanced at an angle that allowed Nura to stand on it without slipping off. From there she searched the rubble for her family as rain fell on her from the sky above. She could smell the faint odor of burned flesh behind the pungency of charred wood, the hint of that stench raising bile in her throat.

She spied the glint of something dirty and white sticking out from beneath the wall on which she stood, her eyes passing over it several times before it caught her attention. When she looked more closely, she saw that it was exposed bone attached to the charred remains of a boot—Babo's boot.

Nura scrambled out of the room, stumbling over scorched timber and debris. She jumped down from the threshold, tripping on the edge of the wheelbarrow and falling into the wet grass.

On all fours, she heaved up what little she had eaten of the saltine paste. She heaved until her stomach hurt and she had nothing more to throw up. The rain fell cold on the back of her neck, her hood having fallen off in her rush to get out of the house. Her face and chest flushed hot with nausea. She was dizzy, and remained on her hands and knees for a long time as she waited for the sickness to pass—waiting for the strength to climb back into the house.

When she was able to stand, she tucked the blankets and string under her arm and made her way back to Babo. She thought her legs might give out as she negotiated over the burned boards and rusted nails. She stood at the edge of the fallen wall and laid a blanket at her side where it would be easy to reach.

The section of wall was no bigger than her dining room table, but it was heavy with plaster, and wood, and rain. She tried to lift it, and the pain in her arms was so great she thought she might collapse. Tears in her eyes, she tried again, screaming as she hoisted it high enough to shove it over.

Nura tried not to look upon her father. Still, she noticed that his hands had curled in on themselves and his hair had burned away. She saw those things in a flash as she spread the blanket over his body, wrapping it around his legs and torso and tying the burial shroud in place with the string. His blanket was blue, which had been his favorite color.

She considered pulling him out through the front door, but it occurred to her that it would be easier to take him out the side of the house where the wall had fallen away. She had to stop thinking of this pile of debris as a house. There was no front door or back door. The path didn't matter; only getting her family out and buried mattered. Respect demanded it of her. Her faith, what little she had left, demanded it. To leave their bodies where they lay—to be picked over by scavengers and rats—would be a cruelty beyond imagination.

She gripped the blanket and pulled, the pain of her wounds causing her to drop him. When she looked down to try again, she saw something that wrenched her heart to the point of stopping it cold. She didn't mean to look, but by the time she saw—and understood—it was too late.

Stanko had lain Babo on top of Danis when he dragged them into the house. Danis's body had hardly been touched by the flames, and he stared up at Nura through slitted eyes, his face pale, his beautiful hair intact.

Nura fell backwards, tripping on fallen boards, the wood scraping against her back and arms, her burns screaming their presence. She felt pinned, unable to move. She turned her face to the sky. She didn't want to see her little brother staring up at her with dead eyes.

When she regained the ability to stand, she picked up a yellow blanket and laid it over Danis. She wrapped the string around his torso and legs to hold the shroud in place like she had done with Babo. Then she returned to the task of dragging Babo out of the house.

She tried to be gentle, but when it came time to lower him to the ground, she had no porch, no steps. Despite her best effort, her father fell to the mud.

She dragged his body around to the back of the house and laid him at the edge of her mother's vegetable garden.

Danis was easier to lift. Nura had carried him a thousand times over the years, and he had never once seemed heavy to her. She eased him to the ground without dropping him and laid him at Babo's side by the garden.

She found Mama in the kitchen. Of all the rooms, the kitchen had been spared the worst of the inferno, the sink and three of the cupboards blackened by smoke, but seemingly untouched by flame. Mama lay near the entrance, obscured by fallen timber. Nura dug down, pulling beams and rafters away until she had uncovered her mother's body.

What she saw would remain seared in Nura's memory for the rest of her life: her mother's flesh burned, her hair singed to stubble, a trickle of blood on her neck from a bullet hole in the back of her head. But unlike her father and brother, Mama had been stripped of her clothing.

Nura covered Mama with a pink blanket and carried her out through the space that had once been the back door, lowering her to the ground at the very spot where Nura had lunged out of the crawl space. She laid Mama next to Danis. They looked so small lying in a row like that, the rain matting their shrouds.

She went to the front of the house to retrieve the spade and pick-axe, and when she bent down to pick them up, something caught her eye. Small and blue. Nura knelt and gently lifted the object out of the grass. It was a blue marble, one of the ten she had given to Danis for his birthday. He had fired it at the bearded soldier, and for that offense, Luka Savić had shot Danis three times in the chest. Her fingers trembled as she held the tiny orb.

Nura drew back to hurl the marble as far as she could throw, but stopped herself. Danis had fired his slingshot to protect his family, an act far braver than anything Nura had done. That marble had been his final testament. She wiped away the dirt and rain, and slid the marble into her pocket. Then she picked up her tools and made her way to her mother's garden.

Nura decided to bury her family where her mother would have planted tomatoes, the topsoil—the mud—sticky and loose from Mama's tiller. But at the depth of one spade blade, the ground turned hard, forcing her to stab at the ground. She stood on the shoulders of the blade with both feet, hopping and wiggling to wedge it between the rocks. Then she pulled back on the handle with all her weight to pry the rocks and the dirt free. Larger rocks, she loosened with the pickaxe and sometimes with her fingers, stacking the stones in a pile.

Rain fell throughout the morning, but Nura ignored it, keeping her focus on her spade and pickaxe. She would bury her family so that Mecca—to the southeast—would align to their right, a custom of her people.

When she'd started digging that morning, she had planned to quarry three separate holes, one for each member of her family, but by the time she had finished the first hole, she realized that she would not have the strength to dig all three. She would have to bury them in a single grave, side by side.

She dug until her hands filled with blisters and her back turned brittle. Her arms cried out as the bandages rubbed like sandpaper against her burns. By evening, she had finished a hole that would be big enough—or at least it would have to do.

The Muslim faith demanded that she clean the bodies before

burying them, and although her family did not follow the dictates of that faith with any rigor, Nura wanted to bury her family with dignity and honor. But she could not bring herself to take that last step, to look upon their charred and mangled bodies, to see betrayal in their lifeless eyes. That would have broken her.

"I'm sorry," she said. "I will come back and do this right...with an imam and Uncle Reuf. Please, forgive me."

Then, one by one, she slid her loved ones into the grave, Babo on one side, Mama on the other, Danis between them. Then she covered her family with dirt.

She had not been raised a strict Muslim, but she knew a prayer. Kneeling in the mud, soaked from rain and barely able to speak, Nura faced Mecca and recited the prayer of her people, hoping to find solace in its words.

In the name of Allah, the Most Beneficent, the Most Merciful.

Praise be to Allah, the Cherisher and Sustainer of the worlds;

Most Gracious, Most Merciful;

Master of the Day of Judgment.

Thee do we worship, and Thine aid we seek.

Show us the straight way,

The way of those on whom Thou hast bestowed Thy Grace,

Those whose portion is not wrath, and who go not astray.

The words drifted with the wind, leaving her empty, her pain untouched, so she added, "Allah...my mama, my babo, and my Danis are with you now. They are in your hands. Protect them from...Please, take care of them for me until I can be with them again."

She could think of nothing more to say.

9

Minnesota

AFTER EVERYTHING

The next morning dawns sunny and warm, and Hana wakes with an idea. Dylan will need clothes, toothbrush, toys, books, and Hana needs to get ahead of Claypool's investigation. A visit to Amina's condo could further both objectives.

Amina had given Hana a key to the condo years ago, a safety measure in case Amina locked herself out. But if she goes under Claypool's supervision, maybe she can ask a few questions while she looks around.

Claypool's number lays on her dresser next to her jewelry box. She dials.

"I was hoping," Hana says, "to pick up some clothing for Dylan. Maybe some toys or books. I have nothing here and I want to make him feel at home as much as I can."

"It's still a crime scene," he says.

"I won't touch anything that you tell me not to touch."

There is a moment of silence—uncomfortably long—before he agrees. The pause plays on Hana's imagination. Maybe he distrusts her. She will need to change that.

After she hangs up, she goes to her closet. She has to get Claypool to open up to her. She has a sense that feigning weak and timid won't get her there.

She flips past her normal ensembles of sweaters and skirts and finds a pair of blue jeans she bought online and never wore because they were just a bit too tight. Now she thinks that might come in handy; Claypool is a man, after all. She finds a blouse that has a hint of femininity, white with a lace collar, casual yet strong—and long-sleeved to hide her scars.

She doesn't put her hair up in a bun, but instead lets it hang in a ponytail, a look that no one at the library has ever seen her wear. When she inspects herself in the mirror, she sees someone trying too hard to make an impression. She almost changes back into a sweater and skirt but doesn't. It is a means to an end.

* * *

Claypool is waiting in his car when she pulls up. He gives Hana a warm smile, the kind normally reserved for greeting an old friend. She sees his eyes drop to her outfit—for just a second, but he'd noticed.

"Hello, Detective Claypool."

"You can call me David."

Familiarity. Good.

"I'd been wanting to do a walk-through with you," David says. "Maybe you can see something we missed."

"And I appreciate you letting me in to get stuff for Dylan."

They stand in the front of the complex: a small yard, no trees. Hana looks up to Amina's balcony, then to the ground beneath it. She envisions her friend falling. She sees Amina on the ground, broken, dying, her hand reaching up to give the blue marble to her would-be rescuers.

"I have to warn you," Claypool says, "it's a mess."

A white-brick exterior with walnut doors gives the building an unmistakable seventies vibe, but the carpeting is new and the hallways smell of recent paint. Hana sees no cameras.

Amina's condo is on the fourth floor with yellow tape stretched across the doorframe. Claypool pulls it down and opens the door.

Hana had prepared herself for a mess, but what she sees goes far beyond the bounds of that word. It is as if a giant hand had shaken the place, knocking all its contents onto the floor. Pictures from the walls lay in heaps beside books and torn cushions from the couch. Furniture is overturned. Every drawer has been pulled and dumped. The drawers lie upside down in the clutter. The cupboards have been emptied of their pans and plates. Ceiling tile that once covered the kitchen area is torn away.

Hana stands frozen just inside the door. Claypool places a hand on the small of Hana's back, urging her forward enough to shut the door. His hand is warm. His touch—or the touch of any man—is foreign against her skin. He leaves his hand pressed against her back for a second longer than necessary, or so it seems to Hana.

"I know it's asking a lot," he says, "but if you could just look around? Let me know if anything jumps out at you."

She steps carefully through the clutter, following a small path probably laid by Claypool and the other investigators.

"Why would they take the pictures off the walls?"

"What he was searching for must have been small—maybe a piece of paper, a disk…thumb drive. Something that can be hidden behind a picture frame."

Hana goes to the living room, where the glass door to the balcony is intact. "I thought you said Amina broke through the door?"

"Landlord fixed it to keep the rain out."

Amid the chaos, a single dining room chair sits upright in the middle of the living room. She points to it. "Is that where…?"

Claypool gives a small nod. "You should have been a detective." He steps through the clutter to the chair. "We believe he tied her to this chair as he searched the place. Her wrists were bound with zip ties."

He points to a broken slat on the backrest. "She must have broken free."

Zip ties. The term summons an image so vivid that Hana subconsciously touches her wrist. To think that Amina had been trussed up that way—again—breaks something in Hana. She stares at the chair as Claypool walks to the glass door and looks out.

"We think she heard the air brakes of Dylan's school bus. She knew he would be coming home. He'd be walking in on...this." He gestures to the destruction scattered around them. "Dylan was in danger...so she broke free...threw herself through the door. We think she was trying to warn him. We're not sure if she fell accidentally or was pushed. Either way...she died saving her grandson."

"Did you find any fingerprints or DNA?"

Claypool seems to debate this question before answering, "No."

"What about video footage...from the area?"

"It's an ongoing investigation, so I'm not at liberty to talk about it... but I can tell you that as of right now, we have no leads."

The answer is both a disappointment and a relief. A lead would be good, but not if it is in Claypool's hands and not hers.

"I need to bury Amina."

"She's still under the custody of the medical examiner."

"She is Muslim. Our religion holds that the body should be cleaned and buried as soon as possible."

"I'll see what I can do," Claypool says.

Hana walks to Dylan's room. It too is turned upside down, his clothing scattered, his mattress cut open and tossed. She digs through the clutter and finds a pair of pants and a few shirts. Claypool nods his approval as she folds them and begins a stack. Shoes and socks. Underwear. When she has enough to last a couple weeks, she loads them into a clothes basket and carries them to her car.

On her second trip, she takes his bedding, a pillow, and a few random items like a baseball mitt and a handheld video game. When she comes back for a third load, Claypool is in Amina's bedroom, looking around. Hana joins him there.

"Is there anything missing as far as you can tell?"

"It's so hard to say." Hana scans the debris. Like the other rooms, all the drawers have been pulled out and emptied. The mattress and box spring are off the bed frame. Pictures are torn from the walls.

She notices a charging cord plugged into an outlet where Amina's nightstand had been. "Did you find her laptop?"

"No. Nor her cell phone. We've subpoenaed her text messages. Should have them in a week or so. I assume we'll find conversations between you and her?"

"We were friends" is all Hana says. There will be text messages, but nothing of value to Claypool. Hana and Amina never discussed their past in such a retrievable forum.

"Did she ever talk to you about what she said to her therapist?"

"That's the second time you've asked me that question. Why?"

"You must have some idea what they talked about."

"Detective Claypool—"

"David."

"David...Amina had a great many tragedies in her life. If you want me to narrow it down for you, you have to help me out. How does this"—Hana waves a hand around the room—"connect to her therapist?"

"It's an ongoing investigation—"

"And you can't talk about it."

"Those are the rules."

Hana spies something in the rubble near her feet. She kneels. It's a picture of her and Amina. She remembers the photograph and how it used to sit on Amina's nightstand. It was taken at Sara's wedding. They were both smiling as they held each other in a loose embrace. Amina wore the necklace, the blue marble held in a setting of four silver prongs. The frame is broken, but the picture is unmarred. "Can I take this with me?" she asks.

"Technically, this is still a crime scene. It's evidence. I shouldn't even be letting you take Dylan's clothes..."

"It would mean a lot to me...David."

Claypool gives her a smile of surrender. "You can take it."

"So, not all of your rules are written in stone," Hana says. She gives David a smile that feels like flirting—but that's part of the plan, isn't it? She is out of practice, but it comes to her more easily than she expects.

"Have you ever heard the expression 'never look a gift horse in the mouth'?"

"An idiom coined by someone trying to pawn off an old nag, no doubt."

Hana is about to stand when she notices a slip of paper that had been caught beneath the picture. It's a receipt with the words *Brake job* written across the top, and it sparks a memory.

"He's a big talker," Amina had said, "but I don't think he's got a pot to piss in."

"How's that?"

"His car needs new brakes, but his credit card got hacked, so he can't use it for a few days."

"If he doesn't have enough cash on hand for new brakes, how's he going to buy you the Ferrari you want?"

"He asked me for a loan." Amina spoke as if she were embarrassed.

"You didn't give him money, did you?"

"I paid it to the mechanic, not to him."

"Amina."

"It's a test."

"How much did this test cost you?"

"Five hundred and ninety-two dollars and six cents."

Hana now stares at the receipt by her knee. $592.06.

Claypool is watching her.

She pinches the receipt to the back of the picture in her left hand as she reaches her right hand out to Claypool. He takes it and helps her to her feet, a gesture she doesn't need but one that distracts him. Standing, she holds his touch a moment longer than necessary as she moves the photo against her leg to hide the receipt. He notices the touch but not the theft. The slight tingle in her chest she attributes to guilt. She lets it pass.

"When are you picking Dylan up?" he asks.

"Day after tomorrow. I called Amina's attorney this morning to get the ball rolling."

"Dylan's lucky to have you. Foster care can be rough."

Hana keeps the photo—and the receipt—against her leg as she makes her way to the door. "It'll be new for us both," she says.

Hana leaves Claypool at the door, where he is reattaching the crime scene tape.

On the way to her car, she contemplates the piece of paper in her hand. It isn't much of a rabbit run, but it is a trail nonetheless.

10

Bosnia

1995

N ura stared at the flowered wallpaper in her uncle's kitchen, her mind numb, her clothes, face, and hair covered with mud, her hands red with blisters, her stomach empty, her body so weak that she had to put her palms on the counter to keep from falling. She knew that she needed to eat even as the thought of food made her want to retch.

Nura scrounged through cupboards and found noodles and some spices. Uncle Reuf had left his propane tank on to feed the stove, water heater, and furnace, the thermostat set just warm enough so that his pipes wouldn't burst if the temperature dropped. She warmed her hands over the stove's flame before setting the pot of water on to boil the noodles.

When they were done, she sprinkled olive oil, garlic, and pepper on the noodles to give them flavor and ate slowly, letting each noodle settle in her stomach before eating another. Despite her best effort, the food held no taste.

After eating as much as she could stomach, she ran a bath. While the tub filled, she found scissors and a mirror and cut the hair on the right side of her head to roughly match the side that had burned away.

Then she peeled her uncle's baggy clothes from her body, unwrapped her wounded forearms, and eased into the bath.

The water rose to her chin, the breath from her nostrils gently rippling the calm surface in front of her face. It wasn't right that she still breathed, still walked, still felt the warmth of bath water against her skin. How had she come to deserve life when her family lay buried in the ground? If she could stop her heart from beating, she could be with them again. In the quiet of Uncle Reuf's bathroom, that small thought grew until it echoed off the walls.

Nura took a breath, held it, and slipped beneath the water. All she had to do was breathe out—and then in—just one time. One small moment of courage and she would be with them and out of this world of pain. She counted to three and let out most of her breath, but couldn't bring herself to inhale the water. Still, if she stayed beneath the water, her body would force her to breathe, her death coming by reflex.

Poisonous carbon dioxide began building in her lungs as she watched Babo fall dead. He had offered himself up to save his family.

Her heart pounded in her chest as she saw Mama run out to save Danis.

Nura sank deeper into the water, committing to her death as Danis shoots his marble at the man who dared to hurt Babo. Even Danis had been more courageous than her.

Her chest heaved as her lungs fought for oxygen. It hurt. It made her dizzy.

They all died for something worthy.

She kicked at the foot of the tub—pushed against the sides to keep beneath the water. Just a couple seconds more and she would be with them as the men who murdered her family lived on. She would die a coward, her death serving no purpose. Those men would never pay a price for their evil act.

Nura bolted up, gasping for breath, coughing, and spitting water. She gripped the side of the tub as an epiphany swirled in her head.

Those men could not be allowed to wash their hands of their crime. If she was going to die anyway, why not die hunting them down?

But she was not a real hunter. She trapped small animals with wire snares. Killing a man isn't like killing a rabbit—or is it? Did these men have a greater claim on life than the animals she hunted? When she came upon a rabbit caught in her wire, his heart still beating, didn't she do the humane thing and slide a knife across his throat? If she had the fortitude to dispatch a hare—who had done her no harm—surely, she could put down the men who had massacred her family.

If nothing else, she would move heaven and earth to find out the answer to that question.

Nura dried herself, rewrapped her wounds, and headed upstairs to Uncle Reuf's bedroom to contemplate what might come next. She was about to climb into bed when the sound of thunder in the distance drew her to the window. The rain had passed, and the clouds were too thin to hold thunder.

She waited, and when it rolled again, she realized that it wasn't thunder. It was the report of artillery, something large being fired in the distance. According to Uncle Reuf, Bosnians were waging their war with mostly small arms—rifles and mortars. What she heard was a gun far too big to belong to her people. She had to be hearing the Serbs, maybe even the same soldiers who had murdered her family.

Nura crawled into bed that night with a reason for being alive— and a destination. Somewhere in the mountains to her west lay her destiny. She would make those men pay for what they did.

* * *

Nura woke hungry. There was something comforting in that hunger, a sense of expectation that one step would follow another and lead her where she needed to go. She put on a pair of Uncle Reuf's socks and went downstairs to scrounge some breakfast, finding a jar of plums and a small bag of rice. That would do.

As she waited for the rice to boil, she snooped through Reuf's kitchen and found a map, unfolding it on his kitchen table. She thought back to the rumble of artillery from the night before and drew a triangle from her home, widening toward where the sound had come from. The roads through the mountains twisted along ridges and valleys like an unsolvable maze. She would need a car.

Babo kept his Yugo in the shed with the tractor. The car had holes in the floorboard and a roll of heavy tape in back because parts tended to fall off on the bumpy drive to Tuzla.

Nura had driven the Yugo up and down the trail to their house, learning to shift on the incline. Babo had even once let her drive it on the blacktop on the way to Petrovo. It was the only time that she got to shift beyond second gear. No one had driven the car since Babo and Uncle Reuf felled the trees to block the trail, but he kept it filled with gasoline just in case they needed to go to the refugee camp in Tuzla.

Nura changed into a clean set of her uncle's clothes and went out into the sun to visit her family's grave. The burial site was not nearly as tidy as she had remembered, her perception having been impaired by exhaustion, darkness, and rain.

She smoothed the mounds with the spade and placed stones end to end, framing the grave. With the frame completed, she found three metal stakes that Mama would have used to hold up her tomato plants. Nura pounded the stakes into the ground at the head of the grave and then knelt. "I will love you always," she whispered. "I will carry you with me for as long as I live, and one day I will join you. I am sorry I was not a better daughter...a better sister. I am sorry, Danis...for breaking my promise. I am sorry that I am here and you are not."

She wanted to cry. She pinched her eyes closed and silently prayed for a tear, but none came. "I am sorry," she said again. Then she stood and walked away.

With the trail to the blacktop blocked by felled trees, the only way off the mountain would be the tractor path behind Uncle Reuf's house. Mama had once joked that the Yugo could no better make it down that bumpy tractor path than it could climb a tree. But Babo had seemed convinced his car could make it.

Nura walked to the machine shed and slid in behind the wheel of the Yugo. Babo kept the key in the ashtray. She moved the seat up to fit her legs and spent a few seconds going over what Papa did to start the car. She pushed in the clutch, pumped the gas four times with her foot, held it down, and turned the key.

The motor croaked twice but started.

Pleased with herself, she put the car in first gear and let the clutch out—a little too fast. The Yugo lurched forward and died.

She wanted to kick herself. She went through the routine again. This time she took the car out of gear and set the hand brake. She got out and walked around the car, inspecting it. The tires had air. The windshield was dusty, but she could see through it. Nothing seemed out of order.

She drove out of the shed and parked next to Uncle Reuf's house. It was time to prepare for her journey.

The overalls she'd worn the day of her family's massacre had dried, and her shoes, though damp, were dry enough to wear. Cold feet meant little to her. She put on one of Reuf's long-sleeved shirts under the overalls, rolling the sleeve up to her wrists, but not so far as to expose her bandaged arms.

To complete her ensemble—and to hide her burned and tangled hair—Nura used the thin curtain in Uncle Reuf's bathroom to make a scarf. Catching her appearance in the mirror gave her second thoughts. If she were stopped at a checkpoint, the headscarf might announce her as a Muslim. If the checkpoint were manned by Bosnians, that would be a good thing, but if they were Serbs... She decided to wear the scarf anyway. She would pull it off her head if she saw a Serbian soldier.

As she headed out of the house, map in hand, she tapped her pocket to make sure that she had Babo's pocketknife. It was there. It would have been nice to have Uncle Reuf's rifle, but he'd taken that with him. She tossed the map into the car and was about to get in when she stopped.

She ran back inside, to the bathroom where she had left Uncle Reuf's clothing that she'd worn to bury her family. In the pocket of the sports pants she had borrowed, she found Danis's blue marble. She kissed it and put it into the breast pocket of the overalls.

In the Yugo again, she eased the shifter into first gear, revved the engine, and carefully let the clutch out. She circled the courtyard three times to get a feel for the car. After the third pass, she headed for the trail behind Uncle Reuf's house.

The drive started easily enough, flat and smooth as she passed her uncle's barn, but it grew more difficult after that. She kept the car in second gear, the transmission whining as the grade grew steeper. It was as if the car were begging to be put into a higher gear. Nura resisted.

The trail was nothing more than two tire tracks on rock, a path meant for the high clearance of a tractor, not a car. The Yugo scraped on small rock ledges as she crawled down the hill. When she neared the creek at the bottom, she stopped.

Beyond the creek, a pasture stretched for half a kilometer before it connected to the blacktop. If she could make it through the creek, she would be good the rest of the way, but the creek had grown with the recent rains.

If the car died in the water, she would be stuck on that mountain alone. Finding that cannon on foot was out of the question, as was walking to Tuzla to live out the war in the refugee camp. She needed to get across the creek, and to do that, she would need speed.

She backed up the hill to get a running start. She rubbed the pocket where she kept Danis's marble, took a deep breath, and charged down the hill.

First gear—second gear—third gear. She punched the gas pedal.

The nose struck the creek hard, slamming Nura chest-first into the steering wheel, water blasting the windshield, blinding her. She kept her foot on the gas, the car jolting left, then right as it careened off rocks. Water splashed up through the holes in the floorboard. Another rock tossed the car so hard that her foot slipped off the gas pedal. She stomped it back down and the car lurched forward, up the opposite bank and into the fallow field.

She stopped, turned on the wipers to clear the windshield, and saw smoke rising from beneath the hood. When she got out and lifted the hood, she found it wasn't smoke at all. It was only steam from water hitting the hot engine. She looked at all four tires. None were flat. She knew very little about cars and engines, but as far as she could tell, her little Yugo had survived the creek just fine.

She was about to get back into the car when she again heard the rumble of artillery being fired to the west. She faced the direction of the sound. The cannon fired again and she adjusted her stance. The Serbs had to be nearly straight west of her.

She pulled her map from the car and laid it out on the ground. With her fingernail, she scratched a line in the direction of the artillery fire. She would crisscross the hills and make her way west, following the sound of the gun as best she could.

She got back behind the wheel of the Yugo, her hands trembling, and drove across the pasture to where the field exited onto the blacktop. There she stopped.

This would be her last chance to change her mind. Turn right and the road would lead her to Tuzla. Maybe she would go as far as Srebrenica and find her uncle. If she turned left, though, she might find Stanko, Luka, and the man with the streaks of gray in his beard. Turn right and become a refugee. Turn left and be a hunter.

Nura turned left.

11

Minnesota

AFTER EVERYTHING

The mechanic's shop is in Midway, a neighborhood aptly named for its location straddling the divide between St. Paul and Minneapolis. A blue stucco building, cracked sidewalks in front. Small tufts of grass grow along the building's foundation. A wooden fence surrounds a parking lot full of damaged cars: smashed fenders, broken axles, dents and rust everywhere. Hana parks out front, gathers the receipt she stole from Amina's condo, and makes her way inside.

The place smells of grease and rubber. It has a small waiting area with a dirty reception countertop, behind which sits a ruddy man with five days of stubble on his cheeks. Receipt in hand, Hana approaches. The man continues to stare at his computer screen, ignoring her for a full minute before he turns to her. "What can I do you for?"

Hana holds out the receipt. "This may sound . . . foolish, I guess, but I need your help."

The man glances at the receipt. "Okay."

"A month ago, I bought a car from this guy. It's this car here." Hana points to the make and model on the receipt: a 1998 Hyundai

Sonata. "I paid cash for it, but... This is so embarrassing. We met in the parking lot of the Aldi. He let me test drive it and it seemed like a good car."

The man behind the counter takes the receipt and begins to read as Hana continues.

"Anyway, I paid cash. He said he didn't have the title on him so he was going to mail it to me. I've never bought a car before. My husband always took care of that stuff. But he's dead now—my husband—and I... Well, I think I may have gotten scammed."

"How's that?"

"I waited for the title to come in the mail, but days went by, then weeks. It never came. So, I called the phone number and... I think it's a dead number, like maybe he was using one of those... Oh, what do you call them..."

"A burner phone?"

"Yeah. I've called and called, but... I get nothing."

"You didn't get the guy's address?"

"Like I said, we met in a parking lot."

"How did you hear about the car for sale?"

"Online. Craigslist, I think."

The mechanic, whose name tag reads *Rick,* scratches his neck. "So, no name. No address. And the phone is a burner."

"That appears to be the case."

"And how, exactly, can I help you?"

"I found this receipt in the glove box. I thought that maybe he has an account here."

Rick gives it a closer look. "He might, but... I can't give out information like that."

"I understand... it's just that... I gave that man my savings. It was all the money I had. If I can't get a title—or if the car is stolen..." Hana makes the sign of the cross—a motion she has seen on TV—but then wonders if she might be overplaying it. "I would hate to think that I might be part of a crime and not even know it."

"Still, I don't think I can help you."

"If this car is stolen, I can't in good conscience keep it. And then where will I be? I'll have no way to get to work. I may lose my job and that guy will get away with it. Surely, there must be an exception when a crime is involved."

Rick appraises Hana with a squint in his eyes. She has done her best to look old and helpless, tipping the corners of her mouth down just a touch. She wants to conjure a tear, but such an act is beyond her ability.

"Please," she says. "If you can give me anything—any clue that might help me…"

With the receipt in his hand, Rick returns to his computer. He types for a few seconds then pauses to read. He looks back and forth between the receipt and the computer screen.

"This receipt…the repair was paid for by a woman."

Amina, Hana thinks. "But I bought it from a man. Is there a man's name associated with the repair?"

Rick purses his lips. "I have the address where we towed it from. It's not a name, but…"

"You have an address?" Hana's words come out too loud—too excited. She pauses to calm down. "If you give me the address…that's not breaking any rules, is it?"

Rick seems to consider this as he glances back and forth between Hana and his screen. She's about to offer him a hundred dollars to tip the scale when he picks up a pen and writes something on a scrap of paper.

"You didn't get this from me, understand?"

"Bless you." She reads the address, folds the paper, and puts it in her pocket.

* * *

The address takes Hana to an apartment building behind a Goodwill store in Frogtown, a neighborhood near Midway. There is no apartment number on the receipt, but the building itself is the kind of run-down eight-plex where a man who can't afford a brake job might live: rusted window air conditioners, torn screens, cracks in the dark red brick from years of settling.

Hana sits in her car long enough to see that there is no one outside the apartment building. She walks to the door. Glass. It opens to a small vestibule with a row of letter boxes along one of the walls. Scanning the boxes, she finds his name. Zaim Galić—apartment number seven. If Amina had ever said his last name, Hana carries no memory of it.

She tries the interior door, but it is locked, a single cylindrical lock on the knob. No dead bolt. She gives the door a shake; it's loose, the latch moving slightly within the strike plate. This is good. She can probably open it with a credit card, but a knife would work better— and Hana is good with a knife.

She gives a quick look around for surveillance cameras. Seeing none, she leaves the building and goes to the Goodwill store. There, she buys a blond wig, a ball cap, thin gloves, and a pair of sunglasses. In the car, she puts her disguise on and drives around Frogtown until she finds a pawnshop.

As she expects, there are cameras at the entrance, as well as one overlooking the knife case, where she finds quite a collection. She has knives at home: butcher knives, paring knives, a menagerie of blades, but none of them suitable for the task ahead. It reminds her how ill-prepared she has allowed herself to become over the years. The lioness tamed by a circus cage.

The case holds big knives that looked menacing but are hard to conceal, as well as tiny blades that could fit in the palm of her hand but won't penetrate deep enough to suit her purpose. And then there are the Goldilocks knives. Not too big, not too small, with blades long enough to be deadly and small enough to fit easily into her back pocket.

As she examines the knives, Hana glances at a scar crossing the inside of four fingers of her right hand, a reminder that a blade can easily slip when it becomes slick with blood. She will need a knife with a quality guard.

She narrows her selection to three and asks the man behind the counter if she can hold them. All three knives have been freshly sharpened. Any of them would do the trick. She holds each. Balances them in her hand. Slides her favorite into the back pocket of her blue jeans. It feels right, so she pays the man in cash.

Back in her car, she takes a moment to invite second thoughts, but none come. She knows his name—Zaim Galić. She will soon know if he is the man who killed her friend. If he did not—she will leave him with a lesson about preying on women. But if he did kill Amina—or if he came to Minnesota in search of Hana's bounty money, she will put an end to his search.

Hana starts her car and heads back to Zaim's apartment.

12

Bosnia

1995

N ura didn't know where she was going, only that the roads she chose twisted in the general direction of the cannon fire. The Yugo coughed as it climbed into the mountains, cutting through passages she vaguely remembered from when Babo had taken the family on a trip to Mount Ozren. They had gone there for a picnic; Nura and Danis had explored a cave. She hadn't paid much attention to the road or the drive, but a few of the landmarks she passed brought the memory back.

She stopped at a high crossroads where a sign pointed the way to Monastery Ozren. She remembered the sign from that trip to the cave. She had asked Babo if they could visit the monastery on the drive back. Babo answered with a somber, "It is a Serbian monastery." She didn't fully understand what that meant at the time, but now she did.

As Nura was about to drive again, she heard the cannon fire. She stepped out of the car and listened. Another boom echoed through the hills. She was getting close. She looked at her map and traced a route with her finger. If she was right, the gun was firing from Mount Ozren itself.

Nura was no soldier, but she imagined that there had to be checkpoints to stop people like her from simply driving up and killing Serbian soldiers. She would need a plan. After ten more minutes of driving, a plan came to her.

She pulled to the side of the road, drew Babo's pocketknife from her pocket, and unwrapped the bandage on her left arm enough to place the open knife against her blistered skin. Then she carefully rewrapped the bandage. From there, she could pull the knife when the time was right. She loosened the scarf from her head and looped it around her neck.

She felt no fear, which bothered her. She should be trembling. She should be second-guessing herself, but instead she breathed in the scent of pine trees and wildflowers. It was a beautiful day, the sky above her a powdery blue. It was a good day to call her last.

Twenty minutes later, the checkpoint came upon her quickly with the turn of a sharp bend on a mountain pass. Two soldiers dressed in camouflage green stood in the road next to a camo-green pickup truck.

Her heart quickened and her breath shallowed. She was certain that her plan would fail, but if she could kill even one of the men who murdered her family, she would join them knowing she had done what little she could. She envisioned the bullet that would end her life, and she prayed that the man's aim would be true.

One of the men, older, maybe Babo's age, held up a hand to order Nura to stop. She parked the Yugo, got out, and ran to the soldiers, wailing, "I must see my father."

"Do not come any closer!" he yelled, pointing his rifle at her chest.

Nura held out her hands, begging, crying, although she could manage no tears. "Please, I must speak to my father. They killed my mother. They burned our house. Please get my father."

"Who is your father?"

"His name is Stanko Krunić. I am his daughter, Jovana. His

wife—my mother—Brina was shot by Muslim traitors. Ratko, my little brother . . . he is badly wounded."

The older soldier waved Nura forward. "Turn around."

Nura did.

He patted down one side and up the other. Then he felt her stomach and breasts, his hand lingering longer than necessary. He started moving his hand down her right arm, and she pulled back.

"Please. I was burned in the fire."

She lifted her sleeves and showed him the bandages. When he didn't react, she peeled back enough of the bandage to show the blisters. At the sight of her burned skin, his expression turned from skepticism to revulsion.

"I escaped the fire. I need to find my father. Please, can I speak to him? I do not know what else to do. I do not know where to go."

"What was his name again?"

"Stanko Krunić. I am Jovana."

The older soldier went to the truck and lifted a radio receiver from inside. He spoke in a low voice so that Nura couldn't hear. The second soldier, a younger man with thick glasses, said nothing but held his rifle with the muzzle pointed at Nura's legs.

After a couple minutes, the soldier in charge returned. "Your father is on the way," he said.

Nura put her hands to her face and sunk to one knee to feign weakness. "Bless you," she said. "Bless you and your children."

She lifted the scarf to conceal her face. She would need Stanko to get close.

In the distance, the whine of a truck engine crept down from the higher elevation.

She waited and listened. As the truck neared the checkpoint, she peeked from beneath her bowed head. It was the same truck that had come to the courtyard in front of her house. There were two men inside, but she could make out no faces.

Carefully, she slid the knife from its hiding place beneath the bandage, inching the handle out until it was unsheathed.

Brakes squealed as the truck came to a stop ten meters away. She kept her face down. Pretended to cry.

Doors opened and closed. Footsteps, running. His voice—Stanko's—calling out: "Jovana!" He stopped in front of her, his muddy boots within her reach. She felt a hand on her shoulder. She stood. Looked into his eyes, his face a mask of confusion, then recognition, then again confusion.

Nura drove the knife into the side of his neck. Stanko didn't react, stunned by the speed of her strike. Blood spurted from the wound as she pulled the knife out and stabbed again, her hand slipping down the blade.

Stanko stumbled backwards, clutching his neck. His mouth moved, but he said nothing. In his eyes she saw fear—or maybe disbelief. They were already the eyes of a dead man begging for life.

She turned and ran.

Out of the corner of her eye she saw the older soldier raise his gun. She dove beside the car for cover as the first bullet shattered the windshield of the Yugo. Rounds pocked the hood with holes. The car was angled just enough to offer cover, but not for long.

Nura rolled, and scrambled to get behind the car as the other soldiers began firing.

Nura had nowhere to go. No place to hide from the attack. She would die soon. Bullets ripped through the back window of the car and pitted the ground around her. She screamed, not out of fear but rage. She had only killed one of them. The man who raped her mother would live. Luka, the man who killed her Danis, would live.

The soldiers stopped firing. Footsteps. The crunch of stones. They were working their way around to her.

She wanted to stand and look at them as they fired the fatal shot, but her legs refused to move. She closed her eyes.

But then, more gunfire, not from the men circling her, but from in front of her. She opened her eyes to see muzzle flashes on either side of the road she had driven up. She didn't understand.

None of the bullets hit her, nor did they hit the car. The soldiers at the checkpoint turned their fire toward the threat coming from down the mountain. The battle raged for only a few seconds before the woods fell silent.

A man stepped from behind a tree on the left side of the road ahead of her. Mid-thirties and fit, he wore a camouflage uniform, his pant legs tucked into leather boots.

"Dammit, Adem!" he yelled as he ran toward her, his attention—and his rifle—fixed on the men at the checkpoint.

Another man, not much older than Nura, stepped out of the woods on the opposite side of the road. He too was dressed in camo, but his clothing didn't seem to fit him well. He too aimed his rifle at the men of the checkpoint, but he looked at Nura.

The second man jogged to where Nura sat crouched behind the car. He put a hand on her shoulder. "Are you all right?"

He was young, practically a boy. He had kind eyes and dark hair that spiked on top. He wore a patch on his arm: a shield with two swords behind it—the army of the Republic of Bosnia and Herzegovina. He was a Bosniak.

He held out a hand to help Nura from the ground. It was the hand of the man who had saved her life, and she held on to it as she steadied her trembling legs.

Behind her a shot rang out. The other Bosniak stood over one of the Serbs, his muzzle pointed at a fresh hole in the side of the man's head.

"Reconnaissance," he yelled back at his young counterpart. "That means we watch. We report. We don't shoot! I can't believe..." His words turned unintelligible as he ducked inside of the truck that had carried Stanko to the checkpoint.

Around them, the four Serbian soldiers lay dead. Stanko had fallen in a pool of his own blood. She had done that. On either side of him, the two checkpoint guards lay dead, shot by the men from the woods. Beside the door of the truck, the driver, too, was dead. Babo's Yugo was riddled with bullet holes, smoke seeping up from the engine.

"Are you all right?" the younger soldier asked again, his words soft and kind.

Nura looked down at her body as if there might be a wound she did not know about. Seeing none, she answered, "I think so."

"You killed that soldier," he said.

Nura looked at Stanko and then at her hands, red with his blood. "He killed my father," she said.

She wiped her hand down the front of her shirt. More blood. She wiped again. That's when she realized that she had cut her fingers on the knife blade.

"Here," the soldier said. "Let me..." He pulled a small first-aid kit from a pocket of his fatigues and wrapped her fingers with gauze, securing it with a piece of tape. "We can tend to this better if you come with me."

The older man started the truck and drove it at Nura's Yugo, the younger man pulling her out of the way. The older man slammed the truck into the Yugo and drove it into the side of the hill. He backed the truck up and angled it to take up as much of the road as possible. Working with the efficiency of a chef, he opened the hood, yanked out a bunch of wires, and fired bullets into the tires. Then he opened the passenger door and retrieved a stack of papers—maps.

"We have to go," he said.

"She needs to come with us," said the younger.

"We leave her. Our mission—"

"They will question her."

The older soldier considered this for only a second before raising his rifle at Nura. The younger man grabbed the barrel and lifted it skyward. "Enes, no. It would make us no better than them. I'll be responsible for her."

Enes looked in the direction from where the Serbs would soon be coming. He gritted his teeth, and said, "Give her your jacket to cover that white shirt." Then he turned and ran down the road. The younger man gave Nura his camouflage jacket and waved for her to follow him.

The three stepped into the woods, escaping the mountain beneath the cover of the trees. Behind her, Luka and the bearded killer still drew breath. She was running the wrong way.

Yet, somewhere deep inside of her, she understood that the path to revenge lay in front of her, with these two men.

13

Minnesota

AFTER EVERYTHING

Back when she killed Stanko, Hana knew his guilt. She had been a witness to his evil act and had no hesitation as she plunged the knife into his neck. Her only question at the time had been whether she would have mettle to match her rage. It turned out, she did.

As she sits in her car, waiting for darkness to fall, she wonders if she still has that mettle—if she is still the Night Mora, the demon of Slavic mythology who can slip through keyholes like a wisp of smoke to kill the men inside. The Serbs had kept that name on her Wanted poster all these years, out of laziness she assumed. Watching the blade of her knife catching the waning light now, she wonders how much of that spirit remains in her. She will find out soon.

A couple men have gone into Zaim's apartment building: one too young to have dated a woman of Amina's age, the other a possible candidate for Zaim Galić. Her palms sweat as she contemplates her plan. Had they been sweaty as she waited for Stanko at that checkpoint? Maybe. It had been so long ago.

Still wearing the blond wig and baseball cap from Goodwill, she wipes the sweat from her hands, slips on her gloves, and gets out of the car.

Traffic on nearby University Avenue masks the sound of her steps on the sidewalk. She enters the vestibule with the air of a person meant to be in that building. No one follows her. She listens and can hear no movement from the corridor within.

She slides the knife from her pocket. It fits easily between the door and the jamb. Gripping the doorknob, she pulls it tight toward her. Presses the blade against the latch bolt. Pushes the door in. The latch bolt gives a couple millimeters. She repeats the movement quickly, each push and pull working the latch bolt back just a little bit further, a millimeter at a time, until ... the door pops open.

Hana enters the building and closes the door behind her. Music bleeds from one of the apartments on the first floor. Beyond that, she hears nothing to give her concern. The building smells faintly of old garbage. The walls are scuffed from years of furniture being hauled in and out. The carpeting is worn down and feels a bit sticky.

She suspects Zaim's apartment, number seven, is on the second floor, so she heads up the stairs. The banister is loose in her hand and rattles a bit, but the carpeted stairs are otherwise quiet beneath her feet. She folds the knife into her palm, hiding the blade against her wrist. Just a small flick and she'll have it ready.

On the second floor, she turns left. There are two doors ahead of her; the one on her left is number seven. She tugs the bill of her cap over her eyes and knocks.

Listens.

She hears no footsteps, but he might be tiptoeing to the door to see who is knocking. *If there is a safety chain, throw all your weight at the door. Force it open before he has a chance to gather his wits.*

She knocks again.

Step in. Move fast. Get your knife to his throat before he has a chance to react. Make him tell you what he did to Amina.

She knocks a third time.

If he's not home, does she wait? Yes, because he is the key to Amina's death—she is sure of it. She'll stake out his place all night if she needs to. She won't squander this opportunity. She needs to be the first to interrogate this man. The first to resolve the question of Amina's death.

She's about to give it one last knock when she hears the sound of a doorknob turning—but it's not Zaim's door. Behind her, the door to unit eight opens.

Hana turns, startled by the little woman peeking her head through the crack in her doorway. The woman is in her late sixties, Black with gray hair and thick eyeglasses. She wears a blue dress with white flowers, the kind of outfit more suited for a church potluck than an evening in front of the TV. Hana reads curiosity in the woman's big, expressive eyes. The knife is curled in Hana's hand, hidden from view, but she slips it behind her back anyway.

"He's not there," the woman says.

"Do you know when he might be back?"

"That depends." The woman steps into the doorway, steady in her ownership of that floor of the building. "Are you here to kill him?"

Hana's knife had been hidden, so how could this woman know? But then a smile cracks at the corners of the woman's lips, and Hana's heart rate steadies. "No, I'm not here to kill him." She tries to lighten her words with a small laugh, but it comes out nervous—guilty.

"You're not as angry as the last one."

"The last one?"

"She beat on his door like she was trying to knock it off its hinges, screaming about how she was going to kill him. Of course, he never opened the door."

"What was she mad about?"

"I didn't talk to her, but I figured he screwed her over somehow. Excuse my French. Are you a girlfriend?"

"No, just a friend, passing through."

"Uh-hum."

"This is the apartment of Zaim Galić, isn't it?"

"That seems to be the question of the day, doesn't it?"

"What do you mean?"

The woman looks over her shoulder into her apartment, then opens the door wide and says, "Come in. I'll show you."

Hana slips the knife into her back pocket and follows.

The tidiness of the woman's apartment stands in contrast to the shabby common areas of the building. A green couch against the wall shows little wear, but the velvet on the recliner facing the TV is worn thin, a blanket flung over the back. Pieces of a jigsaw puzzle lay scattered on the kitchen table, the border completed and waiting to be filled in. The kitchen's counters hold small appliances—toaster, can opener, a cookie jar—but are otherwise clean. No dirty dishes in the sink. No crumbs on the floor. A cat sits on a pillow in the corner of the living room, its face black on one side and yellow tabby on the other.

The woman walks to the cat and picks it up. "This is his cat," she says. "Mr. Galić left three days ago and hasn't come back. Yesterday, I heard this one meowing his poor little head off in there, so I called the landlord. Sure enough—no food, no water, litter box full."

"Three days ago? Did he say where he was going?"

"Oh, we're not friends, honey. No. I didn't call the landlord out of some favor to *him*. I just can't stand to hear one of God's creatures suffer. I'm allergic to cats, so if you really are his friend, I'd appreciate if you take the cat. Give it back to him if he ever shows up."

"You think he might not come back?"

"He's left before—a few days at a time—but he's always taken the cat with him. This time…he didn't. I can't say the man has many admirable qualities, but he did seem to care for his cat."

"You don't like him?"

"God calls on me to forgive the transgressions of others—which I do—but that doesn't stop me from having an opinion, and in my opinion, your friend isn't a very nice man—I think he might even be dangerous."

"What do you mean?"

"He parks in my parking spot. I've been parking in that spot for years. You can ask anyone. Then he moves in last year and thinks he owns the place."

"No, I mean, why do you think he might be dangerous?"

"There was this one time...he was sitting in his car, talking on the phone. I wanted to tell him that he was parked in my spot. I had an armful of groceries and had to carry them from the far end of the parking lot. I know I don't have any legal right to that spot, but it's near the door, and I have bad knees—"

"About him being dangerous?"

"Right. Well, I'm walking up to his car...his window was open, so I can hear him. It's not like I went there to eavesdrop or anything. I couldn't care less. I just wanted to ask him if he could park somewhere else. I mean..."

The woman gives a frustrated huff before realizing that she's fallen off topic again. "Sorry. Like I said, he was on his phone and I heard him say, 'Don't think about double crossing me. I've killed before. So don't...' Excuse my language...but he said 'don't fuck with me.'"

The woman's cheeks flushed with embarrassment. She gives Hana an apologetic smile. "I 'bout dropped my groceries right there. I couldn't believe it. I swear those were his exact words. Well, I backed away and left him alone after that."

"Did he know you were listening? I mean, could he have been saying that to shake you up? Get you to back off about the parking spot?"

"I'm pretty sure he never saw me."

"What about this other woman, the one who said she wanted to kill him."

The woman's eyes cast to the window, as if that is where she might find the memory. "About your age, I'd say. Spoke with an accent like he does—like you do, only thicker."

Amina?

"I don't make it a habit to spy on my neighbors. I only looked out through the peephole because of the yelling."

"Did she have long or short hair?"

"Short. And she was a bigger gal, like me."

Not Amina.

"The one thing that stood out though. She was missing part of her index finger on her..." The woman holds up her hands, fingers spread apart, examining them. "Right hand," she says. "I noticed it when she was slapping her hand against his door."

"When was this?"

"Back around Thanksgiving, I think."

"I don't suppose you know the woman's name?"

"I never opened my door. After a while, she got tired and left."

"Did she give any hint of why she was mad?"

"Just that he had screwed her over. Again, pardon my French."

"I don't suppose you know where he works?"

"You're not his friend, are you?"

"It's important that I find him."

"Did he do someone wrong?"

"Very wrong."

"Nothing would please me more than to help you, honey, but I don't know anything more than what I've told you."

"I appreciate that."

"I don't have the right to ask, but you'd be doing me a real favor if you took that one with you." She points at the cat with the half-and-half face. "He sneaks into my bed at night and I wake up with swollen eyes."

"I'd like to help you, but I have a lot on my plate right now, and a cat doesn't fit into things."

"Well, when you have less on your plate, you know where to find him."

Hana excuses herself and thanks the woman for her help.

On the way out of the building, Hana stops in the vestibule. No one is around. She pulls out the knife, pries open Zaim's letterbox, and takes his mail. Maybe she can find a bread crumb in the stack of envelopes. Otherwise, the trail is at an end.

14

Bosnia

1995

N ura had grown up on a mountain, spent her life climbing hills, jumping creeks, and ducking tree branches, but she had never done it with life-or-death urgency. She pushed tree branches out of her way with blistered arms and only just managed to keep up with the younger man while the older man ran ahead. No one spoke.

At the bottom of the slope, they followed a creek that twisted its way through a long valley until they came to a small bridge. The young soldier climbed out of the creek and helped Nura out. The older soldier stood next to a Range Rover parked in the trees, one of the maps from the Serbian truck unfolded on the vehicle's hood. Beside him lay a stack of branches that they had used to hide the vehicle. As Nura and the young soldier approached, the older man spoke in a harsh but muted voice.

"You gave away our position."

"They were going to kill her. Are we no better than them?"

"You gave away our position!"

The young soldier gave no answer the second time, but turned his attention to the map. "Those are coordinates," he said, pointing to a number written on the map.

"I can see that."

The young man pointed at an X near the top of the mountain. "That's got to be the gun placement."

The older man ran his finger west as if measuring distance. "We can reach it if we can place our mortars along this ridge. We need to get this back to Captain Kovač."

As he folded the map, the younger man opened the back door of the Range Rover and motioned for Nura to get in. She did. The older man drove while the younger man kept watch, his rifle protruding from the front passenger window.

"What is your name?" Nura asked.

"I am Adem," the younger man said. He waited a beat, and when the older man did not say anything, he said, "And this is Enes."

"Pay attention," Enes barked. Adem sat up a little straighter and scanned the hills around them. There was no more talking for the rest of the drive.

They drove for an hour, over roads that Nura had never traveled. When they finally left the blacktop, both soldiers relaxed. The gravel trail they turned onto climbed past a cow pasture that held no cattle and ended at a farm site teeming with men and women in camouflage uniforms. A dozen mismatched trucks sat in the trees around the farm, most of them covered with green netting. Enes parked the Range Rover alongside the other vehicles, gathered the papers and maps, and lit out for the farmhouse.

Nura breathed in the scent of the farm: old manure, hay, mud, and dust—a scent that reminded her of home.

"How is your hand?" Adem asked. He took her hand gently in his and examined the bandage.

"It doesn't hurt."

"What you did up there... it was reckless." He continued to hold Nura's hand even though he no longer looked at the bandage. His eyes were a darker brown than she had ever seen. "It was also brave," he said. "I have never seen anything like it."

"I…" Nura lost her thought as she stared into his eyes.

Adem turned his attention back to the bandage. "You should come with me. Captain Kovač will want to meet you."

Adem gestured toward the farmhouse. Nura hesitated. This captain surely would be mad at her interference in their mission. But Adem stayed with Nura as she walked, and something about his quiet way calmed her fear.

"What is your name?" he asked.

"Nura."

"It is nice to meet you, Nura."

There were two soldiers on the porch of the farmhouse, sitting lazily on chairs, smoking cigarettes. They eyed Nura as she approached, but did not get up. Inside, a man was yelling at Enes.

"What is their troop strength?" the man snarled. "Where have they set up their perimeter? That was your assignment!"

"But we know where the gun is," Enes said. "And this paper here… these coordinates… they must be for the targets in Tuzla. With this, we can hit them and run… then hit them again until that gun is silenced."

Adem put his hand on Nura's shoulder, strong yet gentle. He had disobeyed orders and saved her life, and now he stood as a man who had taken it upon himself to be her protector.

Inside, the man still seemed angry, but he spoke decisively. "Set up mortars here, here and… here. We will have the rest of the company take up positions on either end of the valley. Hit them and move to here. Keep moving. Keep firing until we get that gun off that mountain."

Enes walked out of the house and past Nura, taking no notice of her. After he passed, a woman came out, tall and pretty, her dark hair cut short. She wore fatigues and boots and had a pistol holstered to her hip. When she saw Nura, she stopped and smiled. "Is this the girl?"

Adem nodded.

"Come with me," she said.

Nura's heart quickened to the point that she felt dizzy, but Adem placed his hand on her back and gently moved her forward. She looked at him and he gave her a shy smile. "It will be okay," he whispered. Nura went on without him.

The house had been converted into something of a command center, with the living room cleared of furniture except for a table. On it lay Enes's map. There were other maps on the walls and heavy blankets covering the windows.

The woman in fatigues walked around the table to stand beside a man who appeared to be in his late twenties. He was short, muscular, with a thin beard and a uniform that seemed more complete than many of the others. No civilian shirt beneath his jacket. Black boots instead of sneakers. He had been pacing when they entered, but when he saw Nura, he stopped.

"What is your name?" the man asked.

"Nura...Divjak."

"I am told you killed a Serb."

Nura held up her right hand with Stanko's blood on it. "This is his blood," she said, the fortitude in her voice painting her words with a strength that surprised her.

The man and woman shared a look, the woman letting a small smile escape her lips.

"I am Captain Kovač," he said. "And this is Lieutenant Palić." The woman gave a slight nod. "You interfered with a mission of great importance—are you aware of that?"

"I was not aware of any mission. I went there to kill a man, and I did. What happened after that was not my doing."

"And why, may I ask, did you kill that man?"

Nura pulled up her sleeve to show her bandaged arm. "Two days ago, that man and two others came to my house. They beat my father to death...raped and killed my mother, and shot my little brother. They burned our house not knowing that I hid there. I crawled out of that fire."

She glanced up to see a subtle change in Captain Kovač's demeanor, a shift from anger to respect. It led Nura to straighten her posture and look him in the eye. "That is why I killed that man."

"And the other men," he said, "can you identify them?"

"One of them was Luka Savić. He went to school with me in Petrovo. The other man I do not know, but he has a thick black beard with two gray lines running down his chin."

At that, the captain and the lieutenant shared another glance.

"Is he a big man?" the captain asked.

"He is," Nura said.

Captain Kovač nodded as if to himself. "His name is Colonel Zorić, but he is known as the Devil Dog. What he did to your family...he has done to others."

"Is he on that mountain?" Nura asked.

"Yes."

Nura touched her hand to her pocket and felt the outline of her knife and Danis's blue marble. Her mission was far from over. "Will you take me back there?"

Kovač looked surprised. "Of course I will not."

"Then I shall go there on foot."

"You will not leave this camp!" Kovač's eyes were like fists as he spoke.

"Am I a prisoner...among my own people?"

"You are not a prisoner."

With her heart pounding in her chest, she looked Kovač in the eye and summoned all her boldness. "If I am not a prisoner, then...I will be on my way. You cannot—"

Kovač jammed his finger onto the map. He leaned over the table and barked at Nura. "You see that mark? There is a one-hundred-and-thirty-millimeter gun on that mountain firing on Tuzla. One of the shells landed in Kapija Square. Have you ever been to Kapija Square?"

Nura had been there, a plaza filled with shops and restaurants, where Babo had taken them to a café when Danis was just a toddler. They ate baklava and Babo and Mama drank Turkish coffee. Nura's boldness withered under Captain Kovač's forceful tone.

"There were kids out celebrating the return of the sun after all that rain," he said. "Teenagers. At least fifty are dead now, and they are still counting."

Kovač took a breath as if to calm himself, but when he spoke, his words remained forged in steel. "I am sorry about what happened to your family, but you will not interfere with my orders. Am I clear?"

Nura managed a single, tepid word: "Yes."

Apparently satisfied, Kovač said, "Lieutenant Palić, take her to the medical station. Have Doc look at those arms."

"Yes, sir," Palić said. She motioned for Nura to join her, pulling a green beret from her waistband as they left the house. Nura had hoped to see Adem waiting for her on the porch, but he was not there. Across the lot she spotted him carrying a crate to the back of a truck. He saw her and gave a nod, but didn't deviate from his task.

The farm had come to life in the few minutes that Nura had been inside the house. Soldiers were pulling trucks out of the protection of the woods, standing in a line outside of a machine shed being handed boxes of ammo. Nura could now see that the wood surrounding the farm was filled with tents, and men, and a few women, all wearing military green and making their way to the trucks. She counted their number to be fifty, more or less.

Lieutenant Palić took Nura across the farm to a cow barn that had been converted into a mess hall, the floors scraped clean of manure, the barn doors removed from their hinges and laid out on sawhorses for tables. The stove and refrigerator looked like they had been borrowed from the kitchen of the house and moved to the barn. Palić took Nura up to the hayloft, which stored boxes of canned food, piles of camouflage clothing, boots, field packs. "You have blood on your clothing," she said. "Dig around and find something to wear. If it has Serbian insignia, rip that off." She smiled. "We don't want our men to confuse you for the enemy."

"Thank you ... Lieutenant."

"Call me Nastasja." She turned and started back down the stairs. "When you are dressed, come down and I'll have someone look at your wounds."

Alone, Nura was not sure what to do. Did Nastasja really mean for her to don military clothing? She was not part of their army. She looked around and saw no other option, so she began sifting through the piles.

The boots were the easiest to find. She knew her size and quickly found a pair that fit well enough. The pants were another issue altogether. She held several pairs to her hips, but getting the length and waist correct seemed impossible. Finally, she found a pair that she thought might fit. A little more digging and she found a T-shirt and a long-sleeved shirt to wear.

She looked around for a place to change, but there was none. Below her, men's voices filtered up through the boards of the loft, their serious tone clear even if their mumbled words were not. Nura felt exposed as she undressed out of her bloodied shirt and overalls in the middle of the hayloft.

She slipped the pants on, and they fit well. Nura did a squat, feeling the material against her legs, testing the give at the waist. They were comfortable, the kind of pants she could see herself wearing for a long time.

She found a pair of aviator sunglasses in a pile of belts and canteens and added them to her ensemble. She always liked the way glasses took the emphasis away from her nose, bringing her face into a more conventional proportion. She wanted a mirror to see herself, but there was none there. She started for the stairs but turned back. From her old overalls, she withdrew her father's knife and Danis's blue marble and put them in her new pockets.

Downstairs, Nastasja stood next to a young woman who was similar to Nura in age and stature. She wore a hijab, but otherwise was decked out in army fatigues, a juxtaposition of soft and hard, war and peace. She watched Nura alight the steps as though waiting for her. That's when Nura noticed the satchel in the woman's hand, a large red crescent moon on its face. Was this Doc?

Nastasja waved Nura over.

The woman said nothing but gently went to work, unwrapping the crude bandage on Nura's hand. She cleaned away the blood—some of it Nura's and some Stanko's—and said, "The cuts on your hand are superficial. You will have small scars across your fingers, but it will heal quickly." She wrapped each of the four fingers with a small bandage.

She then unwound the cotton towel bandages from Nura's forearms. "How long ago?" she asked.

"Two days."

"You've been cleaning the wound."

Nura did not know if this was a question or a comment, but she answered, yes. Then added, "I used antiseptic cream."

"I see no infection."

The doctor dug through her satchel and pulled out a tube. "This is silver sulfadiazine." She squeezed a dab onto her finger and gently spread it across the wounds. "I can give you this tube, but we are low on supplies. If you get in a pinch, honey will work as well."

The doctor then wrapped clean gauze around Nura's arms. "How is the pain?"

"It hurts...all the time."

The doctor withdrew a small bottle of pills from the satchel. "Take these sparingly."

When she left, Nura said to Nastasja, "She is young to be a doctor."

"We call her Doc, but in truth she is not one. Her father was a doctor and her mother a nurse. Like you, she is now an orphan, but she learned from her father, helped him in his practice, watched her mother. She may not have a degree, but she knows enough...and she is all we have."

Outside, a steady hum of truck engines mixed with shouts as the soldiers prepared to move out. Nura walked to the doorway of the barn and looked for Adem. At first she didn't see him, but then a man waved to her from the back of one of the trucks. It was him. She gave a wave back. The truck lurched forward and followed the rest of the convoy out.

With the trucks gone, a calm fell upon the camp. About a dozen or so remained behind, including Nastasja, who leaned against the other side of the barn doorway. "This is the hard part," she said. "Waiting."

"How long will they be gone?" Nura asked.

"Hours...or days." She turned to Nura, parted her lips as if to speak, hesitated, then said, "Have you always worn your hair like that?"

Nura self-consciously reached up and touched the charred ends of the hair over her left ear. "This side burned off in the fire. I cut the other side."

"Would you like to have me style it? I worked in a salon before the war."

"I would love that."

Nastasja took Nura to the machine shed where, among other things, furniture from the house had been stored. After finding scissors, Nastasja sat Nura down in a dining room chair, old, wooden, and sturdy, draped a towel across her chest and shoulders, and began cutting.

Nura remained silent at first, nervous, but as Nastasja's fingers gently worked through the knots and tangles, Nura began to relax. Curious, she finally said, "Captain Kovač seems rather young to be a captain."

"He is. But it was part of the bargain he struck."

"Bargain?"

"The Kovač family ran a black market going back as far as World War Two, maybe beyond. He and his brother...Jusuf, operated out of Banja Luka. When the war started in Croatia, they turned their talents to stealing weapons from the Serbs and selling them to the Croats. By the time we declared our independence, the brothers had a following— a militia. The Bosniaks wanted him to join their army, but the brothers did not want to give up their independence, so they made a deal. The Kovač brothers remain in charge of the people, but the Bosnian army sets our missions. Of course, now it is just the one Kovač brother who is in charge."

"Is Jusuf...?"

"My Jusuf was killed last September." Nastasja's words seemed to come from a place far away. She stopped cutting Nura's hair and looked to the light coming in through the door of the machine shed. "I was there. I saw it. We were running, but the Serbs were going to catch us. Jusuf ordered us to keep going. He stayed behind. He fought by himself, buying us time to escape. I was on the opposite side of a valley when I saw him die. He raised his hands, stepped out into the open, and they shot him."

"I'm sorry."

"You understand that death is possible—even likely the way we are outnumbered—but...you always think that it will not come for you. It will not take you or the ones you love."

She began working the scissors again. "But listen to me, going on. You know well what I am talking about—that death comes for us all."

Nura thought of Danis and closed her eyes.

When Nastasja spoke again, it was with a lighter tone. "I was made a lieutenant after that," she said. "I think Kovač gave me the promotion so that he would have a reason to exclude me from going on raids. He said that he needed someone to stay at the camp and be in charge, someone he could trust, and so I am that person."

Nastasja stepped back to inspect the cut, walking in a circle around Nura because the chair didn't swivel. "Yes. I think this will do. Would you like to see?"

"Very much so."

Nastasja stepped into the stack of household furnishing and came out with a full-length mirror. She set the mirror down, and what Nura saw caused her to stand, as if she needed proof that it was really her in the mirror. Her hair was so short she could see the top of her ears, something that hadn't been the case in all of her memory. Nastasja left the top just long enough to be spiky. Nura ran her fingers through her hair, marveling at the feeling of power that short hair gave her.

Then she noticed the fatigues and how they gave shape to her body. She turned to one side then the other, aware of her form—something previously hidden from the world by her loose-fitting dresses and overalls.

"I can't believe it," she whispered. "You are an artist."

Nastasja smiled with satisfaction. "I had good marble to work with."

She handed Nura a beret and Nura put it on along with the aviator glasses. Gone was the awkward kid who mucked the barn and fed the cows. Gone was the girl who slithered through fire to escape that burning crawl space. She had killed a man, stabbed him in the throat, and now she wore the clothing of a warrior, one with a mission to complete. A strange sense of power washed over her, yet in her pocket she carried the small blue marble of a child.

"We need to prepare for the return of the men." Those words came from Nastasja not as a suggestion or request, or even an order, but rather as though Nura had always been a part of their group and now it was time to get to work. "We will need to set up cots for the wounded, get medical supplies ready. They will be hungry and tired. There is much to do."

Nastasja walked Nura back to the barn, where they went to work getting ready for the return of their soldiers.

* * *

Two hours later, they had cots set up in the barn, extra sheets and blankets stacked on a shelf to replace those that became stained with blood. Boxes of medical supplies sat at the ready. They didn't have the facility to care for the worst of the wounded—those soldiers would be driven to Tuzla—but for those who could be patched up and made ready to fight again, the barn would be their place of recovery.

As night fell, the handful of those left behind gathered in the barn to eat, and wait, and worry. Time hung motionless in the air around them. Nura lay on one of the cots to rest, just for a moment. She did not know that she had fallen asleep until the rumble of trucks awoke her.

The barn, in the gray light of dawn, confused her. She had been dreaming of home: her parents, Danis, the garden, her bed; waking up on a cot beneath barn rafters caused her heart to quicken for a second... until she remembered.

The trucks had come to a stop in the turnaround between the barn and machine shed, and soldiers were already climbing down by the time Nura found her way out of her slumber. She saw a man with a thick white bandage wrapped around his leg limping toward the barn. She ran to him, lifted his arm around her shoulder, and helped get him to a cot. Nastasja followed with another soldier wrapped in a blanket, his face and arms patched with bandages.

A few others walked themselves into the barn and took cots to rest. Nura looked at their tired faces. None of them were Adem.

She wandered across the courtyard, picking up bits and pieces of conversations: the attack had silenced the gun; the Serbs were forced to retreat; two comrades had died; four had been taken to Tuzla.

Two had died. The thought that Adem might be one of the dead struck her hard. She had known this man for less than a day, yet the thought of losing him seemed to open a chasm in her chest. She looked in the backs of the trucks, but they were empty. She walked amid the shuffle of ghost-like figures moving toward the tents in the woods. She did not see Adem.

Nastasja, who stood at the opening to the barn, called out for Nura. "We need to prepare the food." It wasn't an order; nor was it a request. It was simply a statement of what needed to be done.

Nura ran to the barn. Inside, she saw a man sitting against the wall, his head tipped back, a bandage patched across his shoulder, a dot of blood seeping through.

Adem.

Nura went to him and knelt.

He opened his eyes, and at first it was as if he didn't recognize her. Then he smiled and said, "You look . . . nice. I like the haircut."

Nura touched the short hair on the side of her head and looked at the ground, unable to keep her smile in check. "Are you okay?"

"Just a cut."

She gently touched the bandage. "I have to . . . help with the food. I'll bring you some."

He leaned his head against the wall, closed his eyes, and whispered, "Moj anđeo."

Moj anđeo—my angel. Nura held Adem's words to her heart as she ran to make food.

15

Minnesota

AFTER EVERYTHING

The mail that Hana stole from Zaim's letter box is useless—past-due bills and credit card demands—the detritus of a parasite straddling the edge of debt. She goes online hoping that having a last name might open a new avenue, but she is surprised to find no hits for the name Zaim Galić. She thinks it impossible for a man to live into middle age without at least one mention on the internet. It takes effort to stay off that radar—Hana knows this well. He too is hiding.

She wakes in the morning with the same pit of frustration gnawing in her gut that had repelled sleep the night before. She eats her usual breakfast, an energy bar, a banana, and a glass of juice, sustenance but not a meal. The taste of the food is lost in a fog of thoughts. How can Zaim Galić be so close and yet so impossibly far away?

Her legs want to run, but it's raining outside, so she puts on a tank top, leggings, and shoes, grabs a bottle of water, and heads down to her basement, one big room with two steel posts supporting the floor above. The walls are painted concrete block. Thin brown carpeting covers the floor and the space emits a slight tinge of mustiness on rainy days like today, a smell that she has grown to ignore.

ALLEN ESKENS

Half of the space holds the furnace, water heater, washer and dryer, and water softener, as well as a collection of stored items that are not prone to rot, like tools and old paint cans. The other half is her exercise area: a treadmill, a weight-lifting machine, a row of dumbbells. In the corner hangs a hundred-pound punching bag.

In those early years, nights alone with her thoughts had become unbearable, too many ghosts visiting her. A constant anger churned in the deepest wells of her memory, an anger that sometimes grew into rage. She just needed to hit something. That's when she bought the heavy bag, which came with a video on proper techniques for punching and kicking—instruction she found to be rudimentary at best.

Her gloves rest atop the heavy bag, padded on the knuckles with Velcro straps that wrap tightly around her wrists for support. She puts them on and starts slow: jab, jab, cross. Again. Again. And again. Her muscles begin to loosen, her shoulders and arms growing warm. One, one, two. Jab, jab, cross.

When the first drop of sweat trickles down her temple, she adds a side kick to the routine. She breathes with purpose, mouth closed, grunting her exertion on the kick. The rhythm feels good.

Articles on trauma call it exercise intervention. What Hana knows is that an hour of hard exercise—the kind that drains her to the point of collapse—calms her. As she had done a thousand times before, she pictures faces on the heavy bag: Stanko, Luka, and Colonel Devil Dog. She puts extra force behind each punch and kick.

She's no longer hitting a bag; she's hitting the men who killed her family. Her jabs go to their throats. Her cross is a blow to their ribs, their kidneys. She kicks their thighs and their knees, the kind of shots that can drop a man to the ground. These aren't the punches and kicks covered by the video; they are things she learned a long time ago, things that stayed with her through the years.

She picks up the pace. Sweat drips down her face. Her arms burn.

112

Jab, jab, cross, kick. Again harder. Crush the larynx. Break a rib. Breathe. Focus. She adds a second kick, one aimed for the side of the head. She dances back on her toes. Regains her balance. Repeats the combination, grunting on each kick.

The Sweater Lady—that's what the children call her behind her back. What would they think if they saw her beating the crap out of that heavy bag, her arms cut with muscle, her left foot pounding the bag high enough to break a man's eardrum?

She can feel fatigue setting in, but she's not ready to quit.

Even though she has no idea what Zaim Galić looks like, she gives him a face and projects it onto the bag. She pictures him tying Amina to that chair. Searching her condo for clues to finding Hana. The assassin in search of a reward.

The thought of Zaim killing Amina gives Hana a final burst of energy. She spins and lands an elbow on the side of his head, then to his ribs. She steps back and front-kicks him in the face, jamming the ball of her foot into his chin. Finally, she unleashes a flurry of punches to his torso and face, the effort draining her of her last ounce of strength.

Spent, she grabs a towel from a shelf above the dumbbells, wobbles to her workout bench, and sits. She gasps for air, her arms barely able to raise a bottle of water to her lips.

Her mind sweeps to Zaim's apartment and the woman across the hall telling her that Zaim has disappeared. Why? The obvious answer is that he is on the run. He didn't find what he was looking for, hadn't expected Amina to throw herself through that glass door to save Dylan. Amina's sacrifice brought attention to his hunt, and now he's found a place to lie low until he can formulate a new plan. He's out there somewhere, and he is the key to solving what happened to Amina. Hana is sure of it.

Claypool thinks so as well. He has resources. He could get phone records, search Zaim's apartment. He could run Zaim's driver's license, put out a call to look for this mystery man. But Claypool doesn't know his name.

If she were to share what she knows, would he help her find Zaim? Maybe she could trade her information to find out how Amina's therapist plays into all this. But what a risky trade that would be.

Hana wets her towel in the sink and puts the cool compress on the back of her neck.

She had warned Amina to not go to a therapist. "No one needs to hear your secrets," she had said. But Amina spoke of PTSD, of nightmares and depression, of rage-filled outbursts that made her want to hurt herself. Amina lived her worst days over and over. She came to tears over nothing and sometimes froze with fear upon passing a stranger on the street. She said that she could no longer live like that, so she started therapy.

Hana, on the other hand, invested in a punching bag, and weights, and a good pair of running shoes. She burns through her rage every day when she comes home from the library, working her body to the point of exhaustion. She finds her therapy in exercise, and it's working, isn't it? She too has nightmares, although they have grown less vivid over the years. She too has felt the chill of panic when a face in the crowd brings back a memory. She has gotten through it without divulging her dark secrets to a therapist. Why couldn't Amina?

But *had* Hana gotten through it? Amina had joined a community of Bosniak refugees in Minneapolis. She had started going to the mosque and the occasional potluck at the community center. She had even dated a few men over the years. Hana, on the other hand, had her farm, and her three cows, and that was all.

Hana stands and takes a long drink from the water bottle. She paces the room to bring integrity back to her shaky legs.

If she tells Claypool about Zaim, it might lead to her Wanted poster. How can Zaim be hunting her and not have that poster saved somewhere? She no longer goes by the name Nura Divjak, but Claypool is a detective; he will put it together. And then what? He will have no choice but to turn her in. He has a duty. She will be deported, face a sham trial, and live out her final years in a Serbian prison while those who committed the true atrocities walk free.

She hobbles up the steps and out onto the front porch, her favorite place to sit when it's raining. A bolt of lightning spikes to earth in the distance, and she counts the seconds it takes for the report to make it to her house. One. Two. Three. Four. *Crack!* She closes her eyes and lets her mind float free, hoping for an epiphany, some plan to pick up on Zaim's trail without bringing Claypool into the loop.

There had been another woman who went to Zaim's apartment looking for him. How did she figure in to this puzzle? A woman with a Bosnian accent and part of a finger missing. A partner? A scorned lover? A refugee? Hana ponders the woman but finds no answers, only more questions. Hana cuts her loose; she is a distraction. Zaim is the key.

As the rain pats steadily against the porch roof, an image comes to Hana. She is standing on a plank extended over a great precipice. Below her, fog obscures the depth of the drop. In front of her, David Claypool stands on the other end of the plank, his weight the only thing preventing her fall. He says nothing, yet he remains on the plank, looking upon her with . . . compassion? Pity?

When she and Claypool met at Amina's condo, he seemed glad that she had called him, his smile, as brief as it was, carrying something more than a cordial greeting—or is she misremembering it? She dismisses the thought. Even if there had been a moment of connection, Claypool would never turn his back on his duty as a cop. If he were to learn the truth about Hana, he would turn her in.

She thinks of Adem. All those years ago when she hid behind her father's Yugo, bullets ripping the ground around her, he had given up his concealment to save her. He had turned his back on what duty demanded of him and done the right thing—or at least the right thing as he had seen it.

But Claypool isn't Adem, and Hana isn't that girl anymore.

Another crack of thunder and rain falls heavily beyond the edge of the porch. Her clothes are damp and the cool breeze chills her.

She remembers the resolve that filled her veins as the Yugo climbed the mountain heading for the Serbian position. Yes, she had been afraid, but she also knew what needed to be done. She had charged toward that end with no hesitation. When had she become the rabbit?

She goes inside and up to her bedroom, where her phone lies on the dresser. She calls David.

David answers with "Hi, Hana." Either he remembered her number or had added her to his contact list. She takes that as a good sign.

"Hi, David. I was wondering if you have time to get together. I came across something...I'd like to discuss it with you."

"Okay." He sounds surprised, almost eager. Gone is the hard, level tone of their first meeting. "But I have a full plate today. What about after work?"

"That would be great. We could do dinner again."

"Um...sure."

"You pick the restaurant," she says. "I'll meet you there."

"In St. Paul?"

"Sure. Text me the time and place."

"I'll do that."

She hangs up and lays her phone down, her mind already turning to what she must do to keep Claypool on that plank. In the mirror she catches her reflection. She thinks back to that day in the barn, to the haircut that Nastasja had given her, to the way the camo fatigues and beret made her feel powerful. She had donned the clothing of a warrior and it made her feel the part. The image that looks back at her from the mirror now fills her with misgivings.

That has to change.

After a shower, Hana drives to the nearest mall and visits three clothing stores before she finds what she is looking for. The blouse is black, form-fitting at the bodice but flared at the hips, giving curves to her runner's body. The most important feature, though, are the sleeves, long and lacy to cover her burn scars. The black pants are easy to find. For shoes, the question is how tall to make the heels. She pictures Claypool—six-one, maybe? She doesn't want to be taller than him, but a three-inch heel should put them eye-to-eye. That's where she wants to be.

With her new clothes in hand, she walks past a salon, posters of stylish women lining the glass wall. Hana gives the posters a glance as she walks past—but then she stops. She walks back.

In the reflection she sees a quiet librarian. No makeup. No jewelry. There is a plainness about her; the crust of middle age that has muted her features. What is the point of hiding behind that dullness now? If someone has tracked her to Minnesota, they will see past any disguise she may throw on.

Hana walks into the salon and asks if anyone has time to style her hair. Something short.

*   *   *

Two hours later, Hana stands in front of a full-length mirror—amazed. Her hair whips toward her chin looking both messy and sculptured at the same time. A touch of makeup gives her cheeks a glow that knocks years off her tally. But more than anything, the new look fills her with a sense of strength. She can almost see that girl in the camouflage fatigues and beret from thirty years ago.

She types the address of the restaurant into her phone's map app and heads out for her dinner with David Claypool.

16

Bosnia

1995

Without signing a document or taking an oath, Nura had become a member of Kovač's band of fighters, waking each day with a new list of tasks to do: cooking, cleaning, mostly light-duty chores that would not irritate the wounds on her arms.

To her surprise, the camp lacked a cohesive set of rules. No bugle to rouse the soldiers in the morning. No muster for inspection. Some soldiers wore boots; others wore sneakers. Anything green passed for a uniform. Some of their number followed salat and prayed five times a day. Others, like her, did not.

On her fourth day at the camp, she noticed that some of the soldiers awoke at dawn to do calisthenics at the edge of the woods. Adem was one of that number, so Nura decided that she would be as well. She watched them for a couple days before joining in. With her arms wounded and wrapped, she focused on exercises that worked her stomach, back, and legs. The soreness that followed told her just how out of shape she was.

She also watched as they drilled on hand-to-hand combat: knife fights, throws, and close-in fighting. Enes led that instruction and talked of martial arts training he had received in Turkey called Krav Maga. Nura watched closely and practiced those moves when she was alone, taking aim on a stack of hay bales outside the barn. She saw Devil Dog in the hay as she punched. He would never expect a simple farm girl to be able to crush his windpipe.

She sought excuses to be near Adem: sitting next to him at mess, sorting supplies in the hayloft together. He seemed to find reasons to be near her as well.

At the end of her first week at the camp, they sat together on the back of a truck as Adem showed her how to use a military-grade compass.

"There is a lot more to it than just which way is north," he said. "It has a lens and a sight so you can find a target on the horizon to follow." He showed her how to line the compass with points on a map. "Say you want to go here. The direction will be one hundred ten degrees off due north." He showed her how to hold the compass to her cheek and use the sight.

In those times that they sat alone, she perceived aspects of both Uncle Reuf's intellectual curiosity and Babo's quiet resolve running through him. He was shy, yes, but his placidity seemed born of strength and patience, like a tide. The more time she spent with him, the more she came to realize that his decision to save her that day had been a deliberate act, not the rash impulse she had thought. He had weighed the options and moved on the Serbs because he saw it as the right thing to do.

Women in Kovač's militia usually drove the trucks and stayed behind with the vehicles to protect the retreat. Nura wanted to help as a driver. She had driven her father's Yugo, but a truck was another matter, so Adem offered to teach her. Every evening for the next several days, they would drive out of the compound and down the road to work on basic control. He had her drive up a mountain pass to give her confidence shifting on hills and rough terrain, learning both the low side and high side of the gearbox. Adem always brought his weapon along just in case trouble found them.

By the end of that week, Nura felt comfortable behind the wheel. The time had come to take the next step in her evolution. On their next trip from the compound, Nura asked Adem to teach her to fire his rifle. She told him that she wanted to fight alongside the men should they ever find themselves in battle. She didn't tell him how it would be easier to kill Devil Dog from a safe distance with a rifle than up close with a knife.

Adem's M70 held little resemblance to her father's hunting rifle. With its metal stock and wooden handguard, her first thought was that Adem's gun was so much prettier than her father's old rifle, but she kept that to herself. Adem showed her how to take the gun apart, explained how it worked, taught her how to clean it. When he finally let her pull the trigger, there were no bullets in it.

"It will spit bullets very fast," he said. "You want to pull and release. Pull and release. Go for three bullets at a time. Reset your aim after each pull. It will kick into your shoulder, but you must maintain control."

The next day, they went out again. This time Adem brought a second magazine and extra bullets. On a hilltop overlooking a long valley, he handed her a magazine. She locked it in just as he had taught her, pulled the bolt to load a bullet into the chamber, and aimed at a tree some fifty meters ahead, a tree that, in her mind, held the face of Devil Dog.

Adem was right about the kick, but it wasn't as bad as she had expected. Four shots and she released, her breath heavy with exhilaration, the echo of her fire coming back to greet her like a cheer from a faraway mountain.

None of her bullets hit the tree, at least not that she could tell. She looked at the gun and then at Adem. "Can I try again?"

Adem nodded and smiled his shy smile.

The second attempt went better. She knew the trigger. She knew the kick. She focused her attention on the tree, controlling her breathing the way Adem had shown her. When she pulled the trigger, three bullets spat out, and in the distance, bark splintered from the tree. She paused, breathed, and fired again: three bullets, three bullets, three bullets. With each pull of the trigger, more bark flew.

"And just like that, you are a soldier," Adem said with a wide smile.

He let her fire the rest of that magazine, but then told her that her lesson was finished. Bullets were precious. She reloaded the magazine and cleaned the gun. She liked letting Adem teach her things.

After watching her clean the gun, he went to the truck and grabbed a pack that he had thrown into the back before they left the compound. Returning to the little nest they had made in the grass, he pulled out a canteen of water and a handkerchief bundle that held ćevapi, a beef mincemeat wrapped in lepinja. He had forgotten to pack cups, so they took turns drinking from the canteen, a small but intimate act. Nura felt a whole new kind of exhilaration.

They had known each other a mere two weeks, yet there had been so many glances between them over that time, their eyes holding on each other just a little longer than usual. Nura wanted to believe that those glances held meaning for him as much as they did for her. And now this shy man had packed a lunch for them. They were on a picnic.

Adem told her about working in a shoe factory in Banja Luka before the war. Serbs took over the city and destroyed his mosque, an edifice that had been built in the sixteenth century, which he described in such loving detail that it almost seemed to be a living thing.

"They began to terrorize us," he said. "Steal from us. My uncle was in his house when soldiers showed up and demanded money. When he didn't have any money to give them, they crushed his hand with a hammer."

Adem stared at his hand, turning it over as if to examine the bones that the Serbs would have broken in his uncle's hand.

"The next day, my father told me to leave. Get out of the city. He said that I would be killed if I stayed. I had heard about Kovač and his men. I knew that they were in these hills somewhere, so I left Banja Luka and walked through the woods until I found them. They took me in like I was a member of their family."

Adem looked at Nura. "As they have done you."

Nura dropped her eyes to hide her shame. She had not joined Kovač's army to fight for her people. She joined to gain the skills needed to avenge her family—her true mission, a calling she kept tamped down in her conversation with Adem. In that moment, she felt unworthy to be sitting with this man, eating the food he had prepared.

"At first we did little more than attack supply caravans," Adem said. "We were not an army as much as we were a band of scavengers. We would hide in the narrows. Used anti-tank grenades and land mines to take out the lead vehicle. Trap them in the pass. And if Allah was with us that day, we would kill them and take their weapons. Then hide again. Every day, more Bosniaks joined us. Now we are over fifty strong."

When Adem spoke about being a soldier, it was as if a switch flipped inside of him. This quiet man had things to say.

"The day we found you," Adem said, "Enes and I were there to scout the troop strength on that hill. Captain Kovač was preparing the attack on the gun. It was the most important mission we have had since I came here."

"And I got in the way," Nura said.

"No. That map we found . . . those documents in that truck . . . we could not have been successful without them. You gave that to us."

In his excitement, Adem put his hand on top of Nura's hand, causing her breath to catch. "Kovač will never say so, but you were the reason we were able to take that gun."

He gave her hand a squeeze, and then, as if he had just realized what he had done, he pulled his hand back, his eyes falling to the ground between them.

Adem would be a distraction from her mission—she knew that— but his touch caused her heart to beat faster. "It's okay," she said. "You can hold my hand … if you want to."

This time his movement was slow and gentle, his hand covering hers as if he were protecting a wounded bird. He seemed unable to speak, so Nura started talking. She told him about her family. She told him about Danis and his love for tiny creatures, about Babo's love of stones and masonry. She talked of her mother's burek and how Nura used to listen to her mama sing when Mama thought no one could hear. The journey tore at Nura's heart, but Adem held her hand the whole way.

As the sun started to sink in the west, Adem said, "We should get back to camp. They might think we got lost … or attacked."

Nura nodded, but added, "This was nice."

When Adem removed his hand from hers, his warmth remained. She could feel where his fingers had wrapped around her palm, his thumb gently stroking the back of her wrist. He packed their things and they walked back to the truck, he carrying the gun and ammo, she carrying the remains of their picnic, one of her hands draped across the back of the other to hold in the warmth of his touch.

17

Minnesota

AFTER EVERYTHING

avid is waiting at the hostess station. He's dressed in his khakis and white shirt, but there are no wrinkles in the hips of his pants, no telltale sign of a day at work, and Hana wonders for a second if he might have gone home to change clothes, spruce up before meeting her. He is talking to the hostess, a short, heavy woman with an electric smile. For a moment, Hana regrets getting the new outfit. She feels overdressed, like a woman trying too hard to make someone like her. She reminds herself that this isn't about attraction, it's about getting information, and if the makeover can put him off-balance, she's happy to use that.

When she enters, David glances at her and then at his watch before returning to his conversation with the hostess. Hana stops a few feet away and waits until he looks at her again. It takes a moment for recognition to set in, and when it does, his eyes can't hold back the surprise.

"Hana?"

"Hello, David." She likes calling him by his first name.

"Holy..." In the second it takes David to appraise her from head to toe, his expression flashes both bewilderment and approval. He reins in his initial surprise and says, "You've been busy."

"I needed a change. It's been a long time coming, and with Dylan on the way, I thought now's as good a time as any."

The restaurant David chose is nice. Wooden columns and arches contrast sharply against the white coved ceiling. Tinted windows give the room the feel of late evening even though the sun won't set for another two hours. High partitions between booths ensure privacy, as Vivaldi's *Four Seasons* floats softly. Hana never goes to restaurants like this; eating alone is best with a bag lunch in the park.

David opens his menu and fixes his attention on the entrées. When he brings himself to glance at her, his eyes linger on the lace of her blouse and the swirl of her new hairstyle. He starts to smile before dropping his focus back to the menu. "If I had known about your... new look, I would have dressed a little nicer."

"Don't be silly," Hana says. "You look great."

A compliment? When was the last time that she'd doled out a compliment—to anyone? What is it about David Claypool that makes it so easy for her to say things like that?

A waiter in a freshly pressed white shirt and black bow tie comes to the table and introduces himself as Jarred. "Can I start you off with something to drink?" That was a more complicated question than Jarred could possibly know.

Hana thought back to the last time she drank alcohol. It had been six years ago, the night that Amina buried her daughter and son-in-law. While Hana has Muslim roots, her aversion to alcohol has nothing to do with religious dogma. Living alone, she has no reason to drink. And does David drink? Is that a part of why he got divorced? If he's on the wagon and she orders a glass of wine, she'll feel foolish.

Hana dismisses the noise in her head. She needs David to be loose. She needs him to let down his guard.

She tries to recall a wine that might go down easily. Chardonnay? Was that what Amina brought to the farm the night of Sara's funeral?

Hana remembers that it had been a white wine that turned all too smooth after the first few sips.

"I'll have a chardonnay," she says.

"Why don't you just bring us a bottle," David says.

The menu has no pictures, which is fine except that many of the dishes are foreign to Hana. She can't help but feel a tingle of excitement at the variety of options in front of her, given that she is a woman who eats the same breakfast every day and carries a bag lunch to work.

David goes back and forth between the menu and his dining companion, holding his gaze on her a little longer each time like a man adjusting to a bright light. Finally, he closes his menu, leans his elbows on the table, and says, "I hope you brought something good."

"Something good?"

"You said you have information."

"Have you found Zaim yet?"

"Is that what you have?"

"Is that what you need?"

David smiles. "I'd like to talk to him."

"Well, I might be able to help you."

The waiter comes with a bottle of wine and two glasses. He shows the bottle to David. David gives a slight nod toward Hana, a polite gesture to tell the waiter that Hana will be approving the wine.

Hana has no experience in such things, but follows the unspoken instructions of the waiter. She nods at the label, not knowing one brand from another. The waiter breaks the seal and uncorks the bottle, handing the cork to Hana. She has seen this in a movie. She's supposed to give the cork a sniff, which she does and then nods again. The waiter pours a little into Hana's glass. She takes a sip—sharp on her tongue, but probably a delight to anyone with a taste for such things. A third time she nods to the waiter, who pours wine for them both.

The waiter leaves without taking their food order, which Hana appreciates because she hasn't yet decided on a main course. To steer the conversation away from Zaim Galić, she asks, "Did the therapist lead pay off?"

David tips his head the way a curious dog might. "That's why you asked me to dinner? And here I thought it was my electric personality and rugged good looks."

He is joking, she knows this, but there is strength in his aging face and kindness in his eyes. She has seen eyes like his before, dark, soft, and compassionate. She had looked into those eyes the first time Adem gently held her hand.

Hana takes a sip of wine as she thinks about how to proceed, then says, "I just find it unusual that therapy notes might be part of an investigation."

"I don't want to leave any stone unturned."

"Routine."

"Exactly."

"And what have you learned from this routine investigation?"

"Nothing yet. We don't have the notes. Dr. Ellsworth is refusing to turn them over."

"Can she do that?"

"She claims that she has an ethical obligation to protect her client even though her client is deceased. She won't give us anything without a search warrant. Personally, I think she's just covering her . . . her keister, ethically speaking. If we get the warrant, she's not breaching ethical rules turning over client information."

"That doesn't sound at all routine to me."

"Well, 'routine' may be a bit off the mark, but I think the notes might be important."

"Are you going to get a warrant?"

"You are a very curious woman," David says.

The waiter steps up to the table with glasses of water and a plate with cucumber slices. David takes a cucumber slice and slips it into his water. Hana follows suit.

"Are you ready to order?" David asks.

She is not, but she orders a salmon dish that had caught her eye. David orders a steak. They give the menus to the waiter and he disappears.

"I really want to solve your friend's murder," David says. "If you have any information that might lead me to Zaim, that'd be a big help. I don't know if he's my guy, but I need to talk to him."

"I want to make a trade. I can help you find Zaim, but I want you to answer a few of my questions first."

"I don't make those kinds of bargains," David says. "I'm the detective and you're the witness."

"And yet I'm the one who found Zaim."

"You...found him?"

"I can give you his last name and where he lives."

"Great."

"In exchange..."

David leans back in his seat. "Why is this so important to you?"

"She was my friend."

"Then help me find her killer. Help me do my job. Tell me what you know."

"In exchange..."

David takes a drink of his chardonnay and stares at Hana. She can tell that he's weighing upsides and downsides. "You tell me first," he says.

"You'll say you can't talk about an open investigation."

"I need to know what you want from me. Some things I simply cannot divulge."

"I'd like to know what the therapist has to do with this case."

"I can't tell you that."

"You *can* tell me. The question is whether you *will* tell me that."

David points to Hana. "Witness." Then to himself. "Detective."

"Good luck finding Zaim...Detective."

"This isn't a game, Hana. If you know something—"

"My friend is dead." Hana speaks impassively but confidently. "I want her killer found. I'm sure you're competent at your job, but this is personal to me. I can help you, but only if you give in return."

"I..." David hesitates, as if choking back his misgivings. "I'll tell you what the therapist has to do with the case if you have what you say you have. You've got my word." He takes another drink and follows with, "You'll just have to trust me."

"Trust..." Hana's tone is scolding. "You use that word as if it is a currency easily found. Something you pluck from a tree as you walk by. I assure you: I do not view trust with such a cavalier sentiment. For me, trust is something precious and rare. It is a black opal. I do not part with my trust easily."

David's eyes turn solemn and still. He reaches across the table and places his hand in hers. "I give you my word...and that's not something *I* part with easily."

He removes his hand, but his warmth remains, as does a slight tickle in her chest. She wants to tell him, but takes a beat to reconsider—to edit her thoughts.

When she tells him the story, she leaves out the part where she lifted the receipt from Amina's condo, replacing it with a recovered memory—Amina telling her about the brake job and the garage. She also leaves out the disguise and the knife.

"That's a fine bit of detective work, but it was dangerous for you to go to his apartment."

Dangerous for Zaim, Hana thinks.

"You should have called me."

"I didn't want to waste your time if it turned out to be a dead end."

"You could have been hurt. Zaim could be a very dangerous man."

"He's hiding," she says. "He hasn't been home since Amina's murder. That has to mean something."

David refills his wineglass and leans the bottle toward Hana. She takes a drink and slides her glass over so he can top it off. The wine warms her chest.

"Now you know his name and where he lives," Hana says. "It's your turn."

David chews on his cheek as if debating whether to keep the bargain. Then he says, "You're right...about the therapist being an unusual part of the investigation. Truth is, there was already an ongoing investigation involving Dr. Ellsworth. A month back, someone broke into her office. They stole a bunch of files; Amina's file was one of them. We didn't know this right away because Ellsworth refused to tell us whose files got taken. Said it was a breach of ethics to give the names. All we had at the time was a report of a burglary."

Like a train switching tracks, Hana's mind veers to the conversation she'd had with Amina when Amina first told her that she would be seeing a therapist.

"There are secrets that must never be shared," Hana had said. "They are too dangerous."

"I will never utter your name," Amina said. "I promise."

"If anyone learns the truth..."

"Nura Divjak died in the war," Amina said. "That will be the truth."

Hana closes her eyes and prays that Amina kept her word. "Why would someone steal files from a therapist?" she asks.

"Blackmail. Some of Ellsworth's clients received a call from a man with an eastern European accent. He threatened to expose secrets if they didn't pay money. Small-time secrets, mostly. People having affairs, that sort of thing. Some of them paid the blackmailer, but one guy came clean to his wife and then called us. Probably figured that divorce is cheaper than blackmail. When I found that letter from Dr. Ellsworth among Amina's things, it struck a chord. I took the letter to Ellsworth and she confirmed that Amina's file was among those stolen. But that's all she would say without a court order."

"If Zaim wanted to blackmail Amina, why kill her? Why tear her condo apart?"

"That's a good question."

"You have a theory?"

"Two of them. One is that she was part of the blackmail scheme. Maybe she took one of the files and Zaim wanted to get it back."

"Amina would never have done that." Hana speaks with the sharp clarity of a bullwhip.

"I don't think so either."

"What is theory number two?"

David leans forward and lowers his voice. "What if he was black-mailing Amina, but Amina put two and two together? Figured out that it was Zaim. What if she had something that implicated him and he needed to find that thing?"

"What thing?"

"I have no idea. Do you?"

"No. None of this makes sense."

"I agree, but the only person who connects Zaim to Dr. Ellsworth is Amina. I can't help thinking that the key lies in Amina's therapy sessions."

Behind Hana, movement again. It's the waiter bringing their din-ners. David reaches across the table and refills Hana's wineglass. Then his. She notices he has nice hands.

The chardonnay has taken on a creamy, almost sweet taste, and she can feel a tingle at the tips of her fingers. Her first bite of the salmon reminds her just how wonderful a well-cooked meal can taste. She savors it before taking a sip of wine. The flavors mix perfectly.

David is looking at her as if he's waiting for an answer to a question. Hana tries to remember the last thing he said. Then it comes to her. "And you think I can tell you what Amina talked to Dr. Ellsworth about."

"You were her best friend."

"I'm afraid I can't help you," she says. Not really the truth, but also not a lie.

David stares at Hana as though trying to figure her out. Hana ignores his stare and takes another bite of the salmon. She has gotten what she came for. Now she will enjoy her meal and do her best to be an engaging dinner date—even though, she reminds herself, this is not a date.

18

Bosnia

1995

Nura and Adem managed one more picnic.

It was on Nura's twentieth day as a soldier, when she and Adem slipped away to that same hilltop and Nura fired Adem's M70 at the same tree, this time hitting it with almost every bullet. After she had emptied her magazine, they reclined in the tall grass and again ate a lunch of ćevapi and shared water from a single canteen.

Finished, Adem leaned back on his elbow, his long, slender body stretching beyond the edges of the blanket. He was taller than she, unlike the boys in her school. He had dark eyes and dark hair, features common to people in her world, yet he wasn't just another Bosniak. His eyes somehow made her forget words, and his hair held a curl that made Nura want to run her fingers through it. There was something in his lanky build and gentle touch that churned sweet in her stomach.

"I overheard Kovač talking," Adem said. "The Serbs are consolidating around Srebrenica. There's talk that the city may fall soon."

Nura pictured her uncle Reuf standing behind a wall, his hunting rifle aimed at the horde that encircled the city, his teeth clenched in desperation. She thought of his kindness when he took her to the library in Tuzla and let her pick out any book she wanted. She thought of the grave where her family lay, a hole dug in the mud—no marker, no funeral—and wondered if her uncle might soon be laid in such a grave.

Adem continued in a whisper as if spies might be lurking in the spruce trees at the edge of the clearing. "We are being reassigned. They want our help."

"Are we going to Srebrenica?" she asked, a shard of hope cutting through her dark thoughts.

"I do not know, but we will be part of the real army."

"What does that mean?"

"It means that we will have weapons and uniforms, not the rags we stole from the Serbs. We will have artillery and tanks." Adem turned to face Nura, his eyes lit with excitement. "We will be real soldiers, fighting alongside men who have been trained and hardened by combat."

"I thought we were the real army."

Adem gave a small chuckle. "We are scavengers. We hit and run. We steal and pester, but we do not fight—not in a way that will end this war. The attack on that gun placement on Mount Ozren was our first real battle. Taking out that gun...stopping the shelling of Tuzla...we were soldiers that day."

"So we will not attack Mount Ozren again?"

"Those troops are gone."

"Devil Dog is gone? Where?"

Adem shrugged. "I think they are the ones moving south to Srebrenica."

Nura had lulled herself to sleep so many times with visions of standing before Devil Dog, Adem's rifle in her hands—or better yet, a rifle of her own. How would she find him now?

"Does the regular army...do they take women?"

"Sure."

Nura wanted to believe him, but what commander would send her out to fight alongside the men—alongside Adem?

"Will they keep Captain Kovač's soldiers together?"

"Enes thinks so—most of us anyway—because we have a bond. We trust each other. He says that is important."

She had been too subtle, so she tried again. "Adem, will I be able to fight at your side?"

He stopped talking, his eyes falling to the woolen blanket between them. She waited for him to speak, and when he didn't, she slid her hand over to his, resting two of her fingers on two of his. He turned his palm up and cupped her hand. Still, he did not speak.

A swift sang out in a nearby tree, its rapid-fire trill filling the heavy silence between them. A light breeze pressed against the tall grass, bending it gently. These things offered proof that time had not ceased, their testimonies a stark contrast to Adem, who seemed frozen. Nura wanted to withdraw her hand. She wasn't prepared for the pain of what she expected to come next, yet she could not move.

Finally, he said, "I do not know what will happen tomorrow, or next week, or next year. I do not know how long this war will last. But I know this... when the war is over... I want you to be by my side."

Nura's heart had stopped and started again with his words. What happened next came from a place deep inside of Nura, a place she didn't know existed until that very moment. She leaned in to him and put her lips to his. Soft. The stubble of his whiskers scratching an itch that had been there since the day she'd first met him.

She held her lips to his, her breath tangling in her chest until she became lightheaded. When she let him go, she settled back on the blanket, shocked by her own boldness. He too seemed addled by what she had done.

She waited for him to speak, afraid that she may have acted rashly, but all he said was, "I liked that."

"Me too," she whispered.

This time it was Adem who leaned in for the kiss, his hand lifting to her face, his long, gentle fingers reaching to the back of her neck. It was a tender kiss, and when it ended, he lay on the blanket, pulled her to him, and wrapped his arms around her. Her head on his chest, she could hear his heart beating as fast as hers.

They lay in each other's arms and talked until the sun faded away and the stars came out to watch over them. And when Nura drove them back to camp, they held hands until the last possible moment, parting at the edge of the farm's courtyard like two comrades returning from a work detail.

Adem wandered away to his tent and Nura climbed up to the hayloft, where she had set up a cot. There, she stared at the barn roof and relived every second of her time with Adem, accepting sleep only after locking the memory away in a place where it would remain for the rest of her life.

19

Minnesota

AFTER EVERYTHING

Hana and David eat at a leisurely pace like two old friends; David is no longer asking about the case. No grilling her on Amina's past. Nothing about Bosnia, or suspects, or witnesses. Instead, he asks her about the food, the wine, her new hairstyle. He compliments her blouse and her eyes and asks her about books and work. It almost seems as though he enjoys her company. And if she were to admit it, she is enjoying spending time with him. It has been so very long since she had such simple conversations with a man.

There had been chances to be with men over the years, of course. Patrons of the library with thoughts of saving Marian the Librarian from a life of old maid–hood. One man in particular had persisted in asking her out only to be shot down—politely—on each occasion. Eventually he found a different library, and probably a different librarian.

She cannot risk bringing a man into her maze of lies. Hana Babić, the woman they see, is herself a work of fiction.

But none of those patrons was nearly as dangerous as David Claypool, a man of the law. Still, she finds herself looking at his lips as he talks—and wondering. She blames it on the wine.

"By the way," he says, "I talked to the medical examiner. He'll release Amina's body tomorrow. I know her funeral won't be within the time prescribed by her beliefs, but it's the soonest I could get him to sign off."

"I appreciate that," she says.

"Do you have someone...to help you through this?"

"Amina was a member of a mosque. A community of Bosnian refugees here in Minnesota. I called them and they agreed to help me with funeral arrangements."

"I'm not talking about funeral arrangements," David says. He taps his fork on what is left of his steak, his eyes soft and still. "I mean *you*, Hana. Is there anyone...you know...in your life that you can turn to for...?"

Hana has done her best to sip her wine slowly over the course of the evening. Still, she can feel a touch of dizziness as she ponders the personal nature of his question. She thinks back to the tall slender man who had kissed her in a field of grass as the world around them fell deeper and deeper into madness.

"I've been on my own for a long time," she says. "I am accustomed to dealing with hardships. How about you? Who is there for you?"

Something easy settles into his demeanor and he puts down his fork. "I've been divorced for..." He looks up at the ceiling for an answer. "Twelve years. It was good while it lasted, though."

"I'm sorry, it's none of my business. I shouldn't have asked."

"Don't worry. It's not one of those stories where we're throwing ashtrays at each other. We actually got along pretty well."

"So..."

"Why did we divorce?" His smile turns sad. "My job, I guess. I never really left the office. When we were together, I was always somewhere else. She deserved better, and one day she figured that out."

Hana feels an urge to reach across the table and touch his hand.

Instead, she moves her wineglass away from her plate. She blames the alcohol for the thought. She's had enough for the night.

"Back then," David says, "I thought I was making a difference. Don't get me wrong—I still want to do my job well—it's just... there used to be a fire in me. I would obsess over my cases. I'd see the victims in my sleep. I spent nights at my desk poring over pages that I'd read a dozen times, hoping that one more read might give me a breakthrough. Day after day. Year after year. And every time I solved a case, another one was waiting for me. I started to feel like... nothing I did really mattered. That fire that used to fuel me... I guess it burned me out."

He turns his attention to a piece of meat on his plate that he swirls in sauce.

"It all came crashing down one day," he says. "Not long after my divorce, I had this case. Gang shooting. A little girl was killed. Her father... a good man... he put his faith in me. Believed me when I told him I'd find the men who murdered his daughter. I had a suspect, but no one would talk. The case went cold. Then one day... this man—this grieving father—went out and shot the guy."

David holds his wineglass by the stem, slowly turning it, the golden liquid holding his stare. "I had to put that little girl's father in prison. It broke me. It just wasn't right. After that case... I guess I never felt like I was making a difference—at least not the right difference. I want to believe that I'm doing more than just going through the motions, but..."

David looks at Hana. He seems not to see her until he shakes loose from his heavy thoughts. "Listen to me. Your friend is dead and here I am saying that it doesn't matter."

"That's not what I heard."

"I appreciate you saying that." He smiles apologetically. "I'm normally much better company." Then he raises his glass in a mock toast. "I pledge that I will avoid self-pity for the rest of the evening."

Hana raises her glass to meet his toast.

* * *

They stay in the restaurant as evening turns to night, talking about things that keep a smile on Hana's face. She even finds herself laughing at times, an expression that feels foreign to her. It's Hana who looks at her watch first.

"Oh, it's almost ten."

David glances at his watch. "I had no idea."

David pays the check and refuses Hana's offer to split it. He holds the door for her when they leave the restaurant and walks beside her until she arrives at her car.

She opens her car door but doesn't get in. Instead, she turns to David. "I haven't..." Her words get lost. She tries again. "It's been a long time...since I've had such a nice meal."

"Me too."

He leans in and puts a hand on top of the car door between them. His fingers are next to her fingers. Touching. Warm. He is so close she can smell the hint of wine on his breath. "You are...an intriguing woman."

Hana can't help but glance from his eyes to his lips. She is certain he is about to kiss her—and if he does, she's almost certain she will kiss him back.

There is a moment—as brief as the life of a spark—when Hana knows that she wants him to move his hand—to lay it atop her hand. She wants him to hold her and kiss her in a way that makes her forget all the reasons she should fear him. That moment comes...and then it goes.

David gives a subtle shake of his head as if admitting a mistake. "It's just my luck."

"Your luck?"

"You're a witness. There are lines..."

"And this..."—she points a finger back and forth between them—"crosses that line?"

David gives another small nod and says, "When this is over... maybe we could have another dinner together."

When this is over. Weren't those the words Adem said to her as she lay in his arms in that field in Bosnia? A rush of emotion hits her and it's all she can do to whisper a thin "Okay."

20

Bosnia

1995

N ura woke the next morning to the sound of trucks moving around the courtyard. She had not yet gotten fully dressed when men came clamoring up the steps to the hayloft. They began to pack up the gear and supplies.

"What is happening?" she asked.

"We're moving out," was the only reply.

Downstairs, she found Nastasja, who was in the mess hall overseeing the packing of food and pans.

"Where are we going?" Nura asked.

"South." Nastasja picked up a box of mixing bowls and headed out. "The Serbs are advancing on Srebrenica."

Nura grabbed a bag of flour and followed her. They stacked the supplies in the back of a waiting truck.

Nura was about to reenter the barn when Nastasja stopped her. "Adem tells me that you are a capable driver."

"I hope so," Nura said.

"You will drive one of the trucks."

Nastasja went back inside, but Nura stayed in the courtyard, taking in the bustle of people and vehicles. Three trucks waited in a line at the machine shed to get loaded with munitions and weapons: mortars, launchers, grenades, and rifles. At the tree line, the rest of the trucks were being loaded with tents and personnel. It seemed both chaotic and organized at the same time.

When the trucks were filled and lined up, the order was given to eat whatever had been left in the kitchen. It didn't take long for the mess to be emptied of what little food remained. Nura ate a couple biscuits and stuffed a couple more into her pocket to give to Adem.

As she went to search for him, Doc came in looking for food. Nura gave her the two biscuits she had saved for Adem.

Doc smiled like the teenager she was. "Thanks," she said. "It's going to be a long day." She walked out of the barn and into the Range Rover at the head of the convoy. Captain Kovač joined her.

Nura climbed into a truck full of medical supplies, second in line behind the Range Rover, and moved the seat forward enough so that her legs could easily reach the pedals. Soldiers filled in what little room remained in the back of the truck. A man she didn't know climbed into the cab next to her, followed by Adem and Enes, pressing Nura against her door. She had practiced driving in the dark and on hills, going fast and slow, but she had never practiced driving when squeezed tight like a bullet in a clip.

She started the truck and—nervous—let the clutch out a little too fast. A man in back hollered, and in the side mirror she saw that a couple of soldiers had fallen off the opened tailgate.

Adem gave her a comforting look as if to say, *You have this.*

Nura took a breath and tried again, her truck making an easy roll forward, falling in behind the Range Rover.

She had only been at Kovač's camp for a month, yet driving away filled her with a sense that she was leaving home. As she watched the barn and farmhouse fade in her rearview mirror, she saw the line of vehicles behind her. They were all leaving. These were her people now, and her home would be wherever they laid their heads at night.

* * *

The column moved south along the same road that she and Adem had traveled when she practiced driving; still, she maintained a death grip on the steering wheel for the first several miles, worried that she might make a mistake.

Captain Kovač, in the Range Rover, set the pace, driving slowly, rarely getting above sixty kilometers per hour, heading south, a direction that might lead her closer to the men she hunted—but also might not. There would come a time when the war would end, because all wars ended, but somewhere, in the deepest recesses of her soul, she understood that she would not lay down her arms until Luka and Devil Dog lay dead.

Enes had his window rolled down, the muzzle of his rifle pointed out. When they drove through a pass where the walls of the valley squeezed in—like those narrow passages that Adem talked about when he described their ambushes—Enes would open his door a crack, ready to jump out.

The man sitting next to Nura slept for the first hour of the trip, waking up to have a cigarette before tipping his head back again. Adem kept watch through Nura's window when they passed through those more dangerous sections of road, his eyes scanning for movement.

Nura concentrated on her truck, keeping it a consistent distance behind the Range Rover. She drove at a steady clip so that the men who had packed into the back with the supplies didn't get jostled. Nura had no idea where they were headed or how long she would be driving that truck. No one talked.

In the silence, a question came to Nura: Was she a soldier now? She had learned to fire a rifle, but was pretty sure that no one other than

Adem knew that. She had joined Enes and the others for their morning calisthenics, learning hand-to-hand combat, but she had never officially trained.

Yet here she was, driving through the mountains with a truck full of men and supplies. Maybe this was how armies formed when you had no country at the start. Just a few years ago, she had been a Yugoslavian, a little girl who loved to watch figure skaters dance on the ice, a child worried about the size of her nose, an adolescent hurt by the sting of rejection as her friends turned their backs on her. Now she was a Bosnian—and a fighter.

She fixed her beret atop her head and nudged her aviators up the bridge of her nose as she watched the hillsides for signs of a Serbian ambush.

The road turned rough as they climbed through the mountains north of Sarajevo, the blacktop pocked with holes and debris from skirmishes in weeks and months past. They were traversing land that had gone back and forth over the course of the war, land that might be in the hands of the Serbs or Bosniaks on any given day. Everyone in the cab of her truck, including the man who had slept most of the way, now kept a close watch.

The road twisted and curved like a piece of fallen string, their serpentine path designed to avoid Serbian territory as much as possible. Nura drove into the sun, then away from the sun. She guided her truck through hairpins as she eased down from the high elevations. She chugged up slopes so steep and broken that she was sure her truck would surrender before cresting.

When they approached a sign that read OLOVO 20 KM, Enes pointed and said, "That is where we are going."

The thought of being near their destination brought relief to Nura's stiff fingers. Her shoulders ached from holding tight to the wheel and working the gearshift as they climbed and descended the mountains.

The cab of the truck had grown hot as the July sun made its way high into the sky. She hadn't had a drink of water since leaving the camp. Twenty more kilometers and she would be able to relax.

They reached a stretch of road that ran straight and level for about a kilometer as it cut through a narrow ravine. Nura loosened her grip to let her hands rest, flexing her right hand a couple of times to work out a cramp. She checked her mirror—the convoy behind her was spaced evenly, as they had been the whole trip.

When she turned her attention back to the road ahead, a puff of smoke spat from the mountainside and the Range Rover exploded. Gunfire lit up the hills on both sides of them.

The man next to her leaned across Nura, stuck his gun through her window, and began firing. Enes fired out the passenger window. "Go!" he yelled.

The Range Rover blocked their way. There was no room to go around it. Nura hit the gas and slammed into the back of the Range Rover. She kept the pedal floored, the tires squealing as her truck pressed forward, the Range Rover skidding sideways and tipping over into the ditch.

The man next to Nura fell into her lap, his head opened by a Serbian bullet. Adem pulled the man up and slumped his dead body forward into the dashboard, his rifle still on Nura's legs. Adem took the man's place firing through Nura's window, the bullet casing bouncing hot onto her legs as they charged through the ravine.

Bullets ripped holes in the truck's hood and destroyed the windshield. Two bullets punched through her door, hitting the floor beneath Nura's legs.

Adem finished one magazine and sat back in his seat just long enough to reload. Then he threw himself across Nura's lap and fired more, his aim turning toward the rear as she charged through the gauntlet.

Nura looked in the mirror to see if any of the other trucks had followed them through. She saw just one.

"Stop here!" Enes yelled. She did.

Enes and Adem jumped out. Two men from the back also leapt to the ground. The four of them ran north into the woods without a word of discussion. Men leapt from the second truck and ran south, heading up the hill opposite them.

Nura slid out of the cab, the dead man's gun falling out of the truck with her. She picked up the M70, grabbed a magazine of bullets from the dead man's pack, and ran into the woods after her men.

The terrain was the same as on her mountain: rocks, trees, roots that could trip you, low-hanging branches to duck beneath. She ran uphill, the rifle heavy in her arms. She could see her men ahead of her, moving fast, but not so fast that she couldn't follow. They moved along the back side of the ridge, working their way behind the Serb position. They were flanking their attackers.

Nura gulped in air as she ran up the slope. Her arms and legs burned, but she kept running.

One of her men began firing, but Nura could not see what he was shooting at until she stepped into a small clearing. Ahead, two Serbs lay dead, probably left on the back side of the ridge to protect the flank. Gunfire opened up in the woods ahead of her. Nura ran toward the sound.

Adem, Enes, and the two men had spread themselves along the top of the ridge and were firing down at the Serbs below, pinning them in a crossfire with the soldiers firing up from the convoy. Nura slid to the ground twenty meters away from Adem. Chaos and bullets filled the woods around her: yelling, smoke, muzzle flashes, splintering trees—yet somehow Nura remained calm.

She saw movement below her. Away from the main battle, two Serbian soldiers climbed the hill working their way to Nura's left flank, their steps light and fast, their guns silent.

Nura took aim and squeezed her trigger the way Adem had taught her. *Bap-bap-bap!* The first man went down and didn't move.

She had shot a man, probably killed him. The notion registered with her but quickly disappeared from her mind as she watched the second man dive behind some trees. He fired at her, his bullets splashing dirt into Nura's face.

She worked her way to a tree, rose to her knees, and fired at the muzzle flashes. Squeeze. Release. Squeeze. Release. She fired until her gun ran dry, then dropped to the ground and loaded the second magazine—her last.

She rose again, aimed, paused. There was no movement from the soldiers below. Had she killed them both? She kept her aim on the last man's location. She had nearly convinced herself that he was dead when he sprang to his feet and ran down the slope.

She fired, and the man fell, sliding limp over the rocks and dirt.

From somewhere on the far side of the slope, one of the Serbs began yelling for his men to retreat. Like mice scurrying through a bean patch, they dashed through the trees, running along the side of the ridge, firing haphazardly up the slope and down, hoping to cover their flight. Nura fired at the sound of voices and the rustle of scrub brush until her clip was empty.

When the guns fell silent, Nura's hands were weak, numb; her fingers trembled with the release of adrenaline.

Enes, Adem, and the other two men rose to their feet, so Nura did as well. Enes turned to Nura. "Get the medical supplies back to the column," he said. Then he nodded to the others and they started making their way down the slope, guns at the ready.

Nura picked up the M70 and ran down the ridge to where she had left the truck. It was filled with bullet holes, yet somehow it started. She managed to get the truck turned around on the narrow road and get it back to the column.

Nura stopped next to the Range Rover, which lay on its side in the ditch. Nastasja knelt beside two bodies on the side of the road. Nura ran to the back of her truck to grab medical supplies. Two of the men who had been in the back of her truck when the shooting started lay dead against the sideboards, their bodies riddled with bullets.

Nura pulled one of the men to the ground to get him out of the way. She climbed into the truck, found a box of bandages, and jumped back out, running to Nastasja.

Nastasja knelt next to a man whose upper torso had been badly burned. It took a few moments for Nura to see that it was Captain Kovač. He tried to raise himself onto his elbows, but Nastasja put a hand on his shoulder and eased him back to the ground. His face was black from the fire and red with blood. His hair had burned off.

Nura froze, the box of bandages clutched to her chest.

"Nura." Nastasja beckoned for the bandages, her sharp tone breaking Nura from her shock. She handed the box to Nastasja and stepped away to where the second body lay in the ditch. It was Doc, black with soot, blood staining her neck and chest. Nura didn't have to look closer to know that Doc was dead.

Others had crowded around the back of Nura's truck. Boxes of medical supplies lay open on the ground as the men took what they needed to help their comrades. Nura went back to the truck, nudged her way through the wall of soldiers, and found a tube of the cream that Doc had spread on her arms and a small bottle of pain pills like the ones Doc had given her. She delivered the cream and pills to Nastasja. "This is what Doc put on my arms," she said. "And the pills for the pain."

Kovač gritted his teeth, his breath ragged as he fought to handle the burn—a pain that Nura knew all too well. She had done this. She had slammed into the Range Rover, pushed it onto its side. She had made it impossible for Captain Kovač and Doc to escape.

A gunshot rang out on the slope above her, causing her to jump. She calmed when she realized that it was Enes and Adem making their way down the mountain. Nura imagined that they had found a Serbian soldier alive and had killed him. The thought sickened her at first, but she looked at Kovač and Doc lying in the ditch. She took a breath. This hadn't been her fault. The Serbs made her do it. They were the ones who held the blame. She'd had no choice. She had to get her men through to the back side of that ridge.

Nura stood. She had something she needed to do. She retrieved her M70 from the cab of the truck, found a full magazine, locked it in, and headed up the side of the slope in search of the men she had shot.

21

Minnesota

AFTER EVERYTHING

Dylan's foster home was in the South Maryland section of St. Paul, a working-class part of town with narrow streets and small front yards, a neighborhood where kids grew up hearing every argument from the houses around them. Amina's lawyer had already filed paperwork with the court making Hana Dylan's legal guardian, and she carries that document in her hand as she steps from her car. The paper, a few words and a judge's signature, feels as heavy as a millstone as she contemplates what lies ahead.

Hana had been at the hospital when Dylan was born. When he was old enough to form words, he called her Ana, the H disappearing in the effort. There had been a time when he would come to her, sit on her lap, and ask her to read books to him. He was a loving child, generous with his hugs and kisses, but recently that had changed and Hana knew why.

Dylan had light hair and dancing blue eyes, but in so many other respects...he was Danis. Hana would hold Dylan on her lap and feel the same warmth that she had felt when she held her little brother beside the pond back in Bosnia. She would rest her chin atop his head the way she did with Danis. When Dylan spoke, she would hear

Danis, his innocent questions and untethered thoughts bouncing from topic to topic. And when Dylan cried, his tears had the power to whisk Hana to a place where abided the deepest pain she had ever felt. Dylan reminded her so much of Danis that it sometimes hurt just to see the child, and as Dylan grew, she saw more and more of Danis in Amina's grandson.

Then came that day—his eighth birthday—when Hana had made her mistake. Amina had brought Dylan to the farm, as she did every year on his birthday. He loved to play in the hay and chase her chickens back when she had some. That year he had been particularly excited to show off the plastic boomerang that a classmate had given him for his birthday, and the open space at the farm made it the perfect place to do so.

He had been throwing the boomerang out behind the house when it went into the barn. Dylan chased it inside, but didn't come back out for several minutes. Curious, Hana and Amina went to check on him. They found him at the bottom of the steps to the hayloft, frozen, his eyes locked onto something above him.

"What are you doing?" Amina asked.

"It's a cat," he whispered. "I want to pet it."

Hana knew of the cat. It had taken up residence in her hayloft that winter and ran away whenever she got near it. She went to Dylan and put her hands on his shoulders to keep him from climbing the steps. "Danis, if you want to pet her, you'll need to tame her first."

Dylan looked at Hana, confused. When Hana realized that she had called him by the wrong name, it was as if a catapult had slung her back in time to the day Danis died. Hana tried to speak, but had lost her voice.

It had been Amina who stepped in to save Hana from her blunder.

"Dylan, why don't you go to the kitchen and get a saucer of milk for the kitty?"

And just like that, Dylan forgot that he had been called by another boy's name. He ran out of the barn and headed for the house.

The next day, Hana would put out a live trap to capture the stray cat—the talisman that had whisked her back to that terrible day—and take her to the pound. That had also been the day that she started making excuses to not come to Amina's home. She called less. Texted less. That had been the day she started building the wall to keep Dylan out.

Dylan hadn't lost his affection for his aunt Hana; she had pushed him away.

There are three children sitting on the sidewalk in front of the foster home: two boys and a girl. They are dressed in stained T-shirts and shorts. The little girl has big freckles, dirty cheeks, and a Kool-Aid smile. The boys are in need of haircuts—in Hana's opinion—their bangs hanging in their eyes. Bicycles lie tipped on their sides in the small lawn nearby.

Hana expects to see Dylan among the group, but he is not there. The children are drawing on the sidewalk with chalk. They look up at her with suspicious eyes and silent lips.

Hana offers them an explanation. "I'm a friend of Dylan's."

None of the children give a reaction.

"Is he inside?" she asks.

The little girl looks at the house but says nothing. Then a boy, older than Dylan, says, "He's a crybaby."

Hana squeezes the paper in her hand. She wants to slap the boy, but she takes a breath instead. This child doesn't know what Dylan is going through. Like all children, the boy sees the world in stark terms of what affects him and what does not.

She relaxes her grip and steps past the children.

The house is older, with a lawn that has been mown but not trimmed. Weeds jut out along the edge of the house and around the chain-link fence that runs along both sides of the property. She steps over metal trucks and toys on the walkway, and once on the porch she has to tiptoe around a couple garbage bags filled with trash.

She knocks on the door.

The woman who answers is young, heavy, her dishwater hair pulled back with hair combs. She wears jeans and a Twins jersey, and she gives Hana a blank stare when she opens the door.

"I'm Hana Babić... I'm here for Dylan?"

"Oh, yeah. Sorry." The woman backs away from the door as an invitation for Hana to enter.

The inside of the house is a little nicer than the outside, the furniture worn but comfortable, the carpets clean for the most part, and very few toys lying out. In the kitchen dishes are piled in the sink, but they are stacked neatly to compact the untidiness. The woman's name, according to the lawyer, is Roselyn.

"They told you I was coming, didn't they?" Hana asks.

"They said someone was coming, but I thought it was this afternoon. He's upstairs."

Roselyn walks to the base of the steps and hollers up. "Dylan! Grab your case and get down here!"

"So he doesn't know I'm the one picking him up?"

"Like I said, I can't remember if they gave me your name."

"Do you want to see the documentation?" Hana holds out the order from the judge.

"Um... sure." Roselyn unfolds the paper, gives it a quick read, and hands it back. She turns back to the steps again and yells, "Let's go, Dylan. She's waiting."

"I'm not in a hurry," Hana says.

"I packed his stuff this morning so he's ready to go."

"Has he been up there... waiting all morning?"

"He didn't want to come down."

"And you just left him...?"

Roselyn puts her hands on her hips and tips her head the way people do when they've been insulted. "I'm sorry?"

"He must be frightened," Hana says.

"He's done nothing but cry since he's been here. Cry and sit on his bed staring at the wall. I did all I could to make him feel at home, but he has no interest in anything. He's just a lump."

Hana takes a step toward Roselyn, her hackles up. "He lost the only family he had left in the world. He's a child. Do you have any idea—"

A creak at the top of the stairs halts Hana's advance. She can't see him, but she can hear Dylan coming down the steps, the *thunk-thunk-thunk* of a suitcase being dragged beside him.

Hana wants to go to the bottom of the steps so Dylan can see her, but Roselyn has planted herself there, and Hana thinks better of pushing the woman out of the way.

Step-*thunk*. Step-*thunk*.

Dylan steps around the corner and past Roselyn, a brown vinyl suitcase in his hands. He seems smaller than she remembers. When he sees Hana, he stops. He doesn't recognize her with the new haircut. She gets down on one knee and holds out her arms. He still doesn't move.

"It's me . . . Hana."

His eyes fill with recognition and tears. The corners of his mouth tug down. He is fighting his cry as he stumbles to her. She folds his tiny, frightened body into an embrace so tight that she is afraid she might hurt him. Then she picks him up, grabs his suitcase, and walks out the door without saying another word to Roselyn.

22

Bosnia

1995

Nura crept up the wall of the ravine, suspicious of every boulder and tree trunk that might hide a Serbian sniper. Halfway up the slope, she saw Enes, Adem, and the other two men. She waved to them but then cut east in search of the two men who had tried to encircle them on the ridge—the men she had shot.

She followed an angle that she would have taken had she been the one trying to get around the side of the ridge, walking slowly, listening intensely with every step.

She found the first man lying on his back, one of his arms caught in the crux of a tree. It gave the appearance that he was leaning—maybe alive. She approached, her steps silent against the hard ground, her rifle aimed at his head, but he did not move. He was tall and thin, maybe in his late thirties, with bullet holes in both his chest and neck. His eyes, open and dry, stared ahead—at her. She had killed this man.

She knelt next to him and saw that he wore a wedding ring. She pictured his wife at home, maybe praying every morning and every night that her man comes home to her. Nura wondered if he had children. Had they cried when he left to go to war?

She felt a seed of emotion begin to grow in her chest, but then she thought about Doc. About Kovač. She thought about her family and the dead men in the back of her truck. This man had tried to kill her. He had tried to kill Adem and Enes. He had been moving to their flank. If she hadn't killed this man, she would be the one dead on the ground. The Serb would have left her there and never wondered about her life before the war.

Nura took his grenades and rifle, and went in search of the second man.

She knew that the second man had been running away when she shot him. She moved through the trees, stepping lightly on rocks and moss, avoiding the twigs and leaves that might give her away.

She found him on his stomach, two bullet holes in his back, one in his right arm, which lay limp at his side, his elbow shattered. His left arm stretched out in front of him as though he had been pulling himself down the hill. She was about to look for grenades when the man took a breath.

She tightened her grip on her weapon, her finger pressing against the trigger. He did not move. She kicked his leg. Nothing, yet his chest rose and fell with breath. His rifle lay on the ground out of his reach.

He gave a light moan and tried to pull himself forward. This Serb could have been the one who launched the grenade that set the Range Rover on fire, or maybe he shot the man in Nura's truck—the one who fell onto Nura's lap. Maybe he was part of Devil Dog's company as they lobbed artillery shells into Tuzla, killing dozens of teenagers. This had been the man who shot at her, the bullets hitting the ground so close that it peppered her face with dirt. She found a strange comfort knowing that this man had tried to kill her.

Laying the grenades and rifle that she'd taken from the first soldier on the ground, she approached the man and put the muzzle of her rifle to the back of his head. "Roll over."

He made no reply, nor did he move.

"I said, 'roll over'!"

"I...can't," he grunted. "I can't...move my legs."

With her M70 aimed at his back, she kicked his shoulder. He stiffened with pain, but did not move. His wounded arm was not a threat, the elbow mostly gone. The hand stretched out in front of him held no weapon. She reached down, grabbed his uniform at the shoulder, and pulled, flipping him onto his back.

He was an older man, early forties, with a scruffy beard and eyes that needed sleep. Her bullets had entered his back and punched two large holes in his front. One bloomed red just below his navel, and the second bullet had pierced the right side of his torso.

Nura put her rifle to his chest. "If you move—even just a twitch—I'll fire." She took three grenades from his belt and tossed them to the side. He had a knife on his hip. She pulled it from its sheath and flung it into the woods.

"Water. Please," he whispered.

"I do not have water."

"My canteen..."

Nura looked around and spotted the fallen canteen up the hill. The impulse to retrieve the canteen came and went quickly. She had never been this close to a Serb—not since the fighting started in earnest at least—and she couldn't resist the need to ask him a question.

Nura sat on the ground and leaned against a tree, her rifle laid across her lap. Birds flitted in the bushes nearby, their world returning to normal after the cacophony of gunfire.

"Water...please..." he repeated.

"First, tell me why you killed my family."

"I...I do not know you. I did not...kill your family."

"My brother, Danis...was only eight years old. He was shot in the chest by a Serb. My father...my mother...you killed them. You and your dead friend up the hill...and all the Serbs lying dead on this mountain. You killed my family, and I want to know why."

"I have a family too." His words gurgled wet from the blood seeping into his lungs and throat. "I have two sons—Stefan and Petar."

"And yet you chose to come here and kill Bosnians instead of staying home with them. That is how much you hate us."

"I do not hate you."

"Then why kill us?"

"I think...it is you doing the killing."

"You will not leave this mountain," she said. "You will never see your sons again."

"You don't have to kill me." The man began to breathe heavily, his face contorted in anguish, and he began to cry. "Please...I don't want to die. I want to go back to my family."

"I want to go back to my family," she hissed. "But you have taken that away from me."

"I'm sorry. I beg you—"

"Don't beg!" The words came out angry. "Is that how you want to leave this world? Begging? My babo did not beg. Nor did my mother and my brother."

"I don't want to die."

"Is your cause not worth your death?"

"I just want to see my sons."

"You are here—a soldier—so you must have thought that killing my family...my people, was worth sacrificing your life."

"I'm so thirsty..."

Blood now mixed with the man's spittle. Nura set her rifle aside and retrieved the man's canteen. She unscrewed the cap and laid it where he could reach it. Then she returned to her tree and her rifle.

He dribbled water into his mouth, washing the blood from his teeth. He swallowed, and coughed, and winced at the pain.

"You have not answered my question."

"Your question?"

"Why did you kill my family?"

"Am I to answer for the acts of others?"

"Yes."

"You can show mercy. You can leave me here with water."

"No one is coming for you. You will die slowly . . . painfully. I will show you mercy if you ask for it. I will put a bullet through your head. It will end your suffering."

He looked at her with fire in his eyes. "You bitch! You . . . balinka!" He coughed and droplets of blood freckled his cheeks. "What about you? When it is your turn to die . . . will your cause be worth your life?"

Nura considered this and said, "My cause . . . is to kill the men who killed my family. I will kill every Serb who gets in my way." She moved and squatted just out of his reach, her rifle resting on her thighs. "I will sacrifice everything for my family. And when the time comes for me to die, I will not cry like a coward. I will not beg. I will accept my fate, just as you must accept yours."

The man coughed again, the blood from his lungs thick and red, his breath gurgling with every exhale. Nura had been talking boldly about him not leaving the mountain, bravado meant to hide her emotions, but now she knew it to be true. He would not be alive to greet his rescuers, but every second he might wait in vain would be one more second of suffering.

Nura took on a compassionate tone. "It won't be long now," she said. "You will soon choke on your own blood. I can make it easy for you, if you ask."

The man shut his eyes, tears trickling down the side of his head. At the bottom of the slope, vehicles began to move. Trucks that were damaged in the fight were being pushed off the road so that others could pass. She would soon be needed to drive again.

"I have no more time," Nura said. "I need to go with my people." She stood and began collecting the rifles and grenades.

The man looked at her through a squint, his quivering lip covered with blood. When he said nothing, she began to walk away.

"Please," he said. "Let me pray first."

She stopped, laid down her weapons—all, that is, except for her M70—and returned to his side. "You may pray."

He closed his eyes. "Lord ... You are my rock and refuge ... my comfort and hope ... my delight and joy ... I trust in Your compassion ... In the name of the Father ... Son ... and Holy Spirit ... Amen." The man turned his head slightly to make his temple an easy target. He pinched his eyes shut and pursed his lips.

Nura stood five meters away, but took care to aim at the soft spot on the side of his head. The man began to cry in earnest, wailing as he waited for the bullet.

Nura fired and his wailing fell silent.

23

Minnesota

AFTER EVERYTHING

Hana has funeral arrangements to make.

She had once dug a hole in her mother's garden to bury her family. She had left dead Serbian soldiers to rot on the side of a hill. She had held Amina's hand as men lowered her daughter and son-in-law into the ground, but Hana, herself, had never planned a funeral. She doesn't know where to begin, so she has contacted the mosque where Amina had been a member.

Her plan that morning had been to pick up Dylan from foster care and drive to the Bosnian Community Center to discuss Amina's funeral arrangements. Now that Claypool and the medical examiner had agreed to release Amina's body, the time had come to finalize those details.

What Hana hadn't planned on is having time to kill between picking Dylan up and her meeting at the center. She had expected to spend more time with the foster mother, but is glad to have left there early.

Dylan sits in the back seat, quietly staring out the window. He's no longer crying, but he seems to be in a daze. Hana tries to start conversations, but he responds with the fewest words he can, or sometimes just a shrug.

When she hits the outskirts of Minneapolis, she detours to a Dairy

Queen. If he ate anything at all for breakfast, he shouldn't be hungry, but Hana doesn't like the silence that has filled the space between them. At least if they're eating, there'd be a reason for the silence.

Dylan chooses a butterscotch Dilly Bar. Hana orders a small cone. They sit at a table outside, across from each other, the metal benches warm from the morning sun.

"Remember coming out to my farm?" she asks.

He nods and takes a small bite of his treat.

"Did they tell you that you'll be living there with me from now on?"

He looks up at her but doesn't answer.

"You liked coming there to visit, didn't you?"

He nods again, but Hana senses reluctance.

"Did they tell you that your Mama Mina is...She's passed away."

He looks at his treat, his eyes glistening, his lips pinching together to hold back yet another cry.

Hana reaches across the table and takes hold of his free hand. "Your Mama Mina was my best friend in the whole world. I loved her." She gives his hand a squeeze. "She wanted me to come get you—to take care of you."

Dylan closes his eyes. His breathing stumbles as a tear escapes and trickles down his cheek.

"She chose me...because she knows how much I love you. She knows that I will never let anything bad happen to you."

Dylan takes a breath to settle himself and rubs his forearm across his runny nose. He opens his eyes and stares at his Dilly Bar but doesn't take a bite. Ice cream drips down the back of his hand.

"It's going to take time, but I want you to know that I'm here for you."

He doesn't move to hold her hand or even make eye contact.

"I called your school. There's only a week left before summer break. Your teacher said that you don't have to attend if you don't want.

You'll be at a different school in the fall, one in Farmington where I live. But if you want me to take you to your school...you know...to say goodbye and stuff, I'd be happy to do that."

Dylan gives a subtle shake of his head.

"Did you know that I had a little brother? I used to tell him stories about the woodland faeries that lived in the land where your Mama Mina and I grew up. Would you like me to tell you one of those stories?"

He nods.

Hana moves around to Dylan's side of the table, sitting close enough beside him that their legs touch. When Dylan doesn't scoot away, Hana gently places her hand on his back. He nibbles at splinters of butter-scotch floating around the bite marks of his ice cream.

"Your Mama Mina grew up in a land filled with mountains and forests. And in those forests there are many faeries, but the greatest of them all is the Golden Faery. She was born when a drop of dew fell from a special tree high up in the mountains. The Golden Faery is very wise and very beautiful. One night, when the Golden Faery was bathing in a mountain pool, she called all the other faeries to her and told them something important."

Dylan licks at the sides of his Dilly Bar to catch the dripping ice cream. When Hana pauses, he glances up at her the same way that Danis used to do when she told him stories.

"The Golden Faery told the other faeries to go throughout the world and take care of the children...especially those who have lost someone they loved. It's their solemn duty. No task is more important than taking care of a child. Now...I'm no faery, but I know what it means to have a solemn duty. So did your Mama Mina. And I will make it my solemn duty to take care of you."

Dylan stares at his ice cream, his bottom lip quivering just enough for Hana to notice. She tries to think of something more to say, something that might comfort him, when, in a tiny voice, he says, "Always?"

"Yes, always."

"Promise?"

It takes all Hana can muster to utter three little words. "Yes," she says, "I promise."

Dylan doesn't say anything further, but his eyes close and his body relaxes as though some small but important weight has fallen from his shoulders.

* * *

The Bosnian Community Center is a small building, single story, yellow brick with a crescent moon above the door. It is a modest structure, a hovel if one were to compare it to the Catholic cathedral and basilica in the Twin Cities. But Babo had always said that small houses hold more warmth than mansions.

Hana doesn't own a hijab, but she brought a scarf from home and ties it over her head before opening the back door of the car for Dylan. Her hand on his shoulder, she leads him into the building.

"Did Mama Mina ever bring you here?" she asks.

Dylan shakes his head.

A woman, probably Hana's age, if not a little younger, greets them at the door. "You must be Hana Babić?"

"Yes."

"I am Berina. I am so sorry for your loss. Sister Amina was such a bright spirit."

"Thank you. This is her grandson, Dylan."

Berina bends down to be at Dylan's level. "Your grandmother spoke of you often. She loved you with a heart as big as the whole world."

Dylan looks down at his shoes.

Berina stands back up. "You'll be meeting with President Fatić in the community room downstairs. You can leave your shoes on."

Berina leads them to a staircase and down to the basement, where rows of tables fill the room. White walls. Tile floor. A ceiling framed with wood trim. An older man with a large belly and crew-cut hair sits at one of the tables, a stack of papers in front of him. When he sees them enter, he stands and holds out his hand to Hana. "Vadim Fatić," he says.

"Hana Babić," Hana says.

Berina adds, "And this is Dylan—sister Amina's grandson."

Fatić tries to shake Dylan's hand, but Dylan doesn't take it. Fatić pats the boy on the head and says, "I don't blame you." Then to Berina, "Would you be so kind as to take this young man to the children's classroom so that Ms. Babić and I can discuss our affairs? Maybe give him a book to read."

Dylan takes ahold of Hana's hand.

"It's okay," Hana says. "I'll be right here."

Dylan seems to weigh her assurance before following Berina out.

Hana and Fatić sit on metal folding chairs across a table from one another. He moves his papers to the side and slides a legal pad in front of him. "I was deeply saddened to hear about Sister Amina's death—deeply saddened. She was a woman of great intelligence and compassion."

"Thank you."

"We are a small community here. Losing anyone is hard on us all, but to lose a light like Amina..." He shakes his head to finish his thought. "Thank you for securing her body for us. We have a professional Islamic burial service that will take care of the ritual washing and shrouding."

Fatić turns his attention to the legal pad, where a checklist lines the left margin, many of the items already checked off. "Is there a cemetery that you would prefer?"

"Um...are there any near Farmington? I would like her grandson to be able to visit when he wants to."

"The Garden of Eden in Burnsville. It is lovely."

"I'm sure that will be fine."

He types a text into his phone and returns to the conversation.

"After the burial, will the gathering be at your home?"

"Gathering?"

"You are Muslim, are you not?"

"By birth," Hana says, "although my family was never observant."

"Are you familiar with Muslim funerals?"

Hana thinks back to the rain and mud when she buried her family. That wasn't a funeral. That was something very different. Dylan's parents were buried in a Christian cemetery. There had been other funerals when she was a little girl, but those memories have been washed away by time.

"No," she says.

"After the burial there is a gathering, normally at the family's home. A meal is served."

"I don't want people in my home."

"We can serve the meal here. There will be a fee, of course...for rental of the space."

"I will pay the cost."

"Sister Amina was truly blessed to have such a friend."

Berina appears at the door and Hana suspects that Fatić had sent her a text.

"Berina, will you contact Masjid and see if they have availability for a funeral tomorrow?"

"Yes, Mr. Fatić."

Berina turns and leaves again.

"There is a mosque near the cemetery. We can gather there for prayer before the burial. Then it's a short drive to the cemetery." Fatić shifts uncomfortably in his seat, then says, "You understand...Muslim tradition holds that only men attend the funeral."

"That would not be Amina's wish. She would want me to be there. She would want me to stand with Dylan."

"I understand. It is unusual, but sometimes an exception can be made. I will talk to the imam."

"Thank you."

"I will have Berina email you the numbers. The funeral home normally asks for a deposit of half."

"That is fine."

"Have you written an obituary?"

"I . . . have not."

"We will need it right away so that we can post it online and put notices in the newspaper. I can have Berina help you with that." He looks at his checklist. "Everything else seems to be taken care of." He gently tears the checklist page from the tablet, leaving the pad and pen on the table. "Do you have any further questions?"

"No . . . I mean . . . I do have one question."

"Yes?"

"There was a man . . . Amina dated him for a little while. She told me that he was Bosnian—a Muslim. His name is Zaim Galić. Is he a member of this community?"

Recognition washes across Fatić's face, his eyes narrowing, his lips drawing tight. He looks like a man holding back a curse. "I know this man," he says.

"He is a member?"

"Why do you ask about him?"

"I think the police are looking for him."

"I am not surprised. He was once a member here, but he is no longer welcomed in our community."

"Why?"

Fatić moves the legal pad to the side, as if what he was about to say would be offensive to its blank pages. He appraises Hana for several seconds before saying, "This man...Zaim Galić, is a fraud...a user of people. He has no honor. We heard from some of the women that he..."

Fatić looks past Hana's shoulder. Hana turns to see Berina standing at the bottom of the steps. Something passes between her and Fatić. In a soft voice, Berina says, "They can hold the funeral at four p.m. tomorrow."

Fatić waits for Berina to leave. He seems unbalanced as he returns to his explanation. "We think that Galić might have been here under less than honorable circumstances. We believe that he might be acting under a false name. It is possible that he is a Serb. We tried to find proof of his existence in Bosnia before the war. All we found was a man by that name who had disappeared from Srebrenica during the siege. Many men disappeared in those weeks. It would be easy for a Serb to steal the papers of a Bosniak. I am sorry that he and Amina were...involved. He is not a man to be trusted. He is not one of us. That is why we asked him to leave."

Fatić stands, picks up his book, and starts to go.

"Wait! Have you heard from him? Do you have any idea where I might find him? It's important."

Fatić pauses at the door. "Zaim Galić is dead to us. You will need to seek him somewhere else. I will send Berina to help you with the obituary."

With that, Fatić leaves.

24

Bosnia

1995

Nura's truck limped its way toward Olovo, smoke rolling from beneath the hood. Adem sat beside her and Enes next to him. No words were spoken.

The man who had been in the cab with them when they left the camp now rode in the back of one of the other trucks, his body lying next to Doc and five other dead soldiers. Hana's truck carried the wounded, including Captain Kovač, who had burns covering much of his torso.

They approached the first checkpoint, their band diminished in size, strength, and spirit. A Bosnian soldier climbed onto the running board to guide Nura to a temporary hospital, the hospital in Olovo having taken so many shells that it was on the verge of collapsing. The new facility lay outside of the city.

Nura followed the soldier's instructions, which took her down a narrow road that twisted its way into a river valley. The guide pointed at what looked like a rock quarry.

"Turn in there."

Nura was sure she had misunderstood. "There? That gravel pit?"

"Yes."

She pulled in but saw no hospital. Three huts lined the north wall of the quarry, their roofs visible but their fronts barricaded with dirt and rocks. Wooden retaining walls made of rough-hewn trees held the dirt in place.

"Stop here," the guide said. He jumped from the running board and ran into one of the huts.

Nura went to the back of the truck, where Nastasja sat with Kovač's head on her lap. "He said that this is the hospital," Nura said.

The door to the hut creaked open and a woman in a white lab coat came running out, climbing into the back of Nura's truck. She quickly examined Kovač before turning her attention to a second man whose uniform was stained red with blood. She opened his jacket to expose a wound to his stomach.

Two men came out of the hut carrying stretchers. When the men got to the back of the truck, the woman with the lab coat pointed at the man with the stomach wound and said, "Take this one first." Then she pointed at Kovač. "Wait on this one until I see what is in the other truck."

She climbed down and, with Nastasja, ran to the second truck to triage the wounded there, leaving Nura alone with Kovač. His eyes were closed, so Nura thought him unconscious. But then he spoke.

"You did well," he said. His words were slurred, his breath heavy and slow. "Nastasja told me...how you pushed through."

"I did not know that you were..." Nura stammered. "Your car exploded...I thought..."

"You did the right thing. We were at their mercy."

"But you...and Doc..."

"There would have been many more dead...had you not done...what you did. You took action...when action was needed. It is better...to be the hunter...not the prey."

"When they killed my family...I did nothing. When the Serbs started firing at us...I did not think. I just..."

"You acted as a soldier...because you are a soldier now."

Kovač's words carried a truth that Nura had been resisting. Three months ago, she lived on her little mountain honing her visions of marriage, and children, and cooking. Now she smelled of sulfur and smoke, her uniform stained with the blood of both her comrades and her enemies. War has a way of finding everyone—that's what Babo had said—but never had Nura dreamed that it would find her as it had on the side of that mountain, or here, kneeling next to Captain Kovač. She treasured his words in silence.

Men from the hospital came to take Kovač inside. He held out his hand without opening his eyes. Nura took it gently.

"Carry on, my little warrior," he whispered.

Nura would never see Kovač again.

*　　*　　*

Commander Hukić of the First Olovo Brigade combined Captain Kovač's remaining band of fighters with an existing unit camped on the south end of Olovo. Nura and Nastasja were billeted in a house that served as the women's barracks, a run-down structure with bullet holes in the walls. Nura moved into a room upstairs with three other women. There were twelve of them sharing three rooms upstairs, all of them vojnici—privates.

Nastasja moved into a room of her own downstairs, she being a poručnik—a lieutenant. Still, Nastasja had coffee with the other vojnici as though she had no rank at all.

There were five other houses and two barns in their little cluster. The other houses had been turned into barracks for the men. One of the barns had been converted into a mess hall and the other held munition and supplies. Enes and Adem roomed together in a tent at the far end of the property.

The women's barracks, for all it lacked in sturdiness, had running water and electricity and fans to circulate the air on those hot July nights. They had a single bathroom and a kitchen downstairs. Compared to the hayloft at the old camp, this little house was heaven.

Life was more regimented here than it had been at the last camp. Chow was served in shifts, and morning calisthenics were mandatory. Nura and Adem were assigned different chow times, but they stood next to one another in calisthenics. And when she wasn't in one training or another, Nura spent her time practicing the hand-to-hand fighting techniques that Enes had taught her, working her movements from thought, to reaction, to reflex. The training made her feel like a real soldier, not just some farm girl wearing a costume. And if she ever came face-to-face with those she hunted, she would need her training to come with the speed of instinct.

On July 6, the soldiers were sent out to join the fight, but Nura was ordered to stay in the camp because of her arms. They were getting better, the healing working its way in from the outer edges toward the center, pink strips of new skin forming scars that crisscrossed her arms, but lines of scab still festered in the center of each burn.

Being left behind infuriated Nura. Did they not know how she had fought on the side of that mountain? How she had protected her men and killed Serbian soldiers? Her wounds had been worse that day, yet she never flinched. She wanted to leave the camp. She wanted to fight. She had a war of her own to wage—men who needed to die for what they did to her family, and here she was, watching a clock tick when she could have been hunting.

She thought of leaving camp, striking out on her own, but how could she leave when Adem was out there fighting? She choked back her rage and stayed, pacing and chewing her fingernails as she waited for her men to come back.

They were gone for three days, and when they returned, their number had been depleted by a third. Adem rolled out of the back of a truck with Enes right behind him. It was all Nura could do not to throw her arms around him. Instead, she walked to him and said, "It is good to see you."

He had blood on his uniform but no wounds of his own. Black soot covered his face, and his teeth shone white against the black when he gave her a slow smile.

They walked through the compound to the mess hall, where Nura assembled a plate of food for him. They took the food into the woods, away from the others, and as he ate, he told her about the fight.

He sat against a tree, his eyes cast far away, his voice weak and shaky. "We never made it to Srebrenica," he said. "We ran into Serbian troops in a valley...thirty kilometers north of Srebrenica. We fought well. Captain Kovač would have been proud. We pushed them into the mountains and they scattered in pockets. We chased them until it was too dark to see. But by morning..."

He put his plate of food on the ground and put his forearms on his knees. "They must have gotten reinforcements. We set defensive positions, but there were too many."

He dropped his head and said no more.

Nura, who had been kneeling opposite him, crawled to his side and wrapped her arms around his head, kissing his hair. She wanted to say something to comfort him, but could not find the words. Then he reached out and embraced her. No words were spoken as they held each other and let the horror of the last three days drain away.

* * *

Three days later, on a warm summer morning in the second week of July, Nastasja got called to the headquarters of the First Olovo Brigade. When she returned, she walked into the barracks like a woman stepping out of a nightmare, shuffling, dazed, to the table in the dining room. Nura was the only one in the house and watched as her friend held the edge of the table to ease herself into a chair. She saw redness around Nastasja's eyes. She had been crying. Nura's thoughts went immediately to Captain Kovač.

Nura walked to the stove to make coffee, hoping that Nastasja might confide her troubles without Nura having to ask. She put sugar, water, and finely ground coffee into the ibrik and lit the stove. When she took a seat at the table, Nastasja didn't look up.

Finally, Nura said, "Is everything okay?"

Nastasja shook her head. "No. Everything is far from okay."

Nura braced herself for the bad news, but it was not what she had expected.

"The Serbs took Srebrenica," she said. "They entered the city . . . told the people to separate. Women and young children on one side, men and boys on the other. They loaded the women onto buses . . . shipped them away. We do not know where. They said that the men and the boys had to stay behind. They were to be interrogated."

Nura thought of her uncle Reuf and her stomach began to churn with dread.

"But they did not interrogate them."

Nura tried to make sense of that statement but couldn't. "I do not understand."

"They locked the men and the boys inside schools and warehouses . . . some of them just children. Then they took them out a few at a time . . . walked them to the woods . . . stood them at the top of pits— graves—and shot them."

Again, Nura saw her uncle Reuf, this time standing over a deep hole, his hands tied behind him, a Serb holding a rifle to his back. She closed her eyes. "That cannot be true. It is a UN safe zone."

"The UN did nothing," Nastasja said. "They watched as the Serbs slaughtered our people. A few survivors made it out. One of them, a twelve-year-old boy, played dead in a mass grave until he could crawl out. He had been shot three times. He walked through the forest until someone found him. He said that before they took him to the woods, he watched the Serbs load his mother onto a bus. Another woman in line had a baby that started crying. A Serb soldier took the baby and ran a knife through it."

Nura felt sick.

"The men who did this... they call themselves the Scorpions. They act on orders from Belgrade."

Nastasja looked around to make sure that they were alone before speaking again in a lowered voice. "There is a village sixty kilometers south and east of here. A large contingent of Scorpions occupy that village. Commander Hukić is launching an offensive there. And... you can tell this to no one, promise?"

"I promise I will not."

"They're sending me there to gather intelligence ahead of the strike."

"Gather intelligence?"

"The village is in the mountains. I will go in with a recon squad. The men will gather what intelligence they can from the forest... but I will walk through the village and find barracks, gun placements, troop strength."

"Why you?"

"A man will stand out, but a woman..."

"You're going alone?" Nura asked.

"They want me to find another volunteer to go with me. Someone I trust with my life." Nastasja gave Nura a look that carried her plea but also unmistakable sadness.

Nura pointed at herself and Nastasja nodded.

Nura stood and walked to the stove to stir the coffee, her mind wrapped around this new detour.

"You need to know," Nastasja said, "this mission carries risks far greater than death. If we are captured, we will not be prisoners of war; we will be held as spies. They will not treat you as a soldier—not even as a human being. The things that they will do... will be unspeakable."

"The things that they will do to me," Nura said, "are the same things they will do to you if you are captured."

"I know."

Nura went to the sink and turned on the faucet just to let the cold water trickle across her fingers. She touched a wet finger to one of her bandages, feeling the scab beneath. She thought about her family. She had to stay alive to avenge their deaths, but she had no right to refuse Nastasja, her friend—her sister.

"Someday I will see my family again," Nura said. "When I stand before them, they will know that I did everything I could to stop the evil that is killing our people."

"They would want you to live—"

"Not as a coward. Not hiding in the rear while people like you take the risks. You, and Kovač, and the others saved my life. You are my family now, and there is no sacrifice I will not endure for my family."

Nastasja stood and walked to Nura, who remained facing the sink. She put her hands on Nura's shoulders. "If I am captured, I will end my own life before I let those animals have me. Are you willing to go that far?"

Nura wanted to believe she could end her own life if it came to that. It sounded easy in the abstract, but to touch a blade to her own skin, cut deep enough to find an artery... Then she remembered killing Stanko Krunić. She had not wavered then. She knew her answer.

Nura turned and took Nastasja's hands in hers. "On that mountain," she said in a voice barely above a whisper, "when Enes and Adem found me—rescued me—I had already surrendered to Allah. My life since that day has been... extra. I was prepared to die then, and I am prepared to die now. The more we know about that village, the better our attack will be. If I can save the life of even one of my comrades— my family—it will be a sacrifice worthy of the extra life that I have been granted."

Nastasja's eyes glistened with tears that refused to fall. "I do not want you to die. I want you to live."

"Just as I want you to live."

Nastasja smiled. "Then we will take care of each other. Make sure that we both leave that village alive."

"Yes," Nura said, "that is what we will do."

25

Minnesota

AFTER EVERYTHING

Hana has never written an obituary. "I don't know where to begin," she says.

"Let's start with loved ones," Berina says. "You know, Amina is survived by..."

"Her grandson, Dylan."

As Berina writes on the legal pad, she doesn't make eye contact with Hana. Her demeanor seems to have flipped from when she greeted Hana and Dylan at the door, a light gone dark.

Hana adds, "Her daughter Sara passed away six years ago."

Hana watches the movement of pen on paper as Berina writes. There's something a little off in how Berina holds her pen, the angle almost straight up and down. Then Hana sees why—Berina is missing part of her right index finger.

"Oh, my God," she whispers. "You know Zaim Galić."

Berina doesn't answer. She lays her pen down and folds her hands together.

"You were at his apartment last fall. You...you threatened to kill him."

When Berina looks up, there is fear in her eyes.

"I need to find him."

"I don't... I can't..."

"It's important."

"Please don't make me talk about that."

"Berina, do you know how Amina died?"

"She... fell?"

"She was thrown off her balcony by a man."

Berina looks at Hana as if searching for a lie.

"The police are looking for Zaim. I'm trying to help them find him. If you know anything—anything at all..."

"They think Zaim...?"

"He's disappeared. Please..."

Berina shakes her head in a sharp and bitter *no*.

"He may have killed Amina."

"It is my darkest shame."

"If you help me find him... I will make sure that no one knows that it came from you. I promise."

Berina folds her arms in and closes her eyes. Then in a tiny voice she says, "I am one of the women Mr. Fatić told you about. Zaim and I dated for a while. I thought he loved me. We made plans, but they were lies."

"Why did you go to his apartment? Why did you threaten to kill him?"

"I didn't mean it. I was... upset."

"Tell me about Zaim."

She looks at Hana, then at the table as if she seeks courage in the thin veneer of its surface. "In the beginning..." She pauses, but then continues: "He was very attentive. He said all the right words. He made me think he cared. He would ask me about my life in Bosnia. I thought he wanted to know me better. But then... I told him something about me, something I had kept secret from everyone. That I was a prisoner at the Vilina Vlas Hotel."

Hana stops breathing. Vilina Vlas? She had never met a survivor of that infamous rape camp.

Berina's voice quivers as she continues. "There was another girl in my room—my cell—her name was Izeta. We became friends."

Berina keeps her head bowed, but Hana can see the shine of a tear etching down the woman's face.

"One day, three guards came to our cell." Berina glances up to see if Hana needs her to spell it out. She doesn't. "They had come for me, but when I saw them...I..." Berina puts her face into her hands and cries, her breath becoming ragged.

Hana goes to the kitchen and finds a roll of paper towels. She tears one off and returns to the table, giving it to Berina.

"Thank you."

Berina wipes the tears away, and when her breath is once again within her control, she continues. "When the guards came, I begged them to take Izeta instead of me. I told them that she was unspoiled." She swallows, takes a cleansing breath, and says, "Izeta never came back. She didn't survive the encounter."

"I am so sorry," Hana whispers.

"I trusted Zaim. I confided in him. But when he learned what I had done, he threatened to contact Izeta's family and tell them the truth of how she died. He demanded that I pay him ten thousand dollars to keep my secret. That was when I went to his apartment. I don't know what I would have done had he been there."

"Did you pay him?"

"I gave him all that I had—a few thousand. I thought it was over, but a couple months ago, he came back. He wanted more, but I had no more to give. I spoke to the imam. I told him what was happening. The imam told me to confess my act to Izeta's family in Bosnia...seek their forgiveness. So, that is what I did."

"That must have been...I can only imagine..."

"After I told Zaim that I'd made peace with Izeta's family, I never heard from him again. I didn't know that he and Amina had been together until today. I'm so sorry."

"This isn't on you, Berina. You're just another victim."

"I would have warned her."

"Mr. Fatić said that Zaim might be Serbian. Why would he think that?"

Berina stares at the table between them. She is no longer crying, but her breath remains shallow. The room is silent except for the hum of the air-conditioning flowing through the vent above them. Hana waits.

Berina does not raise her head when she finally speaks. "He is uncircumcised."

"I see," Hana says.

Berina's evidence cannot rule out the rare exception, but it leaves little doubt that Zaim is no Muslim.

Berina looks up, her eyes wet with tears. "Do you really think Zaim killed Amina?"

"I would like to find him and ask him."

"Did you go to his land in the woods?"

"Land in the woods?"

"He took me there once. It has a little hunting trailer. He told me that it was where we would build our dream house. That was right before he started blackmailing me. He probably used my money to pay off the mortgage. I was such a fool."

"Where is this land?"

"I can..." Berina pulls her phone from her pocket. "I can find it on a map." She taps and swipes at the screen of her phone, and then turns it around to show it to Hana.

Hana reaches for her cell phone to transfer the information, but stops. It would be better to keep those coordinates off her phone in case it was ever searched. "Can I have a piece of paper?"

Berina tears a sheet off the legal pad and slides it and a pen to Hana.

Hana taps the screen to get GPS coordinates. She writes the number down. "This will be very helpful," Hana says, tucking the paper into her pocket.

"I know that I am supposed to forgive my enemies," Berina says, "but if you find him...If he is the one who...hurt Amina, I want him to suffer righteous punishment."

"I promise you, Berina, if I find him...there will be a reckoning."

26

Bosnia

1995

That evening, the food at the camp in Olovo held no taste for Nura. No aroma. The meal could have been beef or rabbit—or cardboard—for all she knew. The food could not steal Nura's attention away from the mission to come. She and Nastasja would leave in the morning along with a four-man reconnaissance team. There would be two additional soldiers whose role it would be to wait at the edge of town and extract the women once they had completed their mission. Nastasja had been tasked with choosing the extraction team. Nura was sure that one of those men would be Enes, the best fighter of their number and a man Nastasja trusted above all others.

Extraction. For Nura, the word brought the notion of a heist, men retrieving a thing of value. If they were successful, they would bring back a map of the Scorpions' barracks and headquarters. They would know where the tanks were stationed and where gun nests had been set up. That knowledge—that map—would not just be a thing of value, it would be priceless.

If they were not successful—if they were captured—the Serbs would want to know why two Bosnian women were in their village.

They would want to know where the Bosnians were camped, their troop strength, equipment, attack plans—details that had been kept from Nura. The Serbs would take her life, but not before they took everything they could from her, and it was that thought that stole the taste from her food.

Nura finished her meal and left the barn to find Adem waiting for her, standing like a statue in the middle of the courtyard, his feet planted, his arms limp at his side, his shoulders slumped. He didn't speak, not even when Nura stood directly in front of him. She wanted to say something but could find no words—her mission being a secret.

Finally, Adem said, "Why did you volunteer?"

He wasn't supposed to know. If it got out that she and Nastasja would be walking through the enemy camp, they would certainly be caught. She played dumb and prayed that Adem was talking about something else.

"Volunteer?"

"I know," Adem said, looking around to make sure that they would not be overheard. "I am going with you. Enes and me... We will be your extraction team."

Adem would be there. His news strengthened parts of her body that had been unsteady for most of the morning. "We should not talk about this here," she said. "Join me for a walk."

A stone trail snaked past the houses and barns and into the woods. Sentries had been posted where the trail came to the crest of the hill, the valley beyond falling to the river bottom. The sentries leaned against their vehicles smoking cigarettes, their guns resting butt-down on the ground. Nura pretended not to notice when one of them gave Adem a wink as they passed.

Nura and Adem didn't speak on the long descent into the valley. They passed an abandoned cornfield, the ears blackened with mold as they clung weakly to the stalks, nearly a year past when they should have been harvested. Once past the field, and out of sight of the sentries, Nura turned them toward the woods. Only then did Adem speak.

"I am worried...about what you are going to do."

Nura reached out her hand and held Adem's, but did not answer.

"It is a small village," Adem said. "You and Nastasja will stand out. You will be stopped, and if that happens..."

She led him to a clearing where the trees opened to the sun, the grass as high as Nura's knee. She stopped walking when she felt the earth turn soft beneath her feet, the rocky terrain giving way to soil. In a nearby tree, a dunnock chirped a song, unaware of concepts like war, and rape, and torture. It was as if they had passed through a curtain to enter a new land, a place of peace. She knelt in the tall grass and brought Adem down with her.

"Should I let someone else go in my place?" she asked.

"You volunteered," he said, as if that explained anything.

"So did you."

"But...I will not be walking through the enemy's camp, out in the open. I will be hiding like a coward. I will be safe...while you—"

"You will be there to bring me home."

"I will bring you home," he said. "I promise."

He leaned in and gave her a kiss, hesitant in his movements until she put her hands to his face and pulled his lips tight against hers, his stubble rough on her skin. They lay in the grass and kissed for a long time, and when they stopped, Nura found a home in the crux of his shoulder, her bandaged arm draped across his chest. He lifted her palm to his lips and kissed it.

"I have scars," she said. "They will always be there...burned into my skin."

"They are a sign of your strength," he said. "It is part of what makes you beautiful."

She had never been called beautiful. It wasn't true, but those were the exact words she wanted to hear. She rolled into him and began to kiss him again.

He wore a T-shirt, army-issue green, tucked into camo pants, and as they kissed, she pulled the shirt free and slipped her hands onto his stomach. He was thin and solid and gave off a slight scent of perspiration that made Nura want to bite his lip. Her fingers moved up his chest.

He followed her lead, his hands carefully following the form of her body, pausing at her hips. He squeezed, but then pulled back, leaving Nura breathless and confused.

"What is wrong?" she asked.

"I have never..." He didn't look at her as he spoke. "I mean, I want to, but I don't know—"

"I don't either," she said. "I haven't either... but I want to."

Nura wanted this man in a way that made her tremble, but there was something else. She did not want to die without knowing a man in that way—without knowing *Adem* in that way. She kissed him before he could read the truth on her face. Then she slid his hand up to her breast. He needed no further encouragement.

He was like a book that had never been read, the pages crisp and fresh, the words pouring over her and through her, filling her mind, her body, her soul, with emotions so powerful they made her writhe and shudder.

When they finished, she lay in his arms, the sun kissing parts of her body that had never lain exposed to its rays. In the silence, she tried to understand the emotion that welled inside of her, a sense of completeness that she had never known before.

In a just world, she and Adem would have fallen asleep in each other's arms and awoken still entwined. They would have lived their days in peace. She would have cooked meals for him—for their children. She would have known the simple joy of turning a house into a home. As Nura lay in Adem's arms, she wanted nothing to do with the war.

She wanted nothing to do with revenge or the mission of the coming day. She wanted only to be with this man.

But she could not have that world, not until the war was over. Not until she avenged her family's murder. Her people needed her. Her family needed her. The mission needed her. So much depended upon her doing her duty.

She tucked herself into Adem as tightly as she could and dreamed of a life after everything, a life she would likely never know.

27

Minnesota

AFTER EVERYTHING

Hana hadn't thought to purchase food for Dylan before going to pick him up from foster care. What do eight-year-old boys eat? When Danis was eight, they had been rationing the beef from the few cows on the farm, supplementing it with snared rabbits and the vegetables that Mama grew in her garden. What Hana has in her refrigerator and cupboards are lean meats, vegetables, and fruits. No cereal. No pastas. No hamburger. So, for their first lunch together, she takes Dylan to McDonald's. After that, they go shopping.

Once home, she walks him through the house. Shows him his room. He stands at the door to take it in, declining her invitation to sit on the bed. She shows him the kitchen, bathroom, and living room before taking him outside.

He had been to her farm before, but on those trips, he had been a visitor, bouncing in the hay, hitting a stick against the tractor tire, climbing the maple tree in the front yard. He had paid no attention to how one thing connected to another. Hana introduces him to her three cows and shows him why the loft is filled with hay. She shows him the pasture behind the barn where the cows go to eat fresh grass. She wants

him to see the farm for what it is, a place to live and grow. She wants him to see it as his home.

At one point, when they are in the pasture with the cows, Dylan reaches out his hand and takes ahold of Hana's. He is nervous around the animals. His hand is so small and she remembers how Danis had held her hand so tightly when he was frightened by the sound of war. "That is far away," she had said. "They will not come to our mountain. There is nothing for them here."

She had been wrong, and when evil came, she had not been ready. She cannot let that happen again. She cannot sit back and wait.

She thinks of Uncle Reuf, how he left the mountain and went in search of the evil that lurked in the dark. He never returned. After the massacre at Srebrenica, the Serbs had buried the dead in mass graves. Later, when they saw that the war would end, they'd dug up the graves and scattered those bones throughout the country. Uncle Reuf's remains had been among those identified. Hana hadn't wanted to believe it until she saw his name in the published list online.

Dylan stays at Hana's side as they walk back to the house, as though he is afraid that if he wanders away from her, she will be gone—like everyone else in his life.

They go to the living room and sit on the couch.

"Want to play a game?"

Dylan shrugs his shoulders.

"Read a book?"

Again, he shrugs.

Hana turns the television on and finds a cartoon channel. Dylan watches but doesn't seem interested.

"Can I ask you a question?" she says.

Dylan doesn't respond.

"Did your Mama Mina ever talk about a man named Zaim?"

Dylan looks at Hana, his brow furrowed with a question.

"Do you know who I'm talking about?"

"I don't like him."

"You met him?"

"He stayed with me when Mama Mina went to the grocery store one time. Mama Mina got mad at him."

"Why did Mama Mina get mad?"

"He used her computer. She came home and got mad."

"What did she say to him?"

"She said he had no business snooping. She told him to leave."

"What else?"

Dylan thought for a moment and shrugged.

"Did she say anything else?"

He thought again. "I don't think so. She was mad though."

Hana turns her attention back to the TV, but her mind mulls over this new information. Zaim Galić—a man who might very well be a Serbian impostor—had been looking for something on Amina's computer. The man who killed Amina tore her condo apart looking for something. He took her computer with him when he fled.

In her pocket, she holds GPS coordinates that might answer all her questions.

Dylan's head has grown heavy against Hana's side. He has fallen asleep. Hana carefully lays him on the couch and sneaks through the kitchen and out onto the back porch, her cell phone in hand.

She could call David, give him the GPS coordinates, but then what? If he found Zaim there with Amina's laptop, that should be enough to arrest him. But if Zaim is a bounty hunter set upon finding Nura Divjak—the Night Mora—he would not keep that a secret for very long. He would use it as a bargaining chip, and she would be the one arrested.

There is something about David that she trusts, but her fate would be out of his hands.

Hana thinks about the child sleeping on her couch. She thinks about the promise she made to be there for him—to protect him—and her decision is made. She dials the phone.

"Hello?"

Hana speaks in a low voice. "Hi Deb, it's Hana."

"Hello, dear. I haven't seen you at the library."

"I took some time off, like you suggested."

"Is everything all right?"

"Remember that friend I told you about...the one who died?"

"Yes."

"I've been named the guardian of her eight-year-old grandson, Dylan. He's here now."

"Oh my. That must be quite the change for you. How is he doing?"

"I have a big favor to ask, and please, feel free to say no."

"You know better than that."

"I have some errands to run, but...I think Dylan's going through separation anxiety. I was hoping that you might see fit to watch him tonight, but I want to wait until he's asleep before I slip out. Does that make sense?"

"It makes sense enough," Deb says. "Why don't you call me when he's down and I'll drive over."

"That would be so great of you. I don't know how long my errands will take, but you can spend the night if you'd like."

"I'll be as quiet as a mouse. He won't even know you've left."

*   *   *

That night, after a meal of chicken strips and fries, Hana plays a game of Uno with Dylan. She reads part of a chapter book to him and tells him more of the faery stories that she used to tell Danis. When night falls hard enough that he can no longer keep his eyes open, Hana tucks him in bed and calls Deb.

Before Deb arrives, Hana picks out her darkest running outfit, making sure that the clothing has no reflective material, and puts the bundle in her car along with the knife she bought at the pawn shop.

She goes on her computer and types in the GPS coordinates she got from Berina, making a mental note that when the mission is over, she will need to destroy her computer and all the tiny microbes of digital evidence floating through its hard drive. The internet is a wonderful thing. With a touch of her finger, Hana is able to see a satellite image of the parcel of land Berina had told her about, a few miles west of the St. Croix River. Marshy, but also wooded, a little over an hour's drive north.

When she zooms in, she can see the outline of what appears to be a trailer home in the woods—the hunting shack. There are no houses or huts close enough for anyone to hear Zaim Galić scream, should it come to that. What a remarkable tool the internet has become, a toy used by voyeurs and busybodies to kill time. If they'd had satellites back in 1995, she and Nastasja would not have had to walk through that pit of Scorpions. How different her life would have been. Such thoughts make her sad; still, she can't help entertaining them.

Hana draws the map on a piece of paper, something that can be easily destroyed to leave no trace of her journey, and tucks it into the pocket of her cardigan sweater just as the headlights of Deb's car flash across the front door.

28

Bosnia

1995

I n the sweltering dark of a July morning, Nura Divjak leaned against
the wall of a burned-out house on the edge of a Serb-held village.
Her team had arrived in the heart of the night, after starting the journey in Olovo that morning.

The first part of the trip had been in the back of a truck, Nura
studying a chart of Serbian military insignia as they rumbled through
the hills. If she saw an officer in the village, she needed to be able to
determine his rank.

When they reached territory where the chances of running into a
Serbian patrol became probable, they abandoned the truck and went
on foot, traversing two mountains along the way. The recon soldiers
led the team, two of them walking far ahead of the others to make sure
there were no Serbian patrols. The remaining two stayed with Nastasja
and Nura. Enes and Adem brought up the rear.

Once at the burned-out house, the four recon men disappeared into
the woods to take up positions around the village, where they would
monitor perimeter security and scout positions for the coming Bosnians to set up mortar nests.

Nura and Nastasja changed out of their fatigues, slipping into civilian clothes of dark pants and blouses, bland attire that would paint them as local peasants. Nura's blouse had long sleeves to cover her arms. The final piece of their ensemble were crucifix necklaces worn outside of their clothing, a masquerade that Nura was sure would fool only the dullest of Serbian soldiers.

As night passed above, she tried to sleep, but her heart beat too hard for that. Instead, she sat against one of the walls, Adem at her side. Neither speaking, they held hands in the dark.

Nura could smell the house in the darkness: charred wood, rotted plaster. She could see stars above them where there had once been a roof. But it wasn't until the gray of morning bled in from the east that she could see the blackened beams above her and crumbling walls all around. Near her feet, she spied the remains of a prayer rug. This had been a Muslim home, which made her wonder about the inhabitants. Had they escaped before the Serbs took over the village? Had they gone to Srebrenica like her uncle Reuf? Did they die there? Did he?

Nura had been given a knife to carry on her walk through the village, its sheath strapped to her right calf, big and bulky, not like Babo's knife, which she still had in her pocket. She thought about the two knives as she waited for the sun to rise. She didn't like having the knife strapped to her leg. She tried to imagine a scenario where she would be able to pull it before a Serb could put a bullet in her head.

At the same time, Babo's knife would need to be pulled and opened before it became a weapon. That wouldn't do either.

As the light of morning began to bleed in through the missing roof, she opened the blade of Babo's knife, slid it into a gap between the floorboards, and kicked the handle until the blade snapped off. She rolled up her sleeve and slid the blade into the wrapping of the bandages—the same place she had hidden the knife when she killed Stanko Krunić.

Nastasja was the first to rise to her feet, patting her thigh where she had attached a map to her leg with an elastic bandage.

Nura rose slowly and looked out through a hole where a window had once been. The house had a small front yard, overgrown by weeds. The road in front of the house, a two-lane blacktop badly in need of repair, rolled in from the mountains on one side and wound past empty pastureland before coming to a small cluster of houses at the edge of the village. Beyond that the road curved left and disappeared.

No goodbyes were said. Nura shared a look with Adem that spoke more than any words could. Enes simply said, "Nightfall." That was when Nura and Nastasja needed to be back. The village had a curfew, and anyone seen out after sundown would be arrested on sight.

Nura didn't need to be a military strategist to understand that the attack would be imminent. Even she could read the bustle of trucks moving around camp the previous morning, the soldiers cleaning their weapons, worried looks hidden behind the thin façade of a smile. For all Nura knew, the attack force might be gathering in the hills above them at that very moment—or it might not.

The two women walked side by side toward the village, a light fog rising from a creek somewhere in the woods. Those first few houses were the ones that made Nura the most nervous. Why would two women, faces unfamiliar to the villagers, be walking down that road at that time of morning? Where had they come from? Who else could they be but spies? Once they got to the center of the village, it would be easier to blend, but not here.

"Lovely morning," Nastasja said in a hushed voice.

Nura linked arms with Nastasja. "Peaceful," Nura said.

They passed the first few houses without incident and followed the road as it curved toward the heart of the village.

The village was long and narrow, bending with the creek as it flowed from north to south. Three roads ran the length: one cutting through the center of the village, one branching east to follow the creek, and one branching west, running along the base of the mountain. They had mapped their course before leaving Olovo: Nura would take the mountain road, Nastasja the creek road. They would rejoin at a church on the opposite side of the village and return along the center street.

When the time came to split, Nastasja gave Nura a small hug. "I'll see you at the church."

Nura nodded, took a breath, and parted from her friend.

The first thing that struck Nura were the roofs on the houses. Some were asphalt shingles, some clay tile, and yet others were cedar shanks. What stood out was that they existed at all. The Muslim villages she had passed on the move south were filled with husks of houses, their roofs burned away. Yet in this village, other than a few structures like their outpost—a Muslim home—the houses were mostly untouched by the war.

Two old women stood in front of one of the houses, one of them hanging laundry on a line, the other talking to the first. They stopped what they were doing and watched as Nura walked by. But once she was past, the women began to chat again, their words lost in the breeze.

Nura came to an empty lot where weeds grew up around a swing set and slide. In the distance beyond the playground equipment, Nura spied a mortar nest with three soldiers sitting on sandbags smoking cigarettes. Their attention was to each other and to the mountain beyond, so they did not see Nura pass. She made a mental note of the location so that she could mark it on the map when she met up with Nastasja.

There were no sidewalks, so Nura walked on the gravel road. Narrow and curvy, it wound its way along the edge of the hamlet, following the contour of the mountain. At one turn she stepped into the path of a dog who snarled at her before limping away with one of its legs raised with an injury.

Around the next turn, she approached a pink building, two stories tall. It looked to be the home of someone wealthy, but military trucks lined the side of the road in front of the house. Nura made a mental note and kept walking.

As she passed the front steps of the pink house, two soldiers came out, eyes half lidded, unshaved faces, rifles slung over their shoulders. They both carried ammo boxes and belts of bullets around their necks, straps that Adem had called bandoliers. One of them was maybe in his late thirties, the other well into his forties. Nura had glanced at them just long enough to see the younger man's eyes light up when he noticed her. They fell in behind her, walking at a gait that matched hers.

"Not much meat on those bones," one of them said. He had said it loud enough for Nura to hear. She tipped her head down and kept walking.

"I do not mind the skinny ones," the second one said, "especially if they are young and pretty."

The first laughed and said, "You call that pretty?"

"Who said I was talking about her?" the second snickered.

For a while they said nothing more, but the crunch of gravel beneath their boots, the clinking of their bullets and ammo boxes, let Nura know that they were getting closer.

"Where are you going?" one of them asked.

Nura didn't answer. They were right behind her.

"I'm talking to you."

A hand grabbed her shoulder and she stopped.

The man with his hand on her shoulder stepped in front of her. He was the younger of the two and smelled of body odor and cigarettes. His lip was pulled up in a smirk but his eyes remained cold and steady.

"I said, 'Where are you going?'"

Nura reached for the crucifix that hung around her neck. She did not look the man in the eye as she answered. "I am going to church."

The second man stepped behind the first, smiling the grin of some-one a bit soft in the head. "Maybe we should give her an escort," he said.

The first soldier kept his eyes on Nura. "Are you hungry?" he said.

"No."

"We have food."

Nura looked up enough to see that he was nodding in the direction of an apartment building across the road. It was three stories tall with a flat roof. Another soldier stepped out of its front door and headed back in the direction from where Nura and the two soldiers had come.

"I am not hungry," she said. "Thank you, though."

"I have wine," he said. "And cheese."

"I have to meet my mother at church," she said. "I am already late."

The man reached out and lifted Nura's chin, forcing her to look at his face. "You are an ugly girl," he said. "But I will be nice to you. You will see."

Nura was sure that the men could see her heart pounding through her shirt, her pulse beating in the veins of her neck. She thought about going for the knife strapped to her leg, but it would only make her situation more dire. She folded her arms across her chest, the fingers of her right hand touching the side of the blade that lay hidden beneath her sleeve and bandage.

The man moved his hand from her chin to her cheek. "Come on up," he said. "Church can wait."

"I . . . do not want to," she said.

"Don't be that way." He turned his palm so that the back of his finger brushed down her cheek to her neck. Behind him, the older man grinned, his yellow teeth dirty with chewing tobacco. He wore a wed-ding ring, and something about that filled Nura with rage.

She slapped the younger man's hand away. "Is this how a soldier treats a woman?"

The man's eyes hardened. The muscles on the side of his jaw flexed.

Before he could react, she pointed to the older man and barked her words, angry and loud, the way a frightened dog will do to cover her fear.

"Is this how you would have your wife treated? Your daughter?"

The older man lost his grin.

"If I were your daughter, would you let this man treat me this way? Would you let him take me?"

The younger man grabbed a fistful of her shirt, twisting the material. His hand was powerful. But the older man grabbed the younger man's arm and pulled him back.

"Come on, Brajan. You've had your fun. Let her go."

Brajan spat at Nura's feet, gave his comrade a snarl, and then stepped away. "Go ahead," he said. "Get your ugly ass to church."

"I will pray for you," Nura said.

"Fuck off," he said. Then he walked across the road, the older man following behind.

Nura also walked away, turning the first corner she came to so that she would be out of sight of the soldiers. In front of her stood a tiny house, its windows busted, its door off the hinges, parts of its roof missing—abandoned. She stepped inside. Piles of rubbish lay scattered about: a washing machine with its back torn off, a sofa with no cushions, a coffee table missing one of its legs. She found a corner that seemed clean enough and sank to the floor, her back to the wall. She shook as she let her fear drain away.

When she felt her heartbeat return to a normal rhythm, she closed her eyes and uttered a silent prayer.

Allah, when the attack comes, please let Brajan be among the first to die.

29

Minnesota

AFTER EVERYTHING

When Deb arrives, Hana is dressed as Hana from the library—as the Sweater Lady—drab cardigan, a long skirt, and sensible shoes. Timid and mousy. Invisible. A disguise she has worn for nearly thirty years. Her hair is shorter, but long enough to be pulled back into a bun, and Deb doesn't notice the haircut.

With Deb ensconced in the job of watching over Dylan, Hana leaves the farm, turning her phone off before pulling out of the driveway. She will not have it track her movements. She will rely on the map she had drawn on the piece of paper, something she can destroy after she finds Zaim.

It is near midnight when she pulls into the parking lot of an abandoned creamery to change her clothes, swapping her library attire for stealth. She wishes she had a pistol. She'd often considered buying one, but was worried that her forged papers might trigger something in a federal background check. She should have had more faith. Now, standing only a few miles from Zaim's hideout, it is too late for such thoughts.

Dressed and ready, she knows it's her last chance to rethink her plan. She mentally shakes thirty years of dust off the training she'd received in Bosnia long ago.

Get in close. If he has a knife, pin his arm to my side. Be willing to take a glancing cut to my back, but make my strike quick and fatal. If it is a gun, move fast. Don't give him time to aim. A person can survive bullet wounds if they are misplaced. She has seen it happen. But then again, she's seen people—friends—die from those wounds too. *Either way, be ready to strike fast and hard.*

She is ready.

She gets back in her car and drives to Zaim's land, pulling past the entrance to a trail that cuts into the woods about half a mile down the road. She parks in the trees where her car will not be seen. The night is hot for late May, and muggy from the recent rains, but the sky above is clear with a gibbous moon to light her way. Stepping out of the car, she pauses to let her eyes adjust to the shadows. She listens. Hearing nothing, she sets off, knife in hand.

She steps lightly on the gravel road, the crunch of pebbles beneath her feet barely loud enough to reach her own ears. When she gets near Zaim's property, she takes to the weeds on the side of the road to be even quieter. No light filters through the trees from the trailer ahead, suggesting either that Zaim isn't there or he is asleep. She looks for trail cameras along the way, but it is too dark. She will have to trust that Zaim Galić isn't one for such careful planning.

She moves with the patience of a wolf spider, stepping, waiting, and stepping again, her eyes fixed on the shadowy outline of the small trailer parked deep into the woods. An animal, probably a ground squirrel, doesn't hear her coming and scurries off only when she's almost on top of it. A choir of frogs croak in the marsh beyond the trailer, masking her steps but also filling the night with unwanted noise.

She stays close to the trees as she makes her way up the rocky path. Every few steps, she crouches in the moon shadow and waits. The night is still. The trailer is dark. And Hana is patient.

A glint of light catches her eye—moon reflecting off glass at the edge of the woods ahead. Hana can't make it out, so she eases ahead, slowly, carefully.

It's the windshield of a car. She sneaks forward until she can see it clearly. A Hyundai Sonata—Zaim's car.

He's here.

Moonlight shimmers off the closed windows of the trailer. No flutter of curtains. No gun muzzle pointing in her direction. She steps forward.

Thirty yards. There are no more trees to hide behind. She is exposed.

Twenty yards. A light breeze licks at the leaves around her, causing the ground to dance with flickering shadows.

Ten yards. She smells something foul but familiar, a stench that takes her back to her mountain in Bosnia. The cow hide that Babo hadn't buried deep enough. The remains of rabbit half eaten by a wolf.

She is at the door of the trailer, a single step for a porch. The odor comes from inside and is unmistakable now.

She slowly reaches for the doorknob with her left hand, the knife ready in her right. Turns the knob. The door is not locked. It unlatches with a tiny click.

When she opens the door, the odor of death hits her like a rogue wave on a calm sea. She covers her mouth and nose. The smell is overwhelming, so much so that Hana is sure Zaim Galić cannot possibly be waiting for her inside—not alive, at least.

She reaches inside, her hand sliding up the wall in search of a light switch. She finds it. Flips it on.

The body of a man sits in a chair facing the door. He is bloated and covered with flies. His putrid flesh gives off a stench so profound that Hana must run into the night to get a breath of fresh air. She wants to throw up, but wills herself to keep it together.

When she has enough fresh air in her lungs, she pulls the collar of her shirt over her nose and mouth, pretty sure that it will do no actual good, and goes back to the door.

The man has a length of cord wrapped tightly around his neck. His face, a muted purple, contrasts sharply with the gray of his rotting skin. He wears a white T-shirt and dirty blue jeans. His feet are bare. His wrists and ankles are tied to the chair with zip ties, and each arm is pocked with round burns the size of a cigar. Blood paints the left side of the chair, where three fingers have been cut from the man's hand.

The path of the blood—down the leg of the chair—leads to the three severed fingers and a bloodied pair of bone shears. Next to the shears lay a wallet. Hana picks it up with her gloved hand and examines it. Empty of everything except for a driver's license.

Hana looks at the picture on the driver's license and then at the grotesque face of the dead man. It is Zaim Galić.

30

Bosnia

1995

Nura did not want to leave the safety of the abandoned house. She relived her encounter with the soldiers, focusing, at first, on how close she had come to getting defiled by a man who smelled so foul that his mere presence made her want to choke. And if he had gotten her into the building, how many more men were waiting there?

It was that thought—that question—that brought Nura back to her mission. How many more men were in that building? Were the Serbs using it as a barracks? And what about the pink house? Was that a barracks as well? It seemed too fancy a building to house common soldiers.

Nura looked for a vantage point from where she might see both buildings. She stepped into a small courtyard protected by a stone wall. She could see the apartment building but not the pink house. A few blocks away, she spied a minaret rising above the trees. With the beginnings of a plan in mind, she left her hiding spot and headed for the mosque.

It was a small mosque, barely bigger than her house had been, built of stone and painted white. The dome had collapsed and one exterior wall was mostly gone, but the minaret stood like a wounded animal refusing to fall. A simple stone spire, the minaret had a hole blown into the side by some powerful munition. No attempts had been made to repair the damage, which told Nura that her people had been run out of the village—or worse.

She was greeted inside by the strong odor of feces and urine. Soldiers—or maybe the townspeople—had made a point of desecrating the inside of the mosque with human waste. The prayer rugs had been ripped out, and water pooled on the stone floor. All the windows had been smashed. Bare wires dangled where lights had once hung.

Nura stepped through the rubble of the fallen dome to the stone steps of the minaret. They seemed sound, rising in a tight spiral around a concrete pillar. She drew her knife from the sheath on her ankle—just in case.

She climbed slowly, listening to the crunch of grit beneath her feet. When she got to the hole in the wall, she paused. Two of the steps had been blown away in the explosion. She pounded her fist on the next nearest step. It showed strength. She stretched a leg across the span of the missing steps and lifted her body over the hole. The stairs held.

A few seconds later, she emerged onto the balcony at the top, the place where the muezzin would stand to call people of her faith to prayer. She stayed low, peeking over the wooden rail of the balcony, working her way around until she could see the apartment building where Brajan and his partner had gone.

The building had a flat roof that held two machine gun nests at the corners facing the mountain. Nura made a mental note.

A truck rumbled past on the road beneath her. She did her best to watch it without sticking her head up too high. It twisted its way through the narrow passages of the village until it came to a clearing at the base of the mountain.

She hadn't noticed them before, but now she saw three long

buildings that reminded her of poultry barns. The truck pulled to the tree line and parked next to other vehicles, green and camouflaged, blending in with the foliage. Eleven … no, twelve vehicles that she could see. Men in camouflage fatigues walked around the barns. Barracks.

Nura sank behind the balcony, closed her eyes, and tried to pinpoint in her mind where the barracks would be on Nastasja's map. Having the location locked in, she turned her attention to the pink house.

Two soldiers approached the pink house, walking up the steps to the veranda, where they exchanged salutes with a man whose back was to Nura. He was a big man, and by the way the others saluted him, she could tell that he outranked them. The pink house had to be their headquarters.

The big man chatted with the other two for a minute before a heavily armored vehicle pulled up on the street out front. The officers exchanged another round of salutes and the big man headed down the steps toward the vehicle.

Before getting in, the big man stretched his back and looked around, his face turning to look up at the minaret.

Nura wanted to duck, but she couldn't move. She had seen his face before. She knew his black beard, with lines of gray falling from the corners of his mouth. It was the man who had killed her mama. It was Colonel Zorić—the Devil Dog.

Then she watched as he stepped into the vehicle and drove away.

31

Minnesota

AFTER EVERYTHING

Hana steps carefully through Zaim's trailer, avoiding the dried blood so as not to leave a footprint. Scattered around the living room are papers and file folders. Hana picks one up. It is the file of a woman named Susan Bloomer. Inside she reads a note from Dr. Ellsworth. Another file—Joyce Herzing—also has dictation from Dr. Ellsworth.

Hana gets on her hands and knees to dig through the clutter, searching for a file with Amina's name on it. Her eyes water from the stench. Paper after paper, file after file—not a scrap of it belonging to Amina.

The cupboards have been emptied, as have all the drawers, everything tossed about. In the bedroom, the same thing. She finds chargers for a cell phone and computer but no devices. When she can no longer stand the smell, she steps outside, shutting off the light and closing the door behind her.

She walks far enough away that she can breathe clean air and think, squatting in the weeds that pass for a lawn. A cloud drifts in front of the moon, casting Hana into darkness.

Did one of Zaim's blackmail victims find him? An unfaithful husband desperate to keep a secret? The severed fingers could have been incentive for Zaim to give back the file—or simply a sadistic treat for the killer.

Or can it be that Zaim has a partner and they turned on each other, the partner killing Zaim for the brass ring they sought? Hana thinks about the bounty on her head. Granted, seventy-five grand can be a lot of money in some countries, but severed fingers? Torture? It seems excessive for such a reward.

She has no doubt that Zaim's killer was searching for something in the trailer. Amina's file? But Hana knows Amina's secrets. Nothing from her past justifies that level of carnage—unless Amina had secrets that Hana doesn't know.

The moon comes out from behind its cloud, and Hana walks back to her car, lost in her thoughts. She strips out of her dark running clothes and back into her library attire, changing from hunter to Sweater Lady in a matter of seconds.

She drives back toward home, and as she reaches the edge of St. Paul, she contemplates telling David what she found.

Why not tell David? Zaim is dead. He can no longer reveal that she is a wanted fugitive. What Zaim might have known about Nura Divjak died with him. And David has crime-scene technicians. He is a detective. It seems like a reasonable plan—maybe even a good plan.

But Hana knows better than most how a good plan can fall apart.

In the end, despite her best rationalizations to keep David out, there is one thing that Hana cannot deny—she wants him in. A monster lurking in the darkness killed Zaim Galić and probably Amina. As much as she wants to keep David in the dark, she needs to protect Dylan, and for that, she will need to tell David about Zaim and the hunting shack—somehow.

Hana pulls off the interstate, taking a random exit into St. Paul.

As she drives through the streets, she contemplates the problems that a call to David will create. She can't tell him how she found Zaim's trailer because she had promised Berina to keep her name out of it. He would want to know why she went there—in the middle of the night. Would he think that she killed Zaim?

She stops at a red light. The streets are quiet as a car pulls up behind her, inching closer and closer until his headlights disappear behind her trunk. She can see the scruffy face of the male driver. Had that car been behind her for long? She hadn't paid attention when leaving Zaim's trailer. This man could have been hiding, watching her as she rifled through Zaim's things. He could have followed her out of the woods with his headlights off.

She looks closely in her rearview mirror. He gives her a creepy smile as if he knows she's looking at him.

A memory flashes through her mind. She sees the face of the soldier who tried to drag her into that apartment building all those years ago. Fear spikes through her before she realizes that the man in the car behind her is far too young to have been a soldier in the war.

The light changes to green, and Hana drives ahead, turning at the next intersection. The man does not turn. The threat was imagined, but the fear is all too real. She has no idea what the monster looks like. She can't protect Dylan from evil if that evil has no face, no form.

She needs to bring David in—but how? Call 911? The responding officers will find Zaim's body. Once they identify him, they'll see that he's wanted for questioning in a murder case. They will alert David Claypool.

But a call to 911 will capture her cell phone number. If only the world still had payphones.

Does the world still have payphones?

Hana pulls into a parking lot and powers up her phone. She types in a search for payphones in St. Paul, and to her surprise, a site pops up with the locations of payphones still in existence in the city, mostly in bars, bus terminals, and a few convenience stores.

Hana drives to one of the bars on the list. She still has the scarf from her visit to the community center. She pulls it from the glove box and wraps it around her head and puts on a pair of sunglasses. It's night, but disguise is more important than visibility.

It is a small bar, dimly lit. She tips her sunglasses down and peers over the top to scan the place for surveillance cameras. There is one watching her from the corner. The payphone is beneath it.

None of the dozen or so patrons notice her as she walks to the phone. She is—once again—invisible.

She dials 911. When the dispatcher answers, she says, "There's a dead man in a trailer."

"Excuse me?"

Hana reads the GPS coordinates to the dispatcher and hangs up.

32

Bosnia

1995

Nura found Nastasja in the cemetery behind the church, kneeling by a headstone as though visiting a long-dead relative. She was late, and she saw relief wash over Nastasja's face as she came into view.

"I was worried," Nastasja said. "I thought maybe..."

"I climbed the minaret so I could see on top of the buildings." She pointed to the tower, which peeked above the rooftops. "I saw barracks."

Nastasja held up a finger to stop Nura. "Come."

Nastasja led Nura through the cemetery, a haphazard collection of crosses, headstones, and flat markers. The terrain dipped on the back side, affording the two women cover. They walked to a stone slab the size of a kitchen table and ducked behind it. Nastasja pulled her slacks down enough to get at the map and pencil that she had taped to her leg. She laid the map on the granite base of the headstone.

Nura pointed. "They converted some old barns into barracks," she said. "I counted at least twelve trucks parked in the woods. I do not know how many men. And there is a building here." She circled the location of the apartment complex with her finger. "I believe it is a barracks as well. There are two machine gun nests on top...here and here, with a mortar nest here."

Nastasja drew circles on the corners of the roof where Nura had indicated and marked them accordingly.

Nura pointed at the corner where the big pink house stood. "I think the house here is being used as a headquarters. I saw soldiers going in and out. And officers. And..." She paused to gather herself. "One of the officers I saw was Colonel Zorić."

Nastasja took a moment to let that settle in. "They needed men without souls to do what they did to those innocent women and children in Srebrenica."

"When the attack begins," Nura said, "we should start with that building. I will pray that Devil Dog has returned by then."

"I will join you in that prayer."

They finished the map, and Nastasja reattached it to her thigh. Then they leaned against the cool slab of granite and ate the energy bars they had carried in their pockets, and drank water that Nastasja bought at a market on her way through the village.

"You did an amazing job," Nastasja said. "We can zero in on their defenses, their barracks, and with Allah on our side, we can turn that pink house into rubble. We will make the Scorpions pay."

Nura gulped her water and savored the compliment. Four months ago, she was a child, playing with her little brother in the woods, setting snares for rabbits. Now she was a soldier—a spy—sitting in the middle of enemy territory, the key to their victory wrapped around Nastasja's leg. All that was left was to get the map out of the village.

33

Minnesota

AFTER EVERYTHING

Hana stops to buy gas on the way home, dropping her running shoes into the trash can by the pump. She is about to drive away when she gives thought to the running outfit. It's one of her favorites, and who knows, she may need the all-black clothing again. But what if she had accidentally brushed up against Zaim's blood or picked up a stray hair as she dug through the mess? She wads the outfit up and throws it into the can as well.

At home, she sees Deb to her car, thanking her profusely for keeping watch over Dylan. When Deb is gone, Hana fits her laptop into a plastic bag and takes it outside. Beside the barn is a pile of dried manure, the product of her last mucking. She has already deleted the computer search that led her to Zaim's trailer in the woods, but she knows that deleting a search doesn't remove it from the hard drive.

Under the light of her jogging headlamp, Hana digs a hole in the manure and buries the laptop—a hiding spot where no one will care to dig.

She cleans up in the bathroom downstairs before heading up to bed. As she passes Dylan's room, she hears a murmur. She pauses. Dylan is talking in his sleep. She listens but can't make out what he is saying. It's nothing more than a quiet mumble. She wants to go into his room. Look at him. Watch over him—the sentinel of a Golden Faery. But she stays in the hallway. What could be more terrifying for a little boy than to wake and find someone hovering over his bed?

She leans against the wall outside his door and sinks down until she is sitting on the floor. Dylan is hers to protect. She has never had such responsibility. Sure, she took care of Danis, but if things went horribly wrong, Mama was there. Babo was there. But now it's just her.

She thinks about Amina, all those years ago when Sara was born. Just the two of them. The circumstances of Sara's conception mattered not a lick to Amina. Nothing mattered beyond taking care of that precious life. Hana should have embraced the way Dylan reminded her of her beloved Danis. Instead, she built walls. Life cannot be lived inside such walls—and death holds no meaning in that desolate place.

In that moment, Hana knows that Amina wasn't thrown off that balcony—she leapt. The person who had cut off three of Zaim Galić's fingers before killing him was in that condo. He had tied Amina to a chair and gagged her, maybe threatened to cut off her fingers as well. Amina couldn't let Dylan walk into that horror. She had heard the air brakes of the bus. She had known that Dylan was in danger. She'd broken free enough to smash through the glass door and over the rail. She had sacrificed everything to save Dylan. Her death had meaning.

Hana had seen such bravery in the war—no, not bravery. Love. To give your life for another can only be an act of love in its purest form.

Hana thinks back to that soldier she killed on the side of the mountain. She had spoken so boldly—so naïvely. *I will kill the men who murdered my family. And I will kill every Serb who gets in my way. I will sacrifice everything for my family. And when the time comes for me to die, I will not cry like a coward.*

But she had sacrificed nothing for her family. She had stayed hidden in the crawl space as her family was slaughtered before her eyes. Killing those Serbs had been born of revenge and hatred, not love. She had been willing to die to assuage her guilt. Love had nothing to do with it.

Dylan mumbles again and Hana closes her eyes.

Something evil found Zaim and Amina, and it killed them both. Now she stands blindfolded in the face of a powerful storm, while she holds in her hand a butterfly so delicate that a tiny puff of breath could cause it injury. It has fallen to her to protect this butterfly—this child— and she has no idea how to do it.

34

Bosnia

1995

They were late starting back to the burned-out house. Nura's trip to the top of the minaret had set them off their schedule and now nightfall—curfew—approached far too quickly.

The road back to the outpost ran through the center of the village, passing little of military importance: a few houses that might also quarter a soldier or two, an old warehouse being guarded that looked to hold supplies—maybe ammo. They walked at a purposeful gait, but not so fast as to attract attention.

Shadows grew long around them as they made their way back through the village. Lights turned on in the houses. Children playing in their yards were called in for the night. The streets steadily emptied as they neared the edge of the village, making the two women stand out even more.

By the time they reached the last occupied dwelling, a shroud of darkness had fallen, the mountain ahead of them a mere silhouette against the pewter sky, the houses behind them visible in shape but not detail. Around the corner, the pasture—a no-man's-land—remained the last obstacle. Nura could barely make out the shell of the burned-out house on the other side.

"We're almost there," Nastasja whispered.

The two women began to jog.

It wasn't until they reached the middle of that no-man's-land that they heard the low rumble climbing down the mountain pass ahead of them. The women turned their jog into a run, but the lights of the truck swung around the bend before they could get to the house. The pasture gave them no place to hide.

Nastasja stopped running, so Nura did as well. They walked arm in arm, well off the side of the road. The burned-out house was only a hundred meters away. They were so close.

Headlights lit the women—but they kept walking.

The truck stopped in front of the burned-out house, so close that Nura could have thrown a stone from one to the other. "Halt!" came an order from a man stepping out of the passenger side of the truck. The driver exited as well, a rifle in his hands.

"Come here," the passenger called out. He shined a flashlight on the women. Nura waited to see what Nastasja would do, and when she walked toward the truck, Nura followed until both stood in the beam of the headlights.

The man giving the orders held a pistol. He had two gold bars stitched to his shoulder, the insignia of a Serbian lieutenant. The driver, a private, stood to the side with his rifle pointed at them.

"You know about curfew," the lieutenant asked.

"Apologies, sir," Nastasja said. She looked at the ground and folded her hands together in front of her chest the way Nura had seen Christians pray. "Our nephew is missing. We have been looking for him. We thought...maybe he came to this house to play. Or maybe he fell and is hurt. Can you come with us to check? We do not have a light."

The lieutenant ran his flashlight beam up to the house, its window dark and empty.

"You are not supposed to be out after dark," he said.

Nastasja looked at the sky as though surprised to see that the sun had gone down. "There is still a little bit of light. Please help us look."

"What are your names?"

"I am Galina," Nastasja said. "And this is my sister Olga."

The lieutenant shined the light in their faces. "You do not look like sisters," he said.

"We have different fathers," she said.

"I could arrest you for violating curfew," the lieutenant said.

"Please—"

"But...maybe we can come to an arrangement."

The lieutenant holstered his weapon and walked up to Nastasja. Shining the light in her eyes, he slid his free hand up her side. "I will need to search you for weapons," he said, a sickening grin lifting at the corners of his lips. "You understand."

He kept his eyes locked on hers as he moved his hands around to her breasts.

Nura gave a side glance to the outpost. Enes and Adem would have the lieutenant in their sights.

The man moved his hands down Nastasja's stomach and onto her hip.

The driver stepped closer to Nura to get a better look at what his lieutenant was doing. His rifle drifted slack as he watched his lieutenant grope Nastasja.

The lieutenant reached a hand between Nastasja's thighs, his cheeks flushing pink with anticipation as he crossed yet another line. But then his hand stopped on her thigh. He gave a squeeze. Nura heard the slight crinkle of paper—the map.

He stepped back and fumbled to free his pistol from its holster. The driver raised his rifle and pointed it at Nastasja, a look of confusion on his face.

Suddenly, a clamor rose from the truck. Two women yelling—screaming—leapt from the back and ran full bore toward the tree line, their hands bound behind them. A soldier jumped out of the truck to give chase, but fell to the ground, clutching his ankle in pain.

As the women neared the trees, the lieutenant yelled, "Shoot them!" And when no one did, he turned his pistol on them and fired, dropping one. At the same time, a soldier behind the truck shot and killed the second.

That's when the world erupted.

Shots rang out from the burned-out house, hitting the lieutenant and causing him to spin and fall. Nura lunged for the rifle of the driver, pushing the muzzle to the ground as he fired a round meant for Nastasja.

"RUN!" Nura yelled.

Nastasja ran. Head down, legs and arms churning.

The driver tried to wrestle his rifle out of Nura's grip, failed, then shifted tactics and grabbed Nura around the neck, using her as a shield, his elbow squeezing and cutting off her air.

Gunfire rang out from the dark windows of the house.

The two men at the rear of the truck fell, but three more men jumped out of the back. Bullets pinged off the truck's frame as the soldiers scampered to find cover.

The lieutenant, holding his side, stumbled to the truck and hid behind the front wheel.

The driver pulled Nura toward the truck, where he too would have cover. She went limp, hoping he would drop her, but he was too strong. She grabbed the knife strapped to her leg, pulled it from its sheath, and stabbed blindly at the driver, catching him on her third attempt, the blade punching deep into the meat of his thigh. He let out a wail.

They toppled backwards, landing at the feet of the lieutenant, who sat sprawled behind the truck's front tire. A boot came down hard on Nura's knife hand as a third man joined the fray. She lost her weapon.

Serbs used the truck as a shield as they fired at the house. A couple of them had taken positions behind some nearby trees. The driver pulled Nura's arms behind her back, his rough grip tearing at the scabs beneath her bandages. He yelled for zip ties.

Nura kicked and twisted with all her strength, but it was useless. Angry hands strapped the zip ties to her wrists as the driver straddled her back.

From where she lay, she could see under the truck. Bullets tore holes across the face of the house. Then, one of the beams caught movement behind the house. It was Nastasja, running up the hill, zigzagging through the trees. Shots rang out from the windows of the house as Adem and Enes covered her escape.

Flashlight beams danced against the side of the house as a second truck charged up the road from the village. It rumbled across the pasture. One of her men, Adem or Enes, moved to a side window and began firing at the new threat as half a dozen soldiers poured out of the back and disappeared into the woods.

Run, Nastasja.

In the penumbra of the second truck's headlights, Nura saw men creeping around the back side of the house, while others fired from behind the truck. Her men were outnumbered. Surrounded. The Serbs closed in from all sides. Bullets ripped the walls.

Then, the muzzle flashes from the side window stopped. Only the man at the front window continued to shoot. He moved across the opening to gain a better angle, and Nura saw that it was Adem. He was alive.

"Adem! Shoot me!" She screamed with all her strength, but with the cacophony of gunfire that filled the night, she knew her plea would not reach his ears. She screamed anyway. "Kill me! Adem, I beg—"

Something slammed into Nura's back, a boot or fist, she wasn't sure. It knocked the wind out of her. She couldn't yell. She couldn't breathe.

The soldiers converged on the house from three sides. One man worked his way to a window and tossed a grenade into the house.

The grenade exploded and the house fell silent.

A tempest broke free inside of Nura, a savage wind that whipped through every fiber of her body. She opened her mouth and let out a scream that filled the sky, hard and raw. She wanted to die. She wanted the earth to open and swallow her.

Serbian soldiers gathered beside the windows and doors, their rifles poised for entry.

Nura wanted to call out to Adem, tell him something to give him peace in those final seconds—if he were still alive. She tried, but all that she could manage was a whisper.

Her *I love you* was lost behind three final shots, the muzzle flashes lighting up the darkness inside the house. Then a Serbian soldier appeared at the window waving to the others. He called out the tally: "Two dead."

35

Minnesota

AFTER EVERYTHING

Hana is in the kitchen, contemplating breakfast: eggs, sausage, toast, and juice. What little boy doesn't like eggs and sausage? Hana doesn't hear Dylan come down the stairs, but he's watching her from the doorway when she turns around.

"Do you like turkey sausage?"

He nods.

"Eggs?"

He nods again, but less enthusiastically.

She turns the stove on and gets to work.

They eat in relative silence. Hana tries to make small talk but it goes nowhere. When breakfast is done, she asks him if he wants to sit on the porch swing with her. He shrugs, and she takes that as a yes, leading him outside.

The porch swing is old-world craftsmanship, not the flimsy stuff you buy at the big box stores. When they're settled, Hana says, "You know that this is your home now, don't you?"

Dylan stares out at the trees.

"I know it's hard ... what you're going through, but this is where you belong now. If you want to watch TV you can. If you want to go look at the cows—they're your cows too. If you want to talk ... we can do that."

"Am I an orphan?"

"What?"

"Kevin—the boy at that house where I was—he called me an orphan ... Am I?"

They sit side by side, a small gap between them. It's only a few inches, but at the same time it's as wide as a canyon. Hana wants to put her arm around Dylan but hesitates, not wanting to fill the space where his Mama Mina should be. But if this were Danis, would she hesitate?

She slides over and puts her arm around Dylan. He leans in to her a little.

"People are fearful creatures at heart, small-minded. Sometimes when bad things happen, it's easier for a kid like Kevin to deal with it by shutting it away. He wants to see you as different from him. If you're different, he can pretend that those bad things will never happen to him."

"I don't understand."

"It doesn't make sense, but just remember that what Kevin thinks, or what any kid like him may think, doesn't matter—not even a little bit."

"I wanted to hit him."

"You have a lot to deal with, Dylan, more than any boy your age should. You're going to be angry, and that's okay—it's okay to feel those feelings. Just remember that people like Kevin aren't important. What's important is that you are loved."

"So ... I'm not an orphan?"

"I don't believe anyone who is loved can be an orphan. When your sweet mother and father died, Mama Mina took you in and loved you as much as anyone has ever loved a child. You weren't an orphan then, were you?"

"No."

"And you're not an orphan now."

Dylan stares ahead at the yard and the trees, silent in his thoughts for a long time before saying, "I miss her."

"I do too," Hana says as she gently strokes his hair.

A gentle breeze carries the sweet scent of corn from a nearby field. The clouds are growing thicker, but the rain is supposed to hold off until nightfall, and Hana is pleased that there will be no rain to sully Amina's funeral. It will be so very different than when her mother, father, and brother were laid to rest. There will be a procession, and mourners, and prayers offered by an actual imam.

Hana is about to slide into a memory of rain and mud and charred wood when a car pulls into her driveway. She doesn't recognize it at first, but then sees David Claypool behind the wheel.

"Honey, can you go watch TV for a little while? I need to talk to this gentleman."

36

Bosnia

1995

Serbian soldiers kicked and punched Nura as she lay on her stomach in the back of the truck. Juiced by the firefight and enraged by the loss of two of their number, they gave one kick that landed so hard that she was sure they broke one of her ribs. Another kick caught her in the face, and everything went dark.

The next thing she knew, she was being pulled from the back of the truck. She had been blindfolded, her wrists still bound behind her back with the zip ties. She couldn't balance on her own, so they dragged her from the truck and up a set of steps. She clenched her teeth to keep from screaming out in pain, yet she counted the steps. Five of them. Her mind went back to those minutes she spent atop the minaret. The pink house had five steps. They were dragging her into their headquarters.

They stopped just inside the door. Footsteps walking away from her. Then voices—distant, muffled, as if coming from a different room or around a corner.

"Report."

"Two Bosniaks dead. One taken prisoner...one escaped. We have deployed units to find her."

"Her?"

"The one who escaped and the one captured are female."

"Casualties?"

"Two dead. Three wounded. Also, the two Muslim prisoners were shot and killed in the fight."

"Colonel Zorić will not be pleased."

At the mention of Devil Dog, Nura came alive, listening more intently.

"I will contact the colonel," the man continued. "He will want to...interrogate the prisoner personally. Take her downstairs."

The men holding Nura moved her forward. With one man in front and one behind, they led her down a narrow staircase. At the bottom she heard a door open. They shoved her. Then a second door opened, accompanied by the grating sound of metal. A steel hinge? Another shove and the metal door banged shut behind her. A lock clicked.

The soldiers walked away, shutting the outer door behind them.

In the black of the blindfold, Nura stepped carefully forward, her head tipped down, until her forehead touched a wall. Rough-hewn stone, the kind Babo had used to build basement walls. She found a stone with a slight edge, turned her back to the wall, and worked the blindfold up until it fell loose.

She could see very little, the only light source being a trace of street-light bleeding through a window outside of her cell. The window had been painted black, but someone had scratched claw marks into the pane. A previous prisoner, maybe.

She was in a cell. The wall behind her was stone, but the other three walls were constructed of iron bars. There were two cells as far as she could tell in the dim light, each about three paces in each direction. No bed or cot, but in the corner was a metal bucket that smelled of urine and feces.

She tried to touch Babo's knife blade beneath her bandages, but the ties dug into her wrists. She gritted her teeth and tried again, but her bindings were too tight.

She leaned against the wall and scraped her arm against one of the stones, hoping to work the blade free, tearing at the scabs beneath the bandage, but the blade did not move. Still, she kept trying. She would gladly scrape her arm to the bone if it meant getting the knife out.

Then, from the shadows in the cell next to hers, a girl's voice, tiny and weak, said, "They are going to kill us."

Nura had thought she was alone, and the small voice startled her. She squinted to see into the cell next to hers. A form lay curled in the corner, knees pulled to her chest, her arms wrapped around her calves, her clothing tattered and dirty. Feet bare. She had long black hair that fell over her face.

"No one who comes here ever leaves," she said, her words sad, as if she were telling this piece of truth to herself.

"Can you help me?"

"It is best not to fight them. They will hurt you."

"Come to the bars. I need your help."

"He will beat me…burn me with his cigar again."

"Please. I won't tell them that you helped."

The girl gave no answer.

"What is your name?"

"Amina," she said.

"Amina, I can help you get out of here, but I need you to cut me loose."

"My sister said she would help me." Her voice, flat and detached, floated on stagnant air. "They hurt her…really bad. Then they killed her."

"I'm sorry, Amina, but I can help. I promise. If you untie me, I can get you out of here."

In truth, Nura had no such plan. They were in the basement of the Serbian headquarters. It would be shelled as soon as the fighting started. Thick walls and a thousand soldiers stood between them and freedom, but Nura had a knife, and that was a start.

The girl rocked gently in her squat as if working up the courage to stand.

"Please, Amina. Your sister would want you to fight—to live."

Amina slowly rose to her feet and walked to the grid of metal that separated them. She was just a child: thirteen, maybe fourteen. She had a swollen lip and traces of blood on her chin.

Nura put her wrists against the bars. "I have a knife blade beneath my bandage on my left arm. Get it out."

Amina ran her fingers up Nura's arm until she felt the blade. Like a child learning to tie a shoelace, Amina fumbled with the bandage, working her fingers beneath one layer at a time. Nura felt the blade move against her skin, and soon it was free.

"Cut the tie," Nura whispered.

Amina worked the blade across the plastic of the tie, gently at first, then with more force. The girl was weak, the ties were thick, and the blade, without its handle, was hard to hold.

The sound of boots coming down steps stopped Amina. She scurried to the corner of her cell, Nura's zip ties still in place. Nura stepped to the center of her cell and planted her feet. She would face the danger with all the resolve she could gather.

The door opened and a guard flicked on the light, blinding Nura for a few seconds. As her eyes adjusted, she could see that she and Amina were in cells that had been built within a larger room. The room was empty except for a single chair near the door. Beyond the door, she could see a corridor and assumed that it led to the staircase and the main floor of the building.

Two soldiers had entered the room. One approached her cell, unlocked a padlock, and flipped the latch. If only Amina had cut through the tie, Nura could have rushed the guards. She could have killed one, maybe both before they realized she had a knife. But Amina had the knife, and Nura's hands were still bound.

The two soldiers stood nervously outside of her cell until another set of footfalls came down the steps. The man entered the room and paused at the door. It was Luka Savić.

Nura turned her face to the floor, offering a false humility to hide the rage that boiled inside of her.

"Did you search her?"

"Yes, Captain."

Captain? Of course he would be a captain. Cruelty is valued among the Serbs, and it had served Luka well.

Luka spied the bandages on her arms. "Did you look under her bandages?"

The two soldiers gave each other a worried glance.

"Idiots!"

Luka entered the cell and spun Nura around, tearing the bandages from her arms, exposing the scabs and scars left by their last encounter. He turned her again and ripped open her blouse, the buttons flying across her cell. He turned her and lifted the shirt as if she might have weapons taped to her back. He roughly patted her legs from ankle to thigh, stopping when he felt something in her left pocket. He shoved his hand in and pulled out a blue marble.

He held it to the light—curious—then looked at Nura. "What is this?"

He didn't recognize her. He had no idea that he held in his hand the grounds for her brother's execution.

"It is a marble," Nura said meekly.

"I can see that it is a marble." He threw it at her, hitting her in the cheek. Nura winced but kept her face to the floor.

"You should consider yourself fortunate," Luka said. "Colonel

Zorić has forbidden me to interrogate you until he returns." He reached out and lifted her chin so he could better see her face. "I think the colonel will be disappointed. You are an ugly—"

Luka stopped. His eyes grew and then narrowed. He turned her to the left, examining the side of her face that held no bruises. "I know you."

Nura stared hard at the face of her friend's brother, now a monster. With a venom more potent than she thought she had in her, she snarled at Luka. "Tanja must be so proud of the man you have become."

Luka raised his hand and hit her hard across the face. She fell to the floor, her ears ringing.

"Private, take a note," Luka said. "The captured spy is a girl named Nura Divjak, a farm girl from the mountains south of Petrovo."

Luka paced in the small cell, his black boots pausing twice near her face. She was sure he would kick her, but both times, he turned and continued pacing.

"You are lucky that I have orders to wait for Colonel Zorić. But when he is finished with you, I will come back…and we will continue this little reunion."

He turned and left her cell, slamming the door as he stomped away. As one of the guards snapped the lock back into place, Nura called, "The great Luka Savić! Killer of women and children!"

He paused at the outer door, his back to her. She prayed that he would draw his gun, spare her what lay ahead. Instead, he turned and motioned for the guards to leave. Alone, he offered her an evil smile and said, "Your last hours on this earth will be long and painful, and before you die, you will beg my forgiveness for that insult."

He shut off the light, closed the door. Once again Nura was in the dark.

37

Minnesota

AFTER EVERYTHING

D avid looks tired, like a man pulled from deep sleep and sent out
into the night to investigate a dead man with missing fingers. He
glances at the trees and the roof of the house, but not at Hana as he walks
toward the porch. He doesn't fix his eyes on her until he climbs the steps.

"Have any trouble finding me?" Hana asks.

"I'm a detective."

At the top of the steps, he pauses and nods toward the porch swing.
Hana pats the seat beside her, and he sits close enough to talk, but
keeps a formal gap between them, a posture to suggest that this is not a
friendly meeting.

"You know why I'm here." It is a statement, not a question.

Hana does not answer.

"Zaim Galić is dead."

Hana thinks about feigning surprise, but it seems disrespectful, so
she simply looks ahead at one of her maple trees, its leaves flickering in
the light breeze.

"At one seventeen this morning, someone made a 911 call from a
bar in St. Paul. A little saloon called Jubee's. Ever been there?"

"I don't spend much time in bars."

"They have a camera inside. We're getting the footage. Should have it in a day or two."

Hana says nothing.

"Aren't you curious how Zaim died?"

"Natural causes?"

"He was tied to a chair and strangled with a garrote."

"That doesn't sound natural."

"Not in the least. We found a single shoeprint—a partial, just a little smudge of dirt on the front stoop—but it appears to be a woman's running shoe. Do you run?"

"Are you suggesting that I killed him?"

David looks at Hana's foot. "It's a size six...about the size of shoe you have on there."

"You have a keen eye for women's footwear."

"If I were to search your house...what are the chances that I might find a shoe to match that print?"

"You have my consent. Search away, but you won't find any such shoe in my house."

"I suspect you're right about that."

David settles into his seat, turns slightly to face her, and puts his elbow on the back of the swing, his fingers brushing softly against her shoulder, his touch, so slight yet nearly enough to turn stone to sand.

"Know what else we found?"

"I do not."

"Dr. Ellsworth's files, the ones stolen from her office. Found them scattered all around the place. All the files were there except one... Amina's. If I were to search your house, might I find that file here?"

For the first time since David took a seat on the swing, Hana looks at him. She wants him to hear the truth in her answer. "I have never laid eyes on her file, nor have I laid a hand on it. I want that file found as much as you do. I want the person who killed my friend brought to justice."

David is silent. He stares ahead like a man contemplating a fateful step. They swing in silence as he works through something. Then he says, "Zaim Galić isn't his real name."

Hana stops the swing.

"We pulled fingerprints," David says, "from his apartment. They didn't match anything in our databases, but, on a hunch, I contacted the FBI. They did an international search. The prints came back to a man named Bosko Ivanović. Does that name ring any bells?"

Hana thinks—delves—but comes up with nothing. "That name means nothing to me."

"He's wanted in Bosnia for war crimes. The name he was living under matches a man who disappeared in the massacre in Srebrenica. The FBI suspects that the real Galić was killed in Srebrenica and this Ivanović took his identity after the war . . . to hide."

Hana thought back to the man she had seen tied to that chair and let the last tiny drop of sympathy she had for him drain away. She wanted to tell David about her conversation with Berina, but she held her tongue.

"We also found a phone at Zaim's apartment. We think it was a burner phone because it only had two numbers in its history. We believe that one of those numbers was another burner phone."

"The other?"

David pauses. He looks at Hana and she can see the doubt in his eyes. He doesn't want to tell her. He doesn't trust her. He turns his gaze back to the maple tree and they rock on the swing as some battle resolves in his head. "For the life of me, I can't figure out why I tell you anything."

"What do you mean?"

"I listened to the 911 call, Hana. Did you think I wouldn't recognize your voice? Your accent? I swear . . ." His tone pitches up in frustration, but he settles himself and continues. "Sometimes I don't know whether to treat you as a witness or a suspect."

"Do you suspect me of something, David?"

"Other than interfering with my investigation?"

"It sounds to me as if the person who made that call is helping, not interfering." Hana turns her attention back to the flickering maple leaves.

David says, "You're playing a dangerous game, Hana."

"I'm not playing a game at all, David...but there are things...secrets that belong to me alone...things that happened a long time ago that I cannot share with you or anyone."

"I'm trying to find the man who murdered your best friend. You have to trust me."

"I do, but..."

"But you won't tell me."

Hana cannot look at David as she slowly shakes her head *no*.

David takes a long pause, gently rocking the swing again before saying, "There are lines you can't cross, Hana. If you do...it won't matter how I feel about you. I'll have no choice but to do my duty as an officer of the law. You understand that, don't you?"

"I expect nothing less."

He moves his hand from where it touches her shoulder, leaning forward in his seat to rest his elbows on his knees, the posture of a man contemplating a futile act. "I know I'm crazy to tell you, but...the call was to New York...we traced it to the United Nations—to the address of the Mission of Serbia. Does that mean anything to you?"

Hana is genuinely confused. Of all the possibilities, that was nowhere near her radar. "I...don't think so."

"I wish I could believe you."

"I swear, David. I don't know any reason..."

David stands, walks to the steps, and stops. He turns. "The one silver lining is that...now that we've found Dr. Ellsworth's files—all but Amina's, that is—we have enough to get that search warrant. By the end of the day, I'll have Dr. Ellsworth's notes. I'll know everything Amina said in those therapy sessions. Whatever secrets she kept—whatever she knew that started this whole mess—it won't be a secret much longer."

He lifts two fingers like he's tapping the brim of an invisible hat. Then he walks back to his car.

As she watches him drive away, her thoughts shift to her computer buried beneath the manure. She'll need to dig it up for one more search, one more thing that David can never know about.

38

Bosnia

1995

Nura's right cheek throbbed from the backhand, the pain matching her left cheek, swollen and sore after being kicked during the truck ride into the village. Once again in darkness, she waited for her eyes to adjust to the thin shards of light that slip through the scratches in the blackened window.

Amina quivered in the far corner of her cell, her whimpering the only sound in the room.

"Amina...I need you."

The whimpering stopped.

Nura worked herself onto her knees and shuffled to where the bars separated her from Amina. "I need you to cut these ties."

"No."

"Please."

"They will know I did it. They will hurt me. You do not know what they can do. You do not know."

"We must help each other. It is just the two of us against all of them."

"You cannot help me," Amina whispered.

"Yes, I can." The lie hurt almost as much as the backhand to her face. Nura could no more save this girl than she could grow wings and fly away, but she needed her hands free for when Devil Dog came for her. "Cut me loose. Please."

Amina again rocked on the balls of her feet, her arms wrapped around her knees.

"Please."

Amina rolled onto her hands and knees and crawled to Nura, who turned her wrists to the bars.

Amina sawed at the plastic, but she had no strength. The blade, with no handle, kept falling from her fingers. Yet every time it fell, she picked it up and worked at the zip tie. When it finally snapped free, blood rushed into Nura's hands.

"Give me the blade," Nura said.

At first Amina hesitated, but then handed the blade to Nura, who cut the second tie away. "You are very brave," Nura said.

"No, I am not," Amina answered, her voice trembling as she spoke. "I sit in terror as I wait for Iblis...He comes for me when it is dark. If I were brave, I would use that blade on my wrists. What he does to me...I want to die, but...I cannot."

"Please, Amina, sit with me."

Amina took a moment before sitting against the wall beside Nura. Nura slid her hand through the bars and Amina took it. The girl's fingers were thin and cold, her nails worn down to nubs.

In another world, they could have been two girls sitting in a café talking about music or boys, showing off the new clothes they bought or comparing notes about a movie. There had to be millions of girls her age—Amina's age—going about their lives unaware that people in a small country called Bosnia were being tortured and murdered. What would it be like to be one of those girls?

It made Nura sad to think that the world would never know that she and Amina had been held captive in that basement. Their graves will be, like so many Muslim graves, just holes in the ground, the only marker of their resting place an imperceptible depression in the terrain. They will be covered with dirt and forgotten. No one to mourn them. No one to remember them.

"How long have you been here?" Nura asked.

Amina considered the question. "Ten days I think."

"Where are you from?"

"I lived on a farm near Sokolac with my sister, Sara, and my babo. We always hid when the soldiers came through. But one day, a truck pulled up to our house. The soldiers were looking for Sara and me. Babo tried to stop them but they shot him. They found us hiding in the barn. I heard one of them say that Colonel Zorić ordered that we be brought here."

Nura thought about the two women who had leapt from the truck during the firefight. Her cell had probably been meant for them, a pen for Zorić's victims.

Nura gave Amina's hand a squeeze and got a squeeze back.

"I'm so afraid," Amina said, her words pinched with emotion. Hana couldn't see the tears, but could hear them in the girl's voice. "Iblis will come. He will hurt me."

"You must have strength, Amina." Nura wanted to say more, but what good were such empty promises?

It was then that Nura saw Danis's marble, close enough for her to reach, its glassy surface reflecting what little light found its way into her cell. She picked it up and handed it through the bars.

"Take this," she said. "It is my amulet."

Amina rolled the marble in her fingers then raised it up to catch just enough of the riffling light to give it a twinkle. "Amulet?"

"It will bring you the courage to face Iblis... just as it has brought me courage. I faced Iblis in the mountains and did not fear him because I had the amulet. Now it is yours."

Amina folded it into her palm and pressed her finger to her chest.

"If Iblis comes for you, think of the amulet...think of me...and you will not be afraid."

"Do you think they will kill us tonight?" Amina asked.

"No." Nura lied. Death was likely on its way. Yet she had the knife blade. She had the element of surprise. With any luck, she might be able to kill Devil Dog before he killed her. Either way, she would die fighting.

"You are my friend," Amina whispered.

"I am your friend," Nura said. "And I will stay your friend until my dying breath. I promise."

39

Minnesota

AFTER EVERYTHING

Hana had left many enemies behind in Bosnia, people who would hunt her down and kill her with or without a reward. Hana knows well how the need for revenge can burn hot. Would Jovana not want revenge if she knew that Hana had been the one to kill her father? And what about Jovana's little brother, Ratko? He would be a man now. Has he discovered her deed? Somehow, it all has to come back to the man she knows as Zaim Galić.

Hana digs her laptop out of the manure pile, takes it to the kitchen, and washes away the dried—and wet—manure that clings to its cover. She opens it and runs a search for Ratko Krunić. She finds nothing on the man. She types Jovana's name and again draws a blank.

Dylan walks in and watches for a little while before he asks, "Who was that man...on the porch?"

"A friend."

"He was talking about Mama Mina."

"Yes." Hana bends down to be eye-to-eye with Dylan. "He is looking for the person who hurt her."

Dylan looks at the floor, but otherwise doesn't move. He doesn't speak. Hana tries to find something to say to fill the void, but her mind is a mess of thoughts, none of them helpful. She sits on the floor and taps her thigh. Dylan hesitates for a moment before sitting. She wraps an arm around him.

"We're going to Mama Mina's funeral this afternoon. Do you know what a funeral is?"

Dylan nods.

"Have you ever been to one?"

He shakes no.

"It's a time for people who loved your Mama Mina to gather together and say goodbye one last time."

"Will she be there?"

"Her body will be there."

Dylan remains motionless and silent.

"I just wanted you to know that if... if you think it might be too hard for you... you don't have to go. No one will think any less of you. You've been so brave."

Hana feels the rise and fall of his chest against her arm. She waits. Then he says, "I want to say goodbye to Mama Mina."

Hana closes her eyes and gives him a light squeeze. "I think Mina would like that."

She feels him swallow, but he does not cry. "We should probably take a bath before we go, don't you think?"

He nods reluctantly.

Hana lifts him off her lap and leads him to the bathroom. She runs a bath and leaves to give him privacy, leaving the soap and shampoo on the edge of the tub.

Back in the kitchen, she returns to her laptop and types in the name Bosko Ivanović. She finds a page that explains that he is wanted by the Bosnian government as well as the International Criminal Tribunal for the former Yugoslavia. He was alleged to have raped and killed several

Bosnian women during the war. Beyond that, she finds nothing on the man.

She runs a search for the UN Mission of Serbia and finds a page of press releases. She reads about delegations being sent to Kosovo to calm tensions between Serbians and Kosovars. She reads about a Serbian delegation presenting their credentials to the UN Secretariat. She reads page after page of diplomatic niceties and mindless protocol but nothing to explain why the man calling himself Zaim Galić would have placed a call to the Mission of Serbia.

"I'm done!" Dylan calls from the bathroom.

Hana goes to his room and picks out some clothes. They have several hours before they have to leave for Amina's funeral. It's far too early to dress him in his good clothes, so she brings him something to wear in the interim, placing the clothes on the floor of the bathroom so he can dress himself.

Back at her computer, she returns to her search, exiting out of the official UN press releases. She finds a site for a Serbian newspaper and types "United Nations" into the search box, getting over one hundred thousand hits. She limits her search parameters to the past year, cutting the hits down to a couple thousand. She looks for articles that focus on personnel, finding only a dozen or so.

When she comes to the sixth article the page opens with a picture. It's a face she hasn't seen in thirty years—and for a moment, she can't breathe.

40

Bosnia

1995

N ura and Amina talked and held hands through the bars. At one
point, deep in the night, a guard entered the room, the rattle of
the doorknob sending Nura to her feet. She pulled her hands behind
her as if she were still tied with the zip ties, but the guard only peeked
in and left.

It wasn't until the soft light of morning began seeping through the
scratches in the window that the door handle rattled again.

Like before, Nura rose to her feet, her hands behind her back, the
blade of Babo's knife pinched between the fingers of her right hand.

A soldier entered and flipped on the light, the bright fluorescence
forcing Nura to look at the floor as her eyes adjusted. When she looked
up again, the Devil Dog stood outside of her cell, his black eyes appraising her from head to toe. The streaks of gray in his beard suggested
a man of some age, although up close he appeared to be barely in his
forties. He held the stub of a cigar in his teeth and his lip rose in a snarl
that gave him the look of a man hungry for a meal but offered only a
handful of tasteless beans.

Nura lowered her eyes to show fear and submission, but visualized the moves she would attempt. He had to be close. She had to be quick. She would get but one chance.

"Leave us," he muttered.

A soldier who had escorted the colonel into the room left.

Devil Dog unbuckled his holster, laying it on the chair by the door. He dropped his cigar to the floor and stepped on it, and walked slowly to Nura's cage.

"So, you are the spy."

Nura didn't answer.

"You will tell me why you came to my village and killed my soldiers."

Nura's hands were sweating. She moved the blade to her left hand and touched her right palm on the back of her pants to dry it.

"What is being planned?" he asked.

Nura's heart pounded in her chest. She took slow breaths to try and ease the terror.

Devil Dog pulled a key from his pocket and unlocked the cell door. This was the man who had raped her mother—the man who had massacred her family.

He stepped into her cell. "You will tell me what I want to know, little girl."

Nura shook the memory of her family from her head, focusing all her attention on the moment in front of her.

He stopped an arm's length away. "I will hurt you in ways you have never imagined, and you will tell me what I want to know."

She needed him closer.

"Or you can tell me and I will only hurt you a little. It is your choice." He took another step.

Nura shook with fear. He was almost close enough. She moved the blade back to her right hand, gripping it tightly in her fingers.

With her buttons torn away, her blouse hung open. Nura glanced up to see Devil Dog looking at the skin exposed by the open blouse.

"So, what will it be? Are you going to make me hurt you? Or will you be nice to me and tell me what I want to know? If you are nice to me, I can be nice to you."

He took one more step. He was close enough now. He reached to her blouse and lifted it open.

Nura attacked.

She thrust her left hand up, grabbing his beard and shoving his chin up with all her strength. With the speed of a striking snake, she pulled the blade across his throat, cutting deep into his windpipe, then stabbed it into the side of his neck—once, twice—before he swung his arm, knocking her to the floor.

He stumbled back against the bars of the cell, his hands clutching his throat, blood pulsing from the side of his neck. His eyes grew large with disbelief. Nura got to her feet. The blade—covered in blood— was slippery in her hand.

He tried to call for help, but only gurgled. When he reached for his sidearm, he found an empty hip, his gun left on the chair by the door.

Nura threw herself against him, knocking him into the wall of her cell. She climbed onto his back and clawed at his face with her fingernails. She bit his ear and tore at it like a jackal pulling meat from bone.

He managed a muted scream, but the guard—likely accustomed to sounds of torture coming from that room—stayed outside.

Blood from his wounded neck stained his hands, shirt, and beard. He punched her in the side of the head, but his blow lacked power. He was already growing weak.

He pushed through the cell door as Nura pulled the blade across his eyes.

Devil Dog, with one hand on his eyes and the other flailing for his gun, ran blindly into a wall. He tried to call for help, but the sound came out wet and flaccid. He dropped to his knees.

Nura fell from his back, rolled to the chair, and picked up the holster. She removed his automatic and chambered a round, pointing it at Devil Dog's head. Blood trickled from his eyes and mouth, and spurted weakly from his neck. She had hit the artery.

She wanted to talk to him, tell him the crime for which he was being executed. She wanted him to know that he would die at the hands of a girl whose family he had massacred—the daughter of a lowly mason and a loving mother. She wanted him to know that he was paying for the life of her eight-year-old brother.

But she said not a word of that. The guard on the other side of the door could hear nothing. He would not come to the Devil Dog's rescue.

*   *   *

Nura dug through the dead man's pockets and found the key to unlock Amina's cell. Amina stepped through the door, but stopped short of the bloody body, as if even in death the monster may still be able to harm her. When the dead man didn't move, she spat on him. Her face grew red and she stepped in and kicked him in the ribs, again, and again, and again, her grunts muffled, tears streaming down her face.

When she had neared exhaustion, Nura put a hand on Amina's shoulder. "You will need your strength for the fight ahead," she whispered.

"What do we do?"

"We get out of here."

"How?"

"I have his gun. That will help." She wiped the blood from the knife blade and handed it to Amina. "Use this if you need to."

Amina took the blade, a look of understanding passing between them. If their circumstance grew hopeless, she would know how to use it.

Nura dragged the chair to the window. Standing on it, she could see through the scratches in the paint. A small cluster of soldiers stood outside.

She climbed off the chair and studied the gun as she contemplated what to do. Amina stood beside her, a mix of hope and fear in her eyes.

"There is a guard on the other side of that door. If we shoot him, the sound of gunfire will bring others. We could run for it, but we will likely be shot."

"I'd rather be shot running than stay here and die the way my sister did."

"Me too. The guard will come in to check on the colonel at some point. We can wait until then."

Amina's left hand was balled into a fist and pressed to her heart. "I trust you," she whispered. Then she opened her fingers to show Nura the blue marble. "And I have courage."

Nura smiled and folded Amina's fingers back around the marble.

A rattle of the doorknob. Nura spun to face the door. How many soldiers would come in? How many could she kill before they overwhelmed her the way they did Adem? She moved Amina behind her.

But then, KA-BOOM! A Bosnian shell slammed into the house, shaking it violently. The attack had begun.

A second explosion just outside the building shattered the black window. Nura pulled Amina to the floor and covered her.

The door opened and a soldier stumbled through, wounded and stunned. Maybe he came looking for the colonel or maybe he sought shelter from the bombing. It didn't matter. Nura shot him in the chest before he could make sense of the scene that lay before him.

Nura grabbed Amina and pulled her to her feet. On the other side of the door, the staircase had been reduced to rubble. Impassable. The air was thick with dust and smoke and the smell of burning wood. Men yelled orders somewhere above them while others screamed in pain.

Nura went back to the window, which had been nailed shut. She stood on the chair and dug glass shards out of what was left of the window sash. Outside, men ran helter-skelter, guns in hand. The sound of explosions peppered the air as Nura climbed through the window. In the chaos, the soldiers took no notice of her. She turned and helped Amina through.

Once outside, Nura took Amina by the hand and ran through the streets as smoke and dust rose into the sky around them. That's when she saw Luka Savić standing in the middle of the street shouting orders to his men. He was close enough that she could have hit him with Danis's slingshot. She raised her pistol. Steadied it with one hand while the other squeezed the trigger.

She fired.

The bullet hit him in the chest, spinning Luka around. He saw Nura, but it was as if his mind refused to believe his eyes.

She fired again.

The bullet hit him in the face and he dropped where he stood.

She fired again, the bullet striking him in the back. He didn't flinch.

A mortar exploded between them, sending a cloud of smoke and dust into the air. Hana started toward him, but Amina grabbed Nura's arm. "He's dead, Nura."

Another mortar exploded near enough that bits of shrapnel zipped past her head. Nura grabbed Amina and ran. She knew where the Bosnian targets lay, so she knew how to find a path devoid of barracks or gun nests, a way out of the village where there would be little or no fighting.

Nura led Amina into the woods. They climbed to the crest of a ridge overlooking the village. From that height, Nura saw smoke rising from the apartment building that had held gun nests and housed Serbian soldiers just hours before. The barracks at the edge of the village—the poultry barns—were also on fire. The pink house lay in ruins, a lifeless Devil Dog buried in the burning rubble.

Soldiers ran, seeking cover from the barrage. Others limped or crawled, wounded by shrapnel. Still others lay dead, like Luka Savić. The man who had killed her brother was now nothing more than a lump of flesh and bone littering the street.

She had completed her mission.

41

Minnesota

AFTER EVERYTHING

Hana stares at the picture of a ghost. His eyes are the same piercing blue, but his golden hair is shorter and thinner than it had been that New Year's Eve night, and he is heavier, his jaw rounder. He has a scar on his left cheek, a reminder of a bullet fired by a seventeen-year-old girl.

But apparently Luka had not died that day.

For thirty years Hana had lived in a world where Luka Savić was nothing more than a name on an archaic military roster, a memory that might occasionally cross the mind of her childhood friend, Tanja. He was just one more soldier buried with the many who had sought her extermination.

The blue marble—Amina was trying to tell Hana that Luka was alive. And not just alive—according to the article, he had been named head of security for the Mission of Serbia to the UN.

He was in the United States.

He had been the one on Amina's balcony. It must have been Luka who tortured and killed Zaim Galić. But why?

Hana steps away from her computer to think.

This can't be about collecting a bounty, not for a man who has risen high enough to be named to a post at the UN. Was it personal? She'd tried to kill him, after all. But why kill Amina? And how did Zaim Galić figure into it? Had they been partners? Then why would he torture and kill Zaim? It doesn't make sense.

Her thoughts swirl and bounce, but nothing lands long enough to gain traction. Dylan pads his way out of the bathroom, his golden hair wet and tossed from drying it with a towel. He is wearing the clothing she had set out for him. He stops at the edge of the kitchen, his innocent blue eyes staring up at her.

"I drained the tub," he says.

"I appreciate—" Her words catch in her throat. She looks at the picture on her computer and back at Dylan. Golden hair. Blue eyes. Amina had dark hair and eyes, as did Sara. Dylan's father had light features, but not the blue eyes. She looks at Luka's picture again as a strange dizziness fills her chest.

"Can I watch TV?" he asks.

"Yes," she whispers, and the boy scampers off.

His light hair. His blue eyes. Were they recessive genes from a grandfather? Luka couldn't be Iblis, could he?

It had to be Devil Dog. Colonel Zorić had been the one to kidnap Amina and her sister. Colonel Zorić smoked cigars. He had been the commander. Amina's reaction—kicking the dead man's body in the basement of the pink house. But maybe Luka also smoked cigars. Maybe her rage at Devil Dog came from the same place as Hana's rage. Devil Dog had been the one responsible for killing both of their families.

Amina had never once uttered Luka's name. But Hana had. She'd spent the last thirty years tending to her ghosts with fierce devotion, holding a special hatred for Luka Savić, a hatred more searing than the fire that had burned her arms. Luka had been her friend's brother.

They had gone to the same school. He had kissed her on the cheek when she was fourteen. When Luka killed Danis, it had been more than just a crime; it had been a betrayal deserving of the greatest suffering that hell had to offer—and Hana had made sure that Amina understood that.

"Of course you couldn't tell me," Hana whispers to herself. "I'm so sorry, Amina."

Pieces of the puzzle start to fall into place. What Luka had done to Amina had been a war crime. That secret would be worth a lot to a petty extortionist like Zaim Galić. He hadn't been Luka's partner; he'd been Luka's blackmailer. He'd stolen Amina's file from Dr. Ellsworth to secure proof of the crime. The call to the UN had been a call to extort money.

Hana closes her laptop and steps outside, hoping the fresh air might clarify her thoughts.

If Zaim blackmailed Luka…and that is what brought Luka to Minnesota…then…he came here to hunt down Zaim…and Amina. He came to bury the evidence of his crime.

"Oh my God." Hana's heart pounds in her chest. She holds tightly to the porch rail as a terrifying realization hits her. The evidence of Luka's war crime swims in the DNA of this child. "Luka is here to kill Dylan."

The world around Hana is suddenly a dangerous place: doors unlocked, no gun in the house, windows uncovered, exposing them to the outside. She scans the courtyard as if she might find Luka hiding behind a tree.

She pulls her phone from her pocket and scrolls to David's number, not thinking what she will tell him. Her hands tremble slightly as she holds her thumb over the call button. In her mind she rehearses what she will say. *Luka killed Zaim to end the blackmail. He went to Amina's to kill the only witness to the rape. He went there to kill Dylan, whose blood carries the truth of Luka's war crime. He'd torn the place apart to make sure Amina didn't have any notes about his evil deed hidden away.*

She will tell David about Luka, the soldier, the rapist, and now the diplomat. When she is finished, David will find Luka and arrest him.

Hana's thumb hovers over the button, but she cannot press it. Something has shaken loose, a word out of place that bounces and pings like it is falling down a deep well.

Diplomat. As head of security for the Mission of Serbia, Luka Savić is a diplomat.

Hana opens a search on her phone and types *diplomatic immunity*. After only a few minutes of reading, Hana turns off her phone. She will not call David.

Luka Savić cannot be arrested. He will never face prosecution for his crimes, not in the U.S., not in Bosnia, and not at The Hague. He will never see the inside of a prison. With diplomatic immunity, he is untouchable. A call to David will only expose Dylan. It will tell this child—and the world—that he is the grandson of the devil himself. Dylan will be destroyed, and Luka Savić, the man who should have paid for his sins thirty years ago, will walk away unpunished, free to return to his hunt. Dylan will never be safe.

But Hana is a hunter too. What had been a shadow a few minutes ago now has a face and a name. He is an animal she understands.

But how to find him?

It is then she hears Babo's voice, whispering the words he had spoken to her when he gave her her first snare. *It is hunting, but you make the prey come to you.*

To hunt a man like Luka she will need bait. A thought crosses her mind. A terrible thought. A dangerous thought.

No! She stands and walks down the steps, hoping to break away from the idea that has latched on to her.

Clouds gather in the distance. A breeze carries the scent of pine, and earth, and cows. She looks to the sky as if another answer—a better answer—may be found in the heavens, but there's nothing there.

Luka lost Dylan's trail when David put the boy in foster care. If she is right, Luka is desperate to find that trail again.

Hana's hands tremble as she takes a deep breath and watches a plan unfold before her. Luka will come to Amina's funeral looking for Dylan. Hana will lead him here—to her farm. In her mind, she watches Luka walk into her barn.

Like it or not, she will need a gun so that Luka Savić never walks back out.

42

Bosnia

1995

Nura and Amina had crossed a deep valley and were climbing the next ridge when they spotted a patrol of Bosniaks. Nura tore part of Amina's shirt away and waved it as a white flag. To her great relief, one of the men in the group had been a member of Kovač's militia. She didn't know his name but recognized him by sight. With the bruises to her face, he didn't recognize her at first, but when he did, he ushered her and Amina through the lines.

They were taken to the hospital in Olovo, the shack built into the wall of a gravel pit where she had left Captain Kovač. But the shack disguised the entrance to a deep cavern that had been converted into a hospital. They took Nura and Amina to a room with brown walls and a brown ceiling. Lights hung from bare wires. But it was cool and dry and it had beds.

A nurse attended to their wounds and brought food and water. After Nura ate her fill, she fell into a deep sleep beneath a wool blanket that smelled of fabric softener.

Later, she awoke confused, unsure of where she was or how she had gotten there. Then she remembered the brown walls and the nurse. Amina lay sleeping in the bed next to her. A familiar voice floated in from somewhere beyond her door, waking her up.

Nastasja stepped into the room, a smile lifting her face when she saw Nura. The friends hugged, although Nura's broken rib cut the embrace short. Nastasja found a stool in the corner and brought it to Nura's bedside; they had much to talk about.

Nastasja told Nura about her race across the mountains, chased by Serbian soldiers. Nura told Nastasja about the firefight. She had to stop several times as she walked through the deaths of Enes and Adem. She told Nastasja about the two women who had been in the back of the truck and about the beating the Serbs gave her on the ride to the pink house. She told Nastasja how she had killed Devil Dog and Luka Savić, and how she escaped with Amina.

"The attack was a great success," Nastasja said. "We shelled the village for an entire day before retreating. Our casualties can be counted in the tens, but the Serbian losses must be in the hundreds. Our map made a difference."

"At a cost," Nura whispered. "I was late. I delayed our escape. And now Adem and Enes..."

"We would not have known about the barracks in the woods had you not climbed the minaret," Nastasja said. She took ahold of Nura's hand. "We would not have known about the gun nests atop the apartment building or the command center at the pink house."

Nura closed her eyes and remembered the way Adem had held her hand in the darkness of the burned-out house, how she'd fit against him as they lay in the grass and watched the stars drift by, the way his naked body felt against hers when they'd made love. She thought about the plans they'd made: evenings on a porch listening to the lowing of cattle in the pasture, children with his beautiful dark eyes and crooked smile running through the house.

He was dead and she was not, and the pain of that injustice consumed her like a fire.

As if she knew Nura's thoughts, Nastasja said, "If you could have given your life to save Adem, would you have done so?"

"In a heartbeat," Nura whispered.

"Do you think that your Adem loved you any less than that?"

Nura did not answer, but gave Nastasja's hand a squeeze.

* * *

Two days later, Nura was given the okay to leave the hospital. As she dressed, Nastasja came in, her face grim.

"What is it?" Nura asked.

Nastasja handed Nura a piece of paper. It had a picture of Nura's face, a photo taken of her last year at the school in Petrovo. Beneath the picture it read:

> ### REWARD—THREE MILLION DINAR
> For the capture or proof of death of
> Nura Divjak—the Night Mora
> Wanted for war crimes.

Nura read on. The Serbs had accused her of killing the two women shot escaping the truck. They claimed that the two women had stumbled upon spies hiding at the edge of the village and that the spies killed the women to keep their mission concealed.

"Who would believe such a lie?" Nura asked. "Those women were Muslim, weren't they? They were being brought to Colonel Zorić. Why would we kill them?"

"Of course it's a lie, but accusing you will muddy the water. They will say that we are the bad ones. We are the ones killing the innocent. It doesn't have to be true, it just has to be said."

"But why me?"

"There are stories being told about you. Serbian soldiers call you the Night Mora."

"Why would they..."

"You were captured. They held you prisoner in the night, but when daylight came, the pink house had been destroyed. Everyone inside had been killed. And you were gone... like an avenging spirit."

"That's crazy."

"Maybe, but your legend is growing in their ranks. Soldiers can be a superstitious lot, so they want to put a stop to it. Thus, the reward is for your capture... or your death. It is the only way to take away your power."

"I will show them my power. I cannot wait to get back—"

"No, Nura. You will not go back to the fight. It is too dangerous. Besides, the legend you have created can serve a purpose. We will whisper your name in the ear of Serbs we capture. We will spread the story of the Night Mora across the country. It is one thing to fight a soldier. It is another to fight a ghost. But you need to stay alive."

"And do what? Cook for the men? Hide and let others fight in my place?"

"You will disappear," Nastasja said. "Commander Hukić is working to get you out of Bosnia. You will go to America, but your legend will stay here."

Nura holds up the Wanted poster. "How will I get to America with this out there? I will be arrested the first time I show my papers."

"You will not travel as Nura Divjak."

Nastasja reached into her back pocket and handed Nura a passport. Opening it, Nura sees the name Hana Babić and the face of a woman she had known only as Doc, the woman who had given Nura pain pills for her arms, the woman who had died at the ambush.

"No one will believe I am her. I am not... pretty."

Nastasja looked around, but not finding what she was looking for, went to a nurse in the corridor. They whispered back and forth, and a moment later Nastasja returned with a small pocket mirror.

Nastasja handed the mirror to Nura, who looked upon her own face for the first time since returning from the mission. Bruises covered so much of her face that she could barely recognize herself. She touched the black and purple that swelled beneath her eyes.

"The swelling will go down in a few days," Nastasja said, "so we need to act fast. We can get you to Mostar. From there you will go to Athens to catch a flight to St. Paul."

"St. Paul?"

"Minnesota. There is a Bosnian community there that will sponsor you and help you start a new life. You will have the documents you need to become Hana Babić in America."

"This is my home. My family is buried here."

"It is best for the cause if you go. It is best for you."

Nura again looked at her face, battered and ugly. Monstrous. This was the face that Amina had been looking into when they pledged their friendship to one another.

In the next bed, Amina watched and listened, her hands balled together against her chest. The expression on Amina's face told a story of heartbreak, abandonment, and fear. Nura remembered her words to Amina as they awaited death. *I will stay your friend until my dying breath. I promise.*

"I will go, but only if I can take Amina with me."

"We don't have a passport for her."

Amina spoke up. "I have a passport. I am from the hills outside of Sokolac. My father hid my passport beneath the floor in our home."

"You can send a soldier for it." Nura added, "I will not go without her."

Nastasja considered Nura's demand, saying, "I will run it by the colonel. I cannot promise, but I will do what I can."

"And," Nura said, "I will need another favor, a very important one."

"If I can, I will."

"I buried my family in a garden next to where my house once stood. Will you give them a proper burial: clean them, pray over them? I did what I could, but..."

"I will see to it. I promise."

Nastasja gave Nura a hug, clinging to her friend, as if knowing she might never see her again. Then she left.

Amina gently unfolded her balled-up fingers, lifted the little blue marble to her lips, and kissed it.

*   *   *

Two days later, Nura rode in the back seat of a red Yugo much like Babo's car. Her last friend in the world, Amina, sat next to her clutching the blue marble to her chest. An older man, a soldier wearing civilian clothing, drove the car, and his wife, also a soldier, sat in the passenger seat, surrogate parents risking their lives to get Nura and Amina to Mostar and then out of the country. Bosnian refugees awaited their arrival in Minnesota, kind people who would help Nura start her life as Hana, people who would give Amina a home and support as she became a mother at the age of fifteen.

Throughout the journey, Nura thought about her family, buried in the dirt of their farm. Would they ever forgive her for living? Would she forgive herself? She would never see them again. She would never again set foot in her beloved Bosnia. For the rest of her life, she would be a woman without a home, without a family, without a true name.

Hana Babić would take refuge in America, but Nura Divjak— the Night Mora—would remain in Bosnia as a whisper floating in the wind, haunting the dreams of her Serbian enemies.

43

Minnesota

AFTER EVERYTHING

At a sporting goods store in Bloomington, Hana takes Dylan to the shoe department, where she asks a female clerk to help him pick out a new pair of shoes and instructs Dylan to wait there for her return. She then walks to the back of the store, where they sell guns.

"I'm in the market for a twenty-gauge shotgun," she tells the man.

He is stocky with a lumberjack's physique and beard. "For you?" he asks.

"Yes."

The man goes to the case and returns with a shotgun. "It's a Benelli. Only six pounds. My wife has one."

Hana lifts the gun. It doesn't seem all that much lighter than the M70 she carried in the war. "This will do."

"I have others that—"

"No. This will be fine," she says. "And am I correct that there is no waiting period?"

"For a handgun, there is, but for this we can run the background check right here. So you can walk out with it today."

Hana fills out the paperwork for the background check and holds her breath as the man runs her name through the system. He looks at his computer screen. He looks at her. Pauses. Smiles.

Hana breathes a sigh of relief. "I also need a trail camera that doesn't emit light," she says, while in her mind, she whispers, *One that cannot be seen by the man I will soon be killing.*

The clerk shows her a no-glow trail camera that uses a frequency of light invisible to the human eye. It has Bluetooth, so she can watch the camera in real time from her phone.

She buys two cameras, the gun, and a box of shells, then takes her purchase to the car.

On her walk back to the shoe department, she again envisions her confrontation with Luka. She sees him sneak onto her property. A light is on in the barn. He checks it out to clear the barn of any threat. A single pull of the trigger and he will be dead. He won't even know what hit him.

She finds Dylan sitting obediently where she left him, a pair of red shoes in his hands.

"You like those?"

He nods his quiet assent.

Luka will come to her farm to kill this child. He has no idea who she is—that she is the girl who put that bullet in his cheek. She will end the threat to Dylan, honoring her vow to protect him, but it hurts her that Luka will die not knowing that his death is also a price paid for murdering an eight-year-old boy thirty years ago.

He won't even know what hit him.

How can she allow Luka to die so peacefully unaware that his long-awaited reckoning has finally arrived? After all the evil he has spread in the world, to have his life taken in a blink—a switch turned off—with no accounting for his sins. It's not right. He needs to know why—and he needs to know who. He needs to remember Danis.

Luka had once vowed to make her beg his forgiveness. Did she not deserve the same from him?

She shook off those impulses. She has a child to protect. *Stick to the plan. Keep it simple. Make the prey come to you. Shoot him and be done with it.*

She gives Dylan a reassuring smile and takes his hand. "Let's go buy you those shoes."

As they walk to the front of the store, they pass the weight-lifting area: benches, dumbbells, gloves, and plates laid out in an enticing display. She has all the weights she needs, but can't help glancing to admire the pristine stack of heavy steel.

In the checkout line, Hana's thoughts drift back to her mountain in Bosnia, to the traps and snares she had set. An idea comes to her and she steps out of line to think it through. Maybe there is a way to make Luka understand who and why.

She takes Dylan back to the weights and examines them as an idea takes shape. How many weights would it take to lift a man of Luka's size? Three hundred pounds of weight should do the trick. Four hundred would be even better. It would snap him off the ground in a flash. She has a hundred feet of steel cable in the barn, something she had purchased a few years back to drag a dead cow—shot by an asshole hunter—out of the tree line. The barn has built-in pulleys for lifting hay bales up to the loft. It would be a simple snare, really.

She calls a clerk over and buys all the barbell plates on display.

* * *

Home again, she goes to work, her first order of business being a call to Deb Hansen to see if Deb can take Dylan once they return from the funeral. If Hana can get Dylan someplace safe, she will go through with her plan; if not, she will abort.

Deb agrees without hesitation. Hana's plan is a go.

Hana makes a lunch of mac and cheese for Dylan, and while he eats, she sets up the trail cameras, one in front of the house, looking out over the front lawn and driveway; the second she sets up behind the barn facing the path that leads up from the cow pasture.

If Luka follows the same script he used when he and Devil Dog came to her mountain, he will favor the back way onto the property. She makes a mental note to lock her cows in the pasture before going to the funeral. She doesn't need one of them stumbling into the barn and messing up her trap.

With the cameras in place, she spends a few minutes with Dylan, settling him into his room with one of his dinosaur books. "Will you be okay here for a while?" she asks. "I need to do some chores in the barn."

He nods without looking up.

The barn has a cow pen running along one side that takes up a third of the ground floor. That narrows the path that Luka can take on his way through. Hana parks her tractor on the other side of the barn to create a bottleneck, a gap of three feet—her rabbit run. That is where she will lay the loop of the snare. He will have to cross that spot unless he climbs across the tractor.

She runs the cable up to a pulley anchored in the center beam just beyond the front edge of the loft. From there, she threads it back to where the center beam extends out of the hayloft through a back door, to a pulley allowing farmers to lift heavy bales up to the loft from the outside.

Now comes the tricky part. The trigger.

She never bothered to hide her snares in Bosnia because rabbits are not clever enough to see a trap, even when it's right in front of them. But Luka is not a rabbit.

She ponders options until she thinks about her vision of standing on a plank with David Claypool on the other end. That will be her trigger—a trapdoor. She will lay a plank in the loft so that it sticks out

265

the back door. A nylon rope will secure one end of the plank to the hayloft floor. She will thread the line through a gap in the planks and tie it off. The weights will be suspended outside of the hayloft on the other end of the plank. Hana will simply hide in the back of the barn with a knife. A flick of her knife and four hundred pounds of steel will snap the cable tight, lifting Luka into the air.

And if that doesn't work, she can just shoot the bastard.

She builds her snare carefully but quickly, burying the loop beneath hay at the place where Luka will have to walk—if she can lure him back far enough. She hides the cable as best she can as it climbs the post to the hayloft.

But what if Luka doesn't show up? Another trap on another day? No. She can't put Dylan in danger again. She needs Luka to come tonight—and he will, she is sure of it. She will lay out bread crumbs for him to follow, a trail that he has been seeking for days. He must be impatient by now. The moon tonight will be hidden behind the clouds, giving him a dark cloak under which to move. His prey will be in mourning, vulnerable. If the funeral goes as she has planned it, Luka won't be able to pass up her enticement.

These are the thoughts she ponders as she stacks hay bales near the back corner of the barn to create her hiding place. She leaves a gap between the top two bales through which she can see the front of the barn. It will also act as an embrasure—a gun hole—to keep her shotgun trained on Luka.

Danis would be proud of her snare. He would understand that this must be done, wouldn't he? Would Mama understand? Would Babo?

Hana hums a song to shoo those thoughts away. For the next few hours, she will need clarity, not ghosts.

44

Minnesota

AFTER EVERYTHING

I f there is such a thing as a good day for a funeral, this day might hit
that mark. Clouds had moved in during the hours Hana toiled in
the barn, and by the time she and Dylan arrive at the mosque, the temperature has fallen to the mid-sixties, perfect weather to wear a sweater.

She covers her head with a scarf and wears sunglasses despite the
overcast skies. The odds of Luka recognizing her after all these years
are minuscule, but not zero. If Luka shows up, he must see Dylan's new
guardian as small. Weak. Easy prey. He must see a quiet librarian.

Dylan wears his best collared shirt and dress pants, but his shoes are
his new sneakers. Holding Dylan's hand, she follows a line of mourners
into the outer prayer room, because women are not permitted in the
mosque itself during the ceremony. As she mills around waiting for
prayers to start, she scans the small crowd for Luka, but he is not there.

A few minutes before four o'clock, two men wheel a silver carrier into
the room. Atop the carrier lies the shrouded body of Amina Junuzović.
Hana places her hands on Dylan's shoulders. They tighten, his breath
holding in his little chest as he sees his grandmother wheeled in. Hana
kneels behind Dylan. "She was a wonderful person," she whispers.

Dylan says nothing.

Wrapped in her white shroud, Amina looks small—weak—like she had that night in her prison cell. Hana wants to shout to the room, tell them about Amina's strength, the enormity of her courage. She wants the men to know that Amina had been braver and fiercer than any ten of them. She wants the people in the room to understand that beneath that tiny white shroud is the body of a woman who leapt from a balcony to save her grandson.

But she says none of that. Muslim funerals are quiet affairs—solemn. Instead, she whispers to Dylan, "No one in all the world was as loving and as brave as your Mama Mina."

Dylan makes no move to suggest that he hears her words.

The imam enters and takes his place in front of the shrouded body. The men line up behind him and the women behind the men, all assembled to face Mecca. Dylan doesn't look at the shroud. His gaze stays on the metal carrier on which his grandmother's body lies.

A program containing Amina's obituary as well as some prayers is handed out. It lists Dylan as Amina's sole surviving family member and Hana as her friend. If Luka manages to get a copy of that program, he will have her name, and as head of security for the Serbian ambassador, he should have no problem finding her address. It is one of the many bread crumbs she is relying on.

Dylan continues to stare at the wheels of the carrier, not at his grandmother's lifeless body. There are no tears on his cheeks, but the breath in his chest has a stammer to it that betrays the battle raging inside of him. Hana gives his shoulder a squeeze, but he offers no response.

When the imam finishes prayers, Mr. Fatić says a few words about Amina. He talks about her spirit and her smile, generalities that tell Hana he didn't know Amina well.

The eulogy complete, Fatić invites the men to form a procession to the cemetery. Hana has received permission from the imam to join them for the burial, but only because she is bringing Dylan.

Dylan walks to the car like a prisoner walking to his cell. He doesn't look at Hana as they drive.

A few minutes later, the procession pulls into the cemetery, a line of only eight cars. Along the way, Hana watches for suspicious vehicles, a car that might have joined the line after leaving the mosque, but Luka is not there. A cold tendril of doubt begins to creep up her spine.

The entrance to the cemetery is divided into an entrance lane and an exit lane, separated by a thin strip of grass. As they pull in, Hana sees a car out of place. It is parked in the exit lane, and a man leans against the hood—but the man is not Luka. It's David Claypool.

Hana pulls out of the procession and parks just inside the entrance. She tells Dylan to stay in the car before walking to David, who has his phone out and appears to be taking pictures of the cars as they enter. With her scarf and sunglasses, he doesn't seem to recognize her, or maybe her presence isn't worth the effort of his acknowledgment.

She removes her sunglasses as she nears him. "I didn't expect to see you here."

He doesn't look at her. "Sometimes the bad guy shows up at the funeral."

"I take it you don't have any new leads?"

Claypool gives Hana a cold stare. "I'm not doing this anymore."

"Doing... what?"

"This... this sharing information. I've been honest with you, but you..."

"But I...?"

"How did you find Zaim Galić?"

"I told you... Amina paid for his brakes to be—"

"How did you find that hunting shack? You were there."

Hana tries to hold his stare, but cannot.

"You know a lot more about this case than you're telling me. You've been playing me this whole time. I thought we were after the same thing."

"And what is that?"

"I want to find the person who killed your friend."

"As do I."

"Then why are you holding out on me? You should be helping me. I'm trying to do my job."

"So am I."

David's tone rises in frustration, but he whispers his bark. "You're dealing with very dangerous people here. You need to stand down. This isn't your business—it's mine. I'm the cop. You're a librarian."

Hana snaps her head, surprised by what he said. "I'm a...librarian? Is that what you see?"

"Don't play that card. It doesn't suit you."

David's phone buzzes. He pulls it from his pocket and looks. When he returns to Hana, his eyes are steady and serious. "The judge just signed the warrant for Ellsworth's files. If there's anything you want to tell me, now's the time."

Her jaw tightens to keep her secrets from spilling out.

David puts the phone into his pocket and, without a hint of emotion, says, "My condolences on the loss of your friend."

He gets into his car and drives away.

Hana returns to her car, subtly glancing around for any strangers in the cemetery. She sees nothing out of place, but there are trees and bushes along the highway. He could be watching from the foliage—or maybe he's farther away, spying through binoculars. If he's watching, she needs him to see Dylan. She needs him to see the bait.

The procession has stopped about a hundred yards ahead. Instead of driving to where the men have gathered, Hana gets Dylan from his seat and they walk.

David will have the search warrant soon. He'll read Amina's notes and learn about Luka Savić. He will read about a girl named Nura who crawled out of a fire and became a soldier, a girl with scars on her arms, a girl who cut the throat of a beast and freed Amina from a hellish prison. But will he put together that Hana and Nura are one and the same? Amina had promised to keep the name Hana Babić out of her sessions with Dr. Ellsworth, but David is a detective.

Hana is the only woman at the burial. Again, there are prayers muttered, knees bent on the grass, foreheads touching the ground. After Amina's body is lowered into the grave, the men, one by one, drop handfuls of dirt into the hole.

Hana holds Dylan's hand as he walks to the side of the grave. He lifts a small handful of dirt and holds it out. Hana waits. Everyone waits. He clenches the dirt in his fingers. His chest stammers with broken breaths. He lowers his hand and drops the dirt back on the pile, not in her grave. He turns and walks hard through the line of men.

Hana follows him, catching up to him when they are outside of earshot.

"Are you okay?" she asks.

His breath comes and goes in stutters, but he doesn't answer.

"Dylan, say something, please."

Dylan blinks. He looks upon Hana's face as if he has just noticed her there. She holds Dylan to her, but he does little more than lean in and accept her hug.

It's then that Hana sees something out of the corner of her eye. In the distance, a man walks in through the cemetery's entrance, hands in pockets, head lowered. Hana turns just enough to keep a side-eye on him. He approaches her parked car and disappears behind it for only a second or two before reappearing and continuing his walk.

She looks hard at the man, but cannot see his face. Is it Luka? Or has he sent a henchman in his place? No, Luka would not send a henchman. He will want to keep his crime a secret from everyone. Killing Dylan is a job he will handle personally.

The man—Luka—never turns to look back. He walks deep into the cemetery, disappearing behind a small grove of pine trees. She watches the trees, but he never reemerges, vanishing like an apparition.

45

Minnesota

AFTER EVERYTHING

Hana resists the urge to search beneath her car before leaving the cemetery. She is certain that she will find a tracking device attached to her frame. These days, anyone can buy a tracker the size of a quarter, so a man with Luka's connections should have access to the best on the market.

She drives out of the cemetery, looking for the man she saw earlier. She can feel him watching her, but she sees nothing. Dylan is quiet in the back seat. The procession turns right, heading to the gathering at the Bosnian Center; Hana turns left and heads for home, traveling along country roads that run long and straight for miles. No one would be able to trail her without her knowing it.

Once home, before getting Dylan out of the car, she walks to the rear and lies down in the gravel. At first she sees nothing out of place. She slides a bit farther under the car and sees it—a box about the size of a garage door opener fixed to her frame. She was right.

Dylan hasn't moved from his seat. She opens his door, unhooks his seat belt, and helps him out.

"Go on inside," she says. "I'll be along in a minute."

Hana walks to the end of the driveway and scans the road. There are no cars on either horizon. Luka hasn't followed her home, but he has no need to follow her. He has the tracker. He is probably parked in a car near the cemetery, watching the tracker dot come to rest. Once he has her location, he will want to get the lay of the land, spend a little time on Google Maps to see how best to approach her farmhouse. He will wait until dark to make his move—at least, that is what Hana would do.

She turns back toward the house to see Dylan standing at the bottom of the porch steps. He's not moving. As Hana gets closer, she can see that he is trembling. His chest is heaving as though he's hyperventilating. Hana steps in front of him and drops to her knees.

"Dylan..." She reaches for him, but he steps back, out of her reach.

"They put dirt on her." His lips wrench into a cry, but he angrily fights back the tears. "Why did they do that? Why?"

"Oh, honey—" Hana inches toward him and he doesn't run, but he doesn't come to her either.

"Mama Mina is scared of the dark. Don't they know that? She can't sleep in the dark. She has bad dreams. They put dirt on her." He can no longer hold back his pain as tears flow down his cheeks.

"Come here, sweetie." Hana puts her hands on his shoulders and he doesn't pull away.

"Why did she have to die? Why? She was good. She..."

"Yes, she was good. She was the best person in the world."

"She was...my only one." His face is red. Spittle webs his lips as he tries to find words. "It just...hurts so much. I can't make it stop."

"I would trade places with her if I could, Dylan. I promise you that. I would rather she be here and not me."

This seems to catch Dylan off guard. He looks at Hana, his reddened eyes searching for answers that she cannot give him. He steps to her and she folds him into her arms. He reaches his arms up and wraps them around her neck. She carries him into the house and sits on the couch. He cries to the point that his body shakes. She holds him and lets him cry.

After several minutes, his breathing settles. Hana strokes his hair and hums a lullaby that her mama used to hum in her quiet moments. The tune had been a salve to Hana when she was little.

Then, without looking up, Dylan quietly sings along. *"You're fly-ing...on the sea of coins."*

Hana stops humming, surprised, and asks, "You know this song?"

Dylan sits up. His cheeks are still red from crying, but there is a light in his eyes that has been absent all day. "Mama Mina used to sing it to me."

"When I was a little girl, my mama used to sing that song to me, too."

"I like it," he says. He lays his head back against her.

Hana is about to hum some more when Dylan whispers to her, his words soft and hesitant as if they hold the power to consume what is left of his courage. "Can I call you...Mama Hana?"

Something inside Hana breaks. Tears that have been absent for thirty years fill her eyes and fall warm against her cheek. She holds Dylan to her as she swallows the lump that squeezes her throat. When she finds her voice, she says, "Of course you can."

Outside, the clouds from earlier have turned dark; the northerly breeze carries a slight chill into the house. Nightfall is coming, and with it, Iblis. She cannot stop what she has set in motion. She cannot postpone her meeting with Luka. Dylan is so warm and tender in her arms, but if she doesn't send him away, her greatest fear will come to pass. Luka will find the child he has come to kill.

"Dylan, I need to take care of some things...about the funeral."

Dylan sits up, confused.

"I don't want to, but...it's something that needs to be taken care of—and it has to be done today. I have a friend named Deb. She's going to come here and pick you up. She's going to watch you at her house while I take care of...my thing. Is that okay?"

Dylan's brow is wrinkled, his eyes wary. "Am I...coming back?"

"Oh, Dylan...of course you're coming back. You'll always come back. This is your home...forever."

"Is she nice?"

"She's very nice. Is it okay...that you stay with her tonight?"

Dylan reaches up and wipes a tear from Hana's cheek. "Okay," he says.

"Can you go upstairs and pack your toothbrush and some clothes for tomorrow?"

Dylan is slow to move, but then he obediently scoots off Hana's lap and heads upstairs.

Hana places her call to Deb Hansen.

As she waits for Deb, a question comes to Hana: What happens if everything goes badly for her? What if Luka somehow kills her instead? She gets a pen and paper from a desk drawer and writes a note to David. She will put the note in her mailbox. An investigation into her death will find it there.

She begins the note with *If you are reading this, I am dead*...She tells David what she has discovered about Luka and Amina and lays out the threat to Dylan. She implores David to do what she had failed to do— protect Dylan from the man who is desperate to kill him. She thinks about telling him about her past in Bosnia, but doesn't. She thinks about letting him know how she feels about him but cannot find the words to explain it to herself. So, she ends by simply asking him to tell Dylan that she is sorry for breaking her promise.

46

Minnesota

AFTER EVERYTHING

With Dylan safely away—and her note tucked into her mailbox—Hana opens the trail camera app on her phone to keep watch as she gets dressed: dark jeans, long-sleeved running shirt, hiking boots, and a black bandanna to keep the hair out of her eyes. She grabs a banana, her knife, and her shotgun and heads out the door.

In the barn, she goes to her little hideaway in the back, sits on a bucket, peels the banana, and eats. She wishes she had the blue marble, not as an amulet of courage but to show Luka before he dies. The memory of Danis Divjak should be on his mind when she pulls the trigger and spreads his brain across the manure-stained dirt.

As the light outside grows dim, rain begins to patter on the roof of the barn. Will that stop him from coming? It shouldn't—it can't. She needs him to come before David Claypool reads Amina's therapy notes. Surely Luka Savić, the killer of women and children, can brave a little rain.

As night falls, the rain stops. She is again alone in silence. The barn has a single light that hangs from the rafters toward the front. The seventy-five-watt bulb barely throws off enough light to reach Hana's little nook, but her phone, with its video feed from the trail cameras, casts an eerie glow around her as she sits and waits.

The barn smells—as it always does—of cows and hay. The night is cool, but in the confines of her hideaway, she sweats. Bothersome flies pester her, but it's not like she's crawling through fire or getting kicked in the face by Serbian soldiers.

The shotgun rests in the embrasure. She peers through the hole every few minutes just in case Luka has managed to sneak past her cameras. The barn door is open and beyond it she sees that she left a light on in the house, the living room light, its hazy glow bleeding through the kitchen and out the back door. That is a mistake. She needs Luka to be drawn to the barn, not the house.

Should she leave her hideout and shut it off? No. Luka could be there already, just outside of the angle of the cameras. She is mentally kicking herself for the mistake when movement flashes on the screen of her phone. It's the camera behind the barn, the one facing the pasture. Hana studies the screen. Something moved; she is sure of it. She waits, and then . . .

The shadow of a man steps carefully along the edge of the tractor path, ducking behind trees after every few steps. Waiting. Listening. Hunting.

Hana turns her phone on silent and picks up her knife. Her hand is sweaty like it was the night she killed the Devil Dog. She wipes the sweat onto her jeans.

The man takes a few more steps.

Hana props her phone against the hay, leaving her hands free to grasp both the knife and the shotgun.

He moves close enough to the camera for his features to become clear. It is Luka. He doesn't look at the camera. He can't see it. As he walks past, he holds his right hand in front of his body, steadily, as if he carries a pistol.

Of course he would bring a gun. The snare was a bad idea.

She shakes the thought away. She's had guns pointed at her before. Besides, she too has a gun—a bigger one—and she has the element of surprise.

Luka steps past the camera, slipping into the darkness beyond its lens. He is out there, just beyond her wall. She hears the tiny click of a single stone scraping against another. His footstep.

She settles her breathing and slips her phone into her back pocket.

The snap of a twig outside—he is near the barn door.

She gets into position, her right hand ready on the shotgun, her left hand holding the knife against the nylon rope—the trigger for the snare. She watches through the gap in the hay.

A head peeks around the corner and then disappears. He's here.

Hana waits, but the head does not peek again. What if he goes to the house? She needs to coax him into the barn, but how?

Hana hums the lullaby that she had hummed for Dylan, the tune rising and floating just enough to reach Luka at the front of the barn. The melody calms her. She is the hunter.

Luka peeks around the corner of the door again—then steps through. He is in the sight of her shotgun.

He walks in a slow crouch, drawn to her humming.

Ten feet from the snare, he pauses.

Hana hums a little softer.

He begins walking again, a tiger stalking its prey, his gun raised, aimed at the wall of hay.

Eight feet.

Five feet.

Two feet.

He pauses again.

Hana's knife is tight against the nylon rope. Her finger presses against the trigger of the shotgun.

Luka steps one foot into the loop of the snare . . . shifts his weight forward.

Hana cuts the line.

The plank falls hard against the side of the barn, the bang of wood on wood startling Luka, freezing him in place. The zing of cable against pulley fills the barn and in a split second, the cable tightens around Luka's left shin. He falls, hitting his head on the dirt floor before being whisked up toward the rafters. Outside, the barbell plates hit the ground with a mighty thud.

Luka swings upside down, his head dangling three feet off the ground. He aims the gun wildly as he spins, but he doesn't cry out. He breathes in heavy gasps as if fighting against a great pain.

Tools hang on nails along the back wall of the barn: a pitchfork, a spade, a shovel, and an old axe. Hana grabs the axe.

Luka has slowed in his spinning. He's wearing a thin rain jacket—unzipped—which hangs down like a small curtain behind his head. When his back is to her, she charges, axe in hand, covering the fifteen feet between them in a flash and swings the axe in an uppercutting arc.

The handle catches him in the forearm, and he lets out a howl that fills the barn. The gun topples from his hand.

Hana kicks the gun toward the barn door, takes a step back, and for the first time in thirty years, looks into the eyes of the man who killed her brother.

47

Minnesota

AFTER EVERYTHING

Luka Savić is crying—well, there are tears in his eyes, but that might be from dangling upside down. He has stopped turning and now faces the front of the barn where Hana squats, axe in hand.

"What are you doing?" He grunts his words. Seeing his pain gives Hana a strange sense of peace, and for a moment, she thinks herself a ghoul. The thought passes as she remembers.

Luka has jowls and a bald spot on the back of his head, imperfections he hid from the photographer who took the picture for his ascendency to the UN mission. She searches for recognition in his eyes, but sees none.

"You broke my arm!"

"Why are you on my property?" she asks in a calm voice.

"My car broke down...I'm just...looking to use a phone." He struggles to sell his lie.

The scene is absurd. He is negotiating with her as if he weren't hanging upside down by his leg, like this sort of thing can happen to anyone—some strange cosmic mistake. Does he think that people set traps in barns as a matter of habit?

"Please, cut me down. I just want to call a tow truck."

She picks up his gun. It is small, no bigger than her hand, a Zastava P25, a gun that Adem once referred to as a Dark Lady, something too small for anything other than a close-in shot. She pulls the slide back far enough to see that a bullet has been chambered. She ejects the clip, checks to see that it is full, and reloads it, tucking the gun into the waistband of her jeans.

"You came into my barn carrying a gun. That is not the conduct of a man seeking help from a stranger."

"I was just being careful. I swear, my car broke down. Please...my leg...it hurts."

"That's how you want this to go? Okay. I've got time."

The arm she hit with the axe hangs limp, but the other one is still dangerous. She walks to the side of the barn and pulls a couple feet of twine from the roll hanging on the wall.

"What are you doing?" he asks.

She squats a few feet from him and makes a slipknot in the twine. When she's finished, she looks hard into his eyes and says, "Give me your hand."

"Please, lady. I was just passing by."

Lady? How can he not recognize her? But then again, the last time they had been together, she had bruises covering much of her face. She was so young. Much has changed since that night at the pink house.

She picks up the axe.

"What are you doing?"

"Give me your left hand or I will break that arm as well."

"What's the matter with you? For God's sake, I just want to use your phone!"

She raises the axe to swing.

"No!" He reaches out his good hand.

She slips the twine around his wrist. When it's tight, she kicks him in the chest, turning him around so she is behind him. Twisting his arm behind his back, she ties the loose end of the twine to his belt. He swings his broken arm at her, but his hand has lost the ability to grip.

Then she looks upon Iblis, pathetic and weak, a snake with no fangs. She has waited thirty years for this.

"Why are you doing this? I don't understand."

Again, she squats to face him. "Then I will make you understand, Luka."

His pleading stops. Anguish is replaced with confusion. Fear. He seems on the cusp of understanding. She gives him one last nudge.

"You are the great Luka Savić, the killer of women and children."

His breath quickens when he recognizes the insult. His eyes are open. Aware. Terrified.

"Do you remember my brother, Danis?"

"I..."

"You shot him in the chest?"

"No... I never knew your brother."

"He was eight years old."

"I didn't kill your brother. I don't know what you heard, but I swear—"

She slaps him across the face so hard that it turns him in a circle. She waits until he swings around to face her again before saying, "Don't insult me."

"How can I prove...whoever told you it was me...they are the one lying to you."

She raises her hand to slap him again. He shuts his eyes, but she holds off. Instead, she pulls the sleeves of her running shirt up past her elbows, lifting the back of her forearm to show him her scars.

"I was beneath the house that day. I watched Stanko Krunić kick my father to death. You placed a wager, remember? I watched you put three bullets into my brother's chest. I endured the horror of my mother

283

being raped and murdered by Colonel Zorić. Then you burned my house to the ground. I crawled through that fire. I vowed to hunt you down and kill you. I thought I had. For thirty years, I believed you were dead. And now...you are here."

"I'm sorry." He starts to blubber like a child. "It was war. I did what I was told. I'm so sorry. Please...forgive me!"

"Forgive you? Did you come here to seek forgiveness? No. You came here to bury the proof of another crime. You came to kill another child like you killed my brother. Like you killed his grandmother— Amina—the girl you raped."

"Please!"

She pulls the Zastava from her belt and points it at his forehead. He shuts his eyes. She feels nothing as she cocks the small hammer back.

But a sound interrupts her—the crunch of gravel.

Hana uncocks the gun and tucks it back into her waistband. She pulls her phone out and opens the app for the trail camera in front of her house.

A car has pulled down her driveway. All she can see are the head-lights. Her thoughts go to Dylan. Has Deb brought him back? Maybe he gave in to his fear of being abandoned and broke down and needed to be brought home.

Luka must have heard the crunch of gravel as well, because he begins to yell. "Help! I'm in the barn! Help me!"

Hana thinks about her knife. Cut his throat and be done with him, but there would be blood. It will spurt. She remembers how cutting the throats of Stanko and Colonel Devil Dog stained her clothing red. How would she explain the blood to Deb—to Dylan?

There is a grease rag hanging on the wall behind the tractor. Hana runs and grabs it. Twisting it into a gag, she ties it around Luka's mouth. He yells, but she tightens it to the point that he nearly swallows his own tongue.

She gives a quick look at the snare around his leg. It's tight. He's not going anywhere. Once she has put Dylan to bed, she will come back and put an end to Luka Savić.

She shuts off the light and heads to the house. On the way, she glances at the camera view on her phone one more time—but it's not Deb who walks onto her front porch. It's David Claypool.

48

Minnesota

AFTER EVERYTHING

Hana crouches on the back porch as she watches David through her camera. He rings the doorbell and waits.

She waits.

He knocks—hard.

She silently begs him to go away.

He paces. Knocks again.

Her car is in the driveway. A light is on inside the house. He knows she's home.

He peeks in the window, pauses, and steps off the porch. Hana breathes a sigh of relief, but then he doesn't go to his car. Instead, he walks toward the side of the house. He's going to come around back, wander within earshot of Luka's muffled screaming.

Hana enters the house and runs to the front door, hitting the porch light and opening the door just before Claypool turns the corner.

"David?"

His gait is deliberate as he returns to the porch. He acknowledges neither his trespass nor her presence until he is face-to-face with her on the porch. He wears his sidearm—this is an official visit—and his eyes seem heavy, sad almost.

"Why didn't you tell me?" he says.

He waits, as if those words are enough to evoke a confession thirty years in the making.

When Hana gives him nothing, he says, "Can I come in?"

"It's late."

"Iblis. You knew this whole time. You lied to me."

"I didn't lie."

"Come on, Hana."

"Not about that."

"Amina spoke about a friend named Nura, a girl whose family was murdered by Serbian soldiers."

Hana feels her jaw tighten. She tries to relax, show no emotion.

"Nura cut a man's throat with nothing but a small knife blade. Helped Amina escape from a rapist named Luka Savić—the man she also called Iblis."

"I...don't know any Nura."

"Stop lying."

David steps closer. She can smell him, clean like the day he first visited her at the library. Someone looking at them from a distance might think them lovers about to share a goodnight kiss. That is far from the case.

"Dr. Ellsworth said that Amina's story shifted over time. At first, she said that Nura died in the war. But one time she let it slip that Nura became a librarian."

Hana's blood turns cold in her throat. She can feel her pulse rise and her breathing deepen. She struggles to control the reaction.

David slowly raises a hand, gently wrapping a finger and thumb around Hana's wrist. "Amina said that her friend Nura hid in the crawl space beneath her house the day the Serbs massacred her family. Burned her arms crawling out of the fire."

Hana pulls her arm in, but David gently keeps his grip and carefully slides one of her sleeves up to expose her scars.

They look at each other, neither saying a word for an eternity. Then Hana says, "Come inside."

49

Minnesota

AFTER EVERYTHING

Hana backs into the house, Luka's gun still tucked into the waist-band of her pants. She motions for David to sit on the couch, and he does. She joins him, keeping her back—and the gun—turned away.

"Tell me about Luka Savić," David says.

"How much do you know?"

"According to Amina's notes—he's the man who raped her."

"What else?"

"That's not how this game—"

"What else!" Hana barks her request.

"I did my research. He's attached to the Mission of Serbia to the UN."

"I didn't lie to you, David...about not knowing who Iblis was. I thought that Amina's rapist had been Luka's commander, a man we called Devil Dog. I didn't know Iblis was Luka until earlier today. I honestly thought he was dead—"

"Shot in the face by a girl trying to escape."

"Yes."

"When we spoke at the funeral, did you know Luka was here...in Minnesota?"

"Yes."

"You should have told me."

"I couldn't."

"Yes, you could have." David's voice turns sharp. "It's easy. You say, 'Hey David, you should be looking for a man named Luka Savić. He might be important to your investigation.' For Christ's sake, Hana, if he's in town, I can bring him in."

"And then what? He has diplomatic immunity. You can't arrest him."

"I can...I can put the fear of God into him. Let him know that we know."

"He shot my brother. I watched as he and another soldier wagered on how many kicks to the head my father could take before he died. He raped a fourteen-year-old prisoner and got her pregnant. Do you really think anything you say will put the fear of God into him?"

"If we can prove that he killed Amina—"

"Do you have any evidence that he killed Amina?"

"Not yet, but—"

"Luka Savić will never stand trial for any of his crimes."

"We can kick him out of the country."

"He'll send someone else back to finish the job. Dylan is a threat to Luka. That sweet child is at the mercy of the man who cut off three of Zaim Galić's fingers before strangling him. One way or another, Luka will find a way to silence that threat."

"But if the world learns what happened—"

"The world doesn't care—don't you see that? It never cared, David. The Serbs slaughtered eight thousand men and boys in Srebrenica— took them into the woods and shot them. The men who pulled the triggers will never face justice. Luka Savić was one of them. He has come here to murder Dylan—and I won't let that happen."

"Exactly how do you propose to stop it? It's not like—" A thought passes behind his eyes that seems to set him off balance. "You have something planned."

"You should go, David."

"I can't let you—"

A sound—something unnatural to a farm—stops David from finishing his thought. Hana hears it too—the raspy cry of a man calling for help.

David stands, his ears perked up. It comes again, a garbled "Help me!"

David looks at Hana, confused.

Hana takes a deep breath and closes her eyes as David charges through the kitchen and out the back door.

50

Minnesota

AFTER EVERYTHING

David stands at the door to the barn, holding his gun in a two-handed grip, the muzzle pointed at the ground. Luka grunts from the darkness inside, sounding like a bear awaking in a cave.

Hana reaches inside and flips on the light.

David points his gun at Luka, then lowers it. "What the...?"

Luka's broken arm wasn't as useless as Hana had thought. He somehow managed to work the gag loose and call out. His face is dark and red from hanging upside down, wet with sweat and tears. One leg stretches up to the cable while the other hangs awkwardly to the side. His good hand is still tied behind his back with the baling twine while the bad one dangles.

"Help me." His voice is weak.

"Christ... Hana, what have you done?" David holsters his gun and walks to Luka.

Defeated, Hana says, "David, meet Luka Savić."

"You can't just..." David walks around the hanging man. "I mean..."

"He came here to kill Dylan. So, here's your chance... put the fear of God into him."

"She's a war criminal," Luka says with great effort. "Her name is Nura Divjak. She is wanted in my country for the crime of murdering civilians."

David looks at Hana, a new question in his eyes.

Hana keeps her eyes on Luka as she speaks. "The night I was captured, his men killed two prisoners—Muslim women they had kidnapped. Those women were shot trying to escape. It was convenient for the Serbs to accuse me of the crime because I had succeeded where those women had not. I got away. I survived. So, yes, there is a bounty on my head, placed there by this man's lies."

"She is the one who lies," Luka pleads. "Get me down. I beg you."

David follows the cable with his eyes up to the center beam and into the hayloft. "We'll sort this out," he says as he heads up the steps.

Luka gives Hana a smile; he thinks he has won.

Hana walks to the hanging man and lifts the gag back into his mouth despite his jerking. He tries to grab her with his bad hand but his fingers are useless.

She squats so she can watch his face as she pulls his gun from her waistband and rests it on her thigh. Luka's eyes grow large. He begins to flail at the end of his tether, a fish trying to shake free.

"You have put me at odds, Luka." Hana keeps her voice low so David doesn't hear. "I promised to kill you...avenge my family—my brother. That is why I should put a bullet in your head."

In the loft, David pulls at the cable. He's trying to lift the four hundred pounds of weights off the ground. He will give up soon.

"I also promised that child that I would be here for him. That I would protect him. I promised that I would be his...Mama Hana. You see the problem, don't you? I can't be here for him if I go to prison for killing you. I am not afraid of prison, mind you. Nothing there can be worse than what I've already lived through. But the thought of leaving Dylan...breaking my promise..."

Hana barely notices Luka as he yells into his gag, his nostrils flaring. She speaks more to herself than to him. "I once knelt beside a dying soldier—a Serb—a man that I had shot. He asked if my sacrifice would be worth it."

Above her, she hears David climbing over the hay, making his way back to the front of the loft. She hasn't much time. She points the gun at Luka's face. He jerks even harder, squealing into the gag, tears glistening against his reddened skin.

"Dylan is a child. He won't understand why I left him, not now, but someday...someday, he'll see that I did this for him, and maybe he'll forgive me."

"Hana! What are you doing?" David is at the edge of the hayloft above her.

"I'm sorry, David."

She cocks the hammer back.

Luka closes his eyes, his muffled scream little more than a nuisance to her. He twists ferociously, hoping to spoil her aim.

"Don't do it, Hana. We'll figure something out."

"There's no other way to save Dylan."

"I'm a cop, for Christ's sake. There are lines I can't cross."

"He killed my family. I won't let him do it again."

"Stop!" David pulls his gun and points it down at Hana. "Don't make me...!"

"We all have our duty, David. You do what you must, and I will do what I must."

"If you kill him you'll spend the rest of your life in prison—that's a guarantee. And then what happens to Dylan?"

"He lives...a long and healthy life."

"Please, Hana, put the gun down."

"David...if you ever had feelings for me, promise that you will find a good home for Dylan."

"Hana I—"

Hana pulls the trigger.

The bullet enters Luka's temple but is too small to fight its way out the other side. Luka stops moving, his eyes bloated and still, his body slowly rocking at the end of her snare.

Hana steps back, lays her gun on the ground, stands with her hands behind her back, and waits for David.

51

Minnesota

TWO MONTHS LATER

The meeting is set for eleven a.m. Detective David Claypool arrives at ten thirty, his investigation folder in hand. The meeting is being held on his home turf, the conference room at the St. Paul Police Department, a simple room: white walls, oak shelves that hold framed pictures of fallen officers, former mayors, and a couple honored K-9s. The oak table in the center has twelve comfortable chairs, the leather armrests scuffed from years of being slid against the table's edge. There are no cameras or recording devices in the room—one of the few demands from the visiting team.

It is not David's show, but he will be the star.

Ten minutes ahead of the hour, Chief Monroe enters with a woman at his side. Short. Plump. The woman carries a black briefcase. Monroe gestures. "Have you met Detective Claypool?" he asks.

"We spoke over the phone," the woman says, holding out a hand. "Delia Vance."

"Nice to finally meet you in person," Claypool says.

He had expected someone taller, younger, sleeker. As he retakes his seat, he ponders why that is. *Movies*, he thinks. Female spies are always tall in the movies. But is she a spy? Head of security for the U.S. embassy in Bosnia sounds like the title a spy might have. And if you want your spy to blend, you would hire someone like Delia Vance, short, stocky, a woman who looks like she would struggle to get through half an hour of water aerobics.

Claypool jettisons his mental ramblings and tries to get back into his headspace for the meeting.

The Serbian delegation arrives fifteen minutes late, three of them. The leader, a grumpy, hunched man in his late sixties named Igor Mitrović, walks in with no smile, no open palm, nothing in the way of greeting other than to say, "Where do I sit?"

Chief Monroe points to the three chairs opposite.

Delia Vance had prepared Claypool for Igor. "He'll stare at you to make you uncomfortable. It's his thing. Stare back if you want, but it's like looking at a rotted tree stump."

The other two men, large, crew-cutted thugs with dark suits and zero facial expressions, take seats to either side of Igor. Once everyone is seated and introduced, Delia Vance nods to Claypool. He stands, if for no other reason than to be able to look down upon Igor and his henchmen as he speaks.

"This investigation began ten days ago when a couple of fishermen found a body in the Mississippi River. It had become tangled in a fallen tree."

The tree hadn't been part of David's plan. If the body had never been found, there would never have been a file to close.

"The deceased," he continues, "was then taken to the office of the Ramsey County medical examiner for identification and examination. The man had a wallet that identified him as Luka Savić. Beyond that—"

Igor interrupts. "This man carried the identification of a Serbian diplomat. Why was my office not notified that day?"

"We wanted to confirm his identification," Claypool says.

"I should have been notified immediately."

Vance steps in. "This man is a detective. He's not responsible for contacting you; the State Department is. If you have a problem with my timing, you can file a complaint with my boss. In the meantime, can we get on with this?"

Igor sits back in his chair, his stare engulfing Claypool like the rising water of a flood.

"Once we identified the man as Luka Savić, we ran a check and found that a rental car had been towed from the Lilydale dog park in St. Paul...along the Mississippi River. The car had been rented by Mr. Savić. When we made that connection, I took a team and searched the area of the park. We found the gun in the water along the levee not far from where the car had been found."

Claypool opens his folder and slides a photo of Luka's gun to the center of the table. Igor pulls it close and examines it.

"It's a Zastava P25. A Serbian-made semiautomatic. They're banned from importation into the United States, so we assume he brought it here illegally."

Vance interjects: "Tell me, Igor, what was your man doing in Minnesota with an illegal firearm?"

When Igor offers no answer, Vance nods to Claypool.

"Savić died as a result of a fatal gunshot wound in his right temple. The evidence suggests that it was self-inflicted. The bullet found in his skull was fired from his own gun—the Zastava. The medical examiner has ruled it a suicide. The only other obvious wound was a compound fracture of the right ulna."

"Excuse me for being blunt," Igor says, "but you are suggesting that he shot himself in the right side of the head while he had a broken right arm?"

"The arm was likely broken after he shot himself," Claypool says.

"The bank is rocky along that stretch of the river. And if he didn't break his arm in the fall, it probably happened during his tumble down the river. The Mississippi has a powerful current and lots of fallen trees. Get tangled up in the crux of a branch and it can cause all kinds of damage."

"Mr. Savić was not the kind of man to take his own life. If you think—"

Vance interrupts him. "You may not know Mr. Savić as well as you think."

Igor turns his cold stare to Delia, holding it on her for a few seconds before returning his attention to Claypool.

"Mr. Savić's body," Claypool says, "being in the river that long offered few clear answers. Fish had been feeding off his exposed skin. Any trace evidence had been washed away."

"You are writing a fairy tale, Detective," Igor says with a dismissive wave of his hand. "This man came all the way to Minnesota just to kill himself?"

Delia gives Igor a thin smile. "There's more, Igor. You might want to hold your questions till the end."

Again, she nods to Claypool.

"We searched his car, which yielded a few nuggets. We found a parking stub for a ramp downtown. Using that as a pinpoint, we asked around at the hotels in the area and found that he had been staying at the Drury Plaza. He never checked out of his room and the hotel held his personal items."

"You will return those to us," Igor says in a matter-of-fact tone.

"In time," Delia answers.

"They are the property of the Serbian people. You have no right to hold on to any of his things."

"Your objection is noted," Delia says.

Claypool continues, "One of the items he left behind was a laptop."

Igor's hands ball into fists. "If you touched that hard drive . . ."

"We took a little peek," Delia says.

"That is highly inappropriate. That laptop is the property of the Serbian government. Mr. Savić was operating under the rules of diplomatic privilege."

"So he was here for official business?" Delia asks. "You sanctioned his trip here?"

Igor must see the box he's building for himself, because he settles back into his chair saying nothing but keeping his stare on Delia.

"Interestingly," Claypool says, "we found that Savić searched for a couple addresses on his laptop. He deleted his searches, but our computer forensics people pulled them up."

Igor's nostrils flare at the news that they had done a forensic search of the laptop, but he holds his tongue.

"One of those searches brought him to the condo of a woman who was murdered just two days after Savić arrived in St. Paul. A Bosnian refugee, she was thrown from her balcony . . . died at the scene. Witnesses saw a man on the balcony after she fell to her death."

Igor seems to grow small in his chair at this news.

"The second address he searched was a hunting shack, where we found a man named Zaim Galić tied to a chair. Dead. Three of Zaim Galić's fingers had been severed—we suspect he had been tortured."

Igor says, "I assume you have a motive? Or are you suggesting Mr. Savić came here to randomly kill two of your citizens?"

"As a matter of fact, we do have a motive. We believe that Galić had been blackmailing Luka Savić," Claypool says. "Galić stole files from a therapist in St. Paul. He used the information in those files to extort money. One of the files belonged to the woman who was thrown from her balcony. It contained evidence of a war crime committed by Luka Savić. He came here to kill both the blackmailer and the witness."

"Which brings us to you, Igor," Delia says. "When Detective

Claypool informed me of his investigation, I thought it best that you and I have a little chat. I think it's important that you understand the gravity of the situation. If this investigation goes public, it will create an international incident. A Serbian spy wandering around Minnesota throwing innocent women out of windows? Cutting off fingers? The head of security for your UN mission, no less. But, as we sit here today, none of this is public."

Delia leans in to the table and laces her fingers together. "I have been assured by Chief Monroe that these two cases can be wrapped up...quietly, with minimal exposure to you and your country. We've managed to be discreet so far, but if this were to get leaked, you'll be getting calls from the *Washington Post* and *New York Times*—not to mention the *St. Paul Pioneer Press Dispatch*. It will be a costly embarrassment for you...and for those you answer to."

"And what will this...discretion cost us?" Igor asks.

"Igor...my friend...this is not the place to discuss price tags." Delia looks at Igor the way a cat eyes a cornered mouse. "That is a discussion we should have in private, don't you think?"

"We will get the laptop back?" Igor asks.

"It's in Chief Monroe's office. You can take it with you when you leave."

"But you will retain a copy of the hard drive?"

"It's only fair."

"I would like to have Mr. Savić's body released to me...so that we may bury him on Serbian soil."

"That can be arranged."

Igor twists his face like he's bitten into spoiled meat as he ponders his options. Then he stands—as do his henchmen. "It is a sad day when a man like Luka Savić...takes his own life in this way. It is an ugly business we are in. Many pressures. I will see to it that this matter is put to rest."

52

Minnesota

EPILOGUE

Hana sits on her porch swing, a cat with a half-and-half face curled on her lap. Although the sun hangs at high noon, she is wrapped in the afterglow of a sunset thirty years in the making. In her heart, she has again buried her family, but this time they rest peacefully, sanctified by atonement. The fire of vengeance that scarred her arms and her soul has gone dead.

Dylan is at the edge of the front yard, a place where the gravel drive curves around to the barn. He is playing with his new slingshot. He has lined cans across the driveway and is firing gravel at them. He has yet to hit one, but he's getting closer.

It is Dylan who hears the car first. He is searching the driveway for a perfect stone to shoot when he stands and faces the highway. The car slows and pulls in—David Claypool behind the wheel.

David gets out and gives a small wave to Dylan, who watches him with a child's curiosity. David is wearing the tweed jacket that he wore that first day he came to the library. At the porch, he climbs the three steps, pauses to slip off his jacket, and takes a seat beside Hana. He hasn't seen her since that night when she drove him back from the river—after they dropped Luka Savić into the current.

David leans back on the porch swing. It is a fine day and there is a smell about the farm: dust, and cows, and hay, but it is a smell that he thinks he can get used to, maybe even grow fond of. Birds flit about in the trees. A dragonfly lands on his knee and sits there as if to welcome him.

Finally, he says, "I met with some Serbians today."

Hana doesn't look at him, but answers, "And?"

"Luka Savić committed suicide. Succumbed to his dark conscience. Apparently, he was a man of many sins."

"You shouldn't have done it."

"I disagree."

"I didn't ask you to get involved."

"I know," he says.

David brings a balance to the movement of the porch swing, the sway forward and back made easy by his weight.

"Why?" she asks.

"Why?"

"Why did you do it?"

"I had to," he says. "Otherwise I wouldn't have been able to look at myself in the mirror."

She gives him a side look to let him know that she doesn't accept his answer.

They rock gently on the swing for a minute more, and then he says, "I know what you and Amina went through in Bosnia at the hands of that man. Dr. Ellsworth explained it in detail. I had the chance to make a difference—to balance a scale that needed balancing."

"You could have gone to jail," she says.

"A wise person once told me that we have both light and dark within us—written on our hearts—and to do what is right, we need only pay heed. Well...I did just that. Iblis is where he belongs."

Dylan hits one of the cans with his slingshot and jumps for joy, waving his arms in the air. "Did you see that? I hit it! Mama Hana, I hit it."

"You have a good eye," Hana calls back.

Dylan picks up another stone and goes back to his task with renewed enthusiasm.

The swing creaks where the chain scrapes along the eyehook, but the sound is comforting to Hana, the music of an old house—a home.

With Luka's death, the tethers that bound her to her past seem to have fallen away. The men who killed her family are gone. The rage that once burned hot is gone, and in the ashes left behind, she has found something incredible and wondrous: a little boy named Dylan. She is Mama Hana now. No words, in all the world, are as sweet as those.

David says, "So now what?"

"Now what?"

He waits a beat. "What I did . . . I did because it was the right thing to do. You don't owe me a thing. You understand that, don't you?"

She nods.

"With that said . . . I guess . . . I like sitting here with you."

Her reply comes to her right away, but she holds the words back for a moment before speaking them. They are the kind of words that one can't unsay once they are spoken. When she is certain of her answer, she says, "I like sitting here with you too."

David reaches into the pocket of his jacket, which lays across his lap, and retrieves something. He holds it out to Hana, his hand balled into a fist.

Unsure of what he wants, she hesitates before placing her hand beneath his. He opens his fingers and something falls into her palm. It is the necklace with the blue marble.

"I thought you would like to have this back."

Hana holds the marble gently in the tips of her fingers, so much meaning in such a tiny bauble, and for only the second time since she left her beloved mountain in Bosnia, her eyes fill with tears. She kisses the marble and hooks the necklace around her neck.

David's hand rests on his leg. Without looking at him, Hana reaches over and lays her hand on his. He turns his palm up and laces his fingers in hers.

The two of them watch Dylan fire stones at tin cans, their swing rocking lightly in the breeze, effortless in its motion.

ACKNOWLEDGMENTS

I wish to acknowledge, and thank again, Dr. Erma Nezirević and Mr. Elvir Mujić who guided and helped me understand the culture and the war in Bosnia. Without them I could not have written this novel. I also wish to acknowledge and thank my wife, Joely, whose literary opinion I trust beyond measure.

I want to thank my agent, Amy Cloughley, and my editor, Helen O'Hare, who encouraged me to write what is a departure from my previous nine novels. I want to thank my proofreaders, Joely, Nancy Rosin, and Terry Kolander, for their attention to detail — far superior to my own. And I owe a great debt of gratitude to my team at Little, Brown/Mulholland: Michael Noon, Alison Kerr Miller, Bryan Christian, Gabrielle Leporati, Liv Ryan, Gianella Rojas, Josh Kendall, Lucy Kim, and everyone else at Little, Brown/Mulholland Books who have had my back all these years.

Finally, I want to thank you, my readers, for making my dream of becoming a writer come true. I enjoy, beyond words, the hours I spend conjuring up stories and putting those stories on paper, but it is you and your support that made this a career for me and not just a hobby. For that, I am forever grateful.

ABOUT THE AUTHOR

Allen Eskens is the *USA Today* bestselling author of *The Life We Bury*, which has been published in twenty-six languages, and eight other novels, most recently *Saving Emma*, *Forsaken Country*, *The Stolen Hours*, *The Shadows We Hide*, and *Nothing More Dangerous*. His books have won the Barry Award, the Rosebud Award, the Silver Falchion Award, and the Minnesota Book Award. Eskens is a former criminal defense attorney and lives with his wife, Joely, in Greater Minnesota.